DIRTY WORK

Also by Stuart Woods in Large Print:

Chiefs ✓
Cold Paradise ✓
Dead Eyes
✓Deep Lie
✓ Grass Roots
Heat
L.A. Times ✓
✓ Orchid Blues
Santa Fe Rules ✓
✓Under the Lake

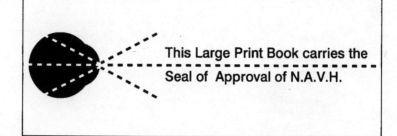

This Large Print Book carries the
Seal of Approval of N.A.V.H.

(DIRTY WORK)

STUART WOODS~

WHEELER
PUBLISHING

Published in 2003 by arrangement with G. P. Putnam's Sons, a member of Penguin Group (USA) Inc.

Wheeler Large Print Hardcover Series.

The text of this Large Print edition is unabridged.
Other aspects of the book may vary from the original edition.

Set in 16 pt. Plantin by Christina S. Huff.

Printed in the United States on permanent paper.

Library of Congress Cataloging-in-Publication Data

Woods, Stuart.
    Dirty work / Stuart Woods.
    Waterville, Me. : Wheeler Pub., 2003.
        p. cm.
    ISBN 1-58724-440-3 (lg. print : hc : alk. paper)
    1. Barrington, Stone (Fictitious character) — Fiction.
2. Private investigators — New York (State) — New York —
Fiction.   3. New York (N.Y.) — Fiction.   4. Large type books.
5. Mystery fiction.   I. Title.
PS3573.O642D58 2003b
    813′.54—dc21   2003052537

THIS BOOK IS FOR
CHARLTON AND LYDIA HESTON.

As the Founder/CEO of NAVH, the only national health agency solely devoted to those who, although not totally blind, have an eye disease which could lead to serious visual impairment, I am pleased to recognize Thorndike Press* as one of the leading publishers in the large print field.

Founded in 1954 in San Francisco to prepare large print textbooks for partially seeing children, NAVH became the pioneer and standard setting agency in the preparation of large type.

Today, those publishers who meet our standards carry the prestigious "Seal of Approval" indicating high quality large print. We are delighted that Thorndike Press is one of the publishers whose titles meet these standards. We are also pleased to recognize the significant contribution Thorndike Press is making in this important and growing field.

Lorraine H. Marchi, L.H.D.
Founder/CEO
NAVH

* Wheeler Large Print is an imprint of Thorndike Press.

1

Elaine's, late.

A big night — a couple of directors, a couple of movie stars, half a dozen writers, an assortment of journalists, editors, publicists, cops, wise guys, drunks, hangers-on, women of substance, and some of considerably less substance. And this was just at the tables; the bar was a whole other thing.

Stone Barrington pushed his plate away and sat back. Gianni, the waiter, snatched it away.

"Was it all right?" Gianni asked.

"You see anything left?" Stone asked.

Gianni grinned and took the plate to the kitchen.

Elaine came over and sat down. "So?" she said. She did not light a cigarette. To Stone's continuing astonishment, she had quit, cold turkey.

"Not much," Stone replied.

"That's what you always say," Elaine said.

"I'm not kidding, not much is happening."

The front door of the restaurant opened, and Bill Eggers came in.

"Now something's happening," Elaine said. "Eggers never comes in here unless he's looking for you, and he never looks for you unless there's trouble."

"You wrong the man," Stone said, waving Eggers over to the table, but he knew she was right. For ordinary work, Bill phoned; for more pressing tasks, he hunted down Stone and usually found him at Elaine's.

"Good evening, Elaine, Stone," Eggers said. "Your cell phone is off."

"It didn't work, did it?" Stone replied.

"I gotta be someplace," Elaine said, getting up and walking away. She got as far as the next table.

"Drink?" Stone asked.

Michael, the headwaiter, materialized beside them.

"Johnnie Walker Black, rocks," Eggers said.

"I have a feeling I'm going to need a Wild Turkey," Stone said to Michael.

Michael vanished.

"How's it going?" Eggers asked.

"You tell me," Stone said.

Eggers shrugged.

"If I had to guess," Stone said, "I'd say, not so hot."

"Oh, it's not so bad," Eggers replied.

"Then what drags you away from home and hearth, into this den of iniquity?"

"You remember that big Irish ex-cop, used to do little chores for you from time to time?"

"Teddy? He dropped dead in P. J. Clarke's three months ago."

"From what?"

"How many things can an Irishman in an Irish bar drop dead of?" Stone asked, rhetorically.

"Yeah," Eggers admitted.

"And why would I need somebody like Teddy?" Stone asked.

"You remember telling me about that thing Teddy used to do with the water pistol?" Eggers asked.

"You mean, after he kicked down a door and had his camera ready, how he squirted his naked subjects down low, so they'd grab at themselves and leave their faces open to be photographed in bed with each other?"

Eggers chuckled. "That's the one. I admire that kind of ingenuity."

The drinks came, and they both sipped for a long, contemplative moment.

"So, you're in need of that kind of ingenuity?" Stone asked at last.

"You remember that prenup I tossed you last year?" Eggers asked. Bill Eggers was the managing partner of Woodman & Weld, the very prestigious New York law firm to which Stone was of counsel, which meant he sometimes did the work that Woodman & Weld did not wish to appear to be doing.

"Elena Marks?" Stone asked.

"The very one."

"I remember." Elena Marks was heiress to a department store fortune, and she had married a member in high standing of the No Visible Means of Support Club.

9

"You remember that funny little clause you wrote into her prenup?"

"You mean the one about how if Larry got caught with his pants around his ankles in the company of a lady other than Elena, he would forfeit any claim to her assets or income?" Lawrence Fortescue was English — handsome, well educated, and possessed of every social grace, which meant he didn't have a receptacle in which to relieve himself.

"The very one," Eggers said.

"Has Larry been a bad boy?" Stone asked.

"Has been, is, and will continue to be," Eggers replied, sipping his Scotch.

"I see," Stone said.

"Now that Teddy has gone to his reward, who do you use for that sort of thing?"

"It's been quite a while since that sort of thing was required of me," Stone replied edgily.

"Don't take that tone with me, young man," Eggers said, raising himself erect in mock dudgeon. "It's work, and somebody has to do it."

Stone sighed. "I suppose I could find somebody."

Eggers looked at him sharply. "You're not thinking of doing this yourself, are you? I mean, there are heights involved here, and you're not as young as you used to be."

"I am *not* thinking of doing it myself, but I'm certainly in good enough shape to," Stone said. "What kind of heights are we talking about?"

"The roof of a six-story town house, shooting

10

through a conveniently located skylight."

"There is no such thing as a conveniently located skylight, if you're the one doing the climbing," Stone said.

"You'd need someone . . . spry," Eggers said, "and the term hardly applies to the cops and ex-cops you mingle with."

At that moment, as if to make Eggers's point, Stone's former partner from his NYPD days, Dino Bacchetti, walked through the front door and headed for Stone's table.

"If you see what I mean," Eggers said.

Stone held up a hand, stopping Dino in his tracks, then a finger, turning him toward the bar.

"I get your point," Stone said. "I'll see who I can come up with."

"You don't have a lot of time," Eggers said. "It's at nine o'clock tomorrow night."

"What's at nine o'clock tomorrow night?"

"The assignation. Larry Fortescue has an appointment with a masseuse who, I understand, routinely massages more than his neck muscles. Elena would like some very clear photographs of that service being performed."

"Let me see what I can do," Stone said.

Eggers tossed off the remainder of his Scotch and placed a folded sheet of paper on the table. "I knew you would grasp the nettle," he said, standing up. "The address of the building is on the paper. I'll need the prints and negatives by noon the day after tomorrow."

"What's the rush?"

"Elena Marks is accustomed to instant gratification."

"But not from Larry?"

"You *are* quick, Stone. Nighty-night." He slapped Dino on the back as he passed the bar on his way to the door.

Dino came over, licking Scotch off his hand, where Eggers had spilled it. He flopped into a chair. "So what was that about?" he asked, pointing his chin at Eggers's disappearing back.

"Dirty work," Stone said.

2

Dino patted the rest of the spilled Scotch off his hand with a cocktail napkin. "Is there any other kind?"

"Sure there is, and they give me plenty of it," Stone said defensively.

"How dirty?"

"Just slightly grubby; I don't have to kill anybody."

"And who are you going to get to do it?"

"Well, Teddy's dead, so I guess I'd better call Bob Cantor," Stone said, digging out his cell phone and switching it on.

"Bob's your man, as well as your uncle," Dino observed.

Stone dialed the number and got a recording. He left a message, then dialed Cantor's cell phone.

It was answered instantly. "Speak to me!" Cantor's voice shouted over a babble of voices and steel-band music.

"It's Stone. Where the hell are you?"

"Saint Thomas, baby!" Cantor yelled.

"Like in the Virgin Islands, Saint Thomas?"

"I'm not talking about the church."

"Bob, I need some help. Are you sober?"

"Certainly not! I've had enough piña coladas to fill that hot tub at your house."

"It's not a hot tub; it's just a big bathtub with the Jacuzzi thing."

"Whatever. Why don't you come down here, Stone? You wouldn't believe the women."

"I'd believe them."

"What d'ya need, that you would interrupt a man's drinking?"

Stone looked around and cupped a hand over the cell phone. "I need a second-story man who's good with a camera."

"You running a badger game?"

"Close, but not quite. And the shots have to be taken on a roof, so I need somebody who's in good enough shape not to fall off the building and embarrass everybody."

"Got a pencil?"

Stone dug out a pen. "Shoot."

"Herbie Fisher."

"Who's he?"

"My sister's boy. He's young and bold and agile, and he's a pretty good photographer."

"The light may not be very good."

"It never is in those situations, is it?"

"Right."

Cantor gave Stone the number, and he wrote it on a cocktail napkin. "Tell him I sent you and not to screw it up."

"Does he make a habit of screwing up?" Stone asked. But Cantor had punched off and returned to his piña coladas.

"I heard that," Dino said, "but I didn't hear it."

"Good," Stone said, punching in the number Cantor had given him. The phone rang five times before it was picked up.

"What!" a young man's voice said, panting.

"Herbie Fisher?"

"Who wants to know? Jesus, can't a guy get laid anymore?"

"My name is Stone Barrington. Your uncle Bob said to call you."

"Gimme your number, I got something to finish here."

Stone gave him the number, and he hung up.

"I think I interrupted him," Stone said.

"In the saddle?"

"That's what it sounded like."

"These kids!" Dino said, laughing. "Nobody would ever have caught you or me doing that."

"Nah," Stone agreed. Then he looked toward the door and froze. "Look over your shoulder and tell me if I'm seeing what I think I'm seeing," he said.

Dino looked over his shoulder. "Carpenter!"

She was standing there in a beautiful cashmere coat that set off her dark brown hair, looking around, looking lost; she hadn't seen him. Stone grabbed Michael, the headwaiter, as he passed. "The lady at the door," Stone said. "Go over there and say, 'Miss Carpenter? Mr. Barrington is expecting you.' Then bring her here."

Michael nodded and went to his work. Stone watched her face; no sign of surprise. Carpenter had never given much away. Michael led her back toward the table, and Stone and Dino stood up.

"What took you so long?" Stone said, embracing her and kissing her on the cheek.

"I came as fast as I could," she said, her British accent smooth and creamy. "Dino, how are you?" She hugged him.

"Better now," Dino said.

Stone took her coat, hung it up, and held a chair for her, then he sat down and waved Michael over again. "What would you like to drink, Carpenter?" He didn't know her first name, nor her last name, for that matter. Carpenter was a handle, a moniker, a code name. They had met in London the year before, when he had gotten himself into a mess that required the assistance of British intelligence. Dino had been there, too.

"Bourbon, please," she said, "no ice."

"You get that, Michael?"

Michael nodded and went away.

"Since when does a limey girl drink bourbon?" Dino asked.

"Since Stone extolled its virtues," she replied. A glass was set before her, and she sipped appreciatively.

"And what brings you to New York?" Stone asked. "Besides me, I mean."

"Well," she said drolly, "you were the most important consideration, of course, but there is

16

a little job I have to do with an agency of your government that will require every waking moment that I can tear myself away from your presence."

"I'll see that there are not many of those moments," Stone said. "Dare I ask which agency of my government?"

"The FBI," she said.

"Oh, yes, they would be the folks who are roughly analogous to your own outfit, wouldn't they?"

"Perhaps," she said coolly.

"C'mon, Stone, she's not going to tell you anything," Dino said.

Elaine came back and pulled up a chair.

"Elaine Kaufman," Stone said, "let me introduce . . ." He waited for Carpenter to fill in the blank.

"Felicity," Carpenter said, offering her hand to Elaine and shooting Stone an amused glance.

"Really?" Stone asked.

"Sometimes," Carpenter replied.

Stone's cell phone rang.

3

Stone stood up. "Excuse me for a moment," he said to Carpenter. He walked toward the kitchen and turned into the empty dining room that Elaine used for parties and overflow. "Hello?"

"This is Herbie Fisher. You called?"

"Yeah, I spoke to your uncle Bob a few minutes ago, and he recommended you for a job."

"What kind of job?"

"It involves a camera."

"I'm up for photography," Herbie said. "Tell me more."

"The job's tomorrow evening, so clear your schedule. Come to my office tomorrow morning at ten." Stone gave him the address. "It's the professional entrance of the house, lower level."

"What's it pay?"

"I'll talk to you tomorrow morning." Stone hung up and went back to his table. Elaine had moved on to somebody else's.

"Late date?" Carpenter asked.

"Business," Stone said.

"Ah, business."

"How long are you in town for?"

"A few days, unless I can think of a reason to stretch my stay."

Dino stood up. "I'll leave you two to work on some reasons."

"Good night, Dino," she said. "I hope I'll see you again while I'm here."

"Count on it," Dino said, then he left.

"Sweet man," Carpenter said.

"If you say so. Felicity, huh? I like it."

"It's just as well; I'm not going to change it."

"Have you had dinner?"

"I had a business dinner earlier."

"Where are you staying?"

"With friends."

"Where, with friends?"

"In the East Forties."

"Very near me. Will you come to my house for a nightcap?"

"All right."

They got into their coats and, outside, Stone started to hail a cab.

"Don't," she said. "I have a car, courtesy of my firm." She nodded toward a black Lincoln idling at the curb.

"All the better," Stone said, opening the door for her. He gave the driver his address.

"That's in Turtle Bay," she said.

"You know Turtle Bay?"

"I can read a map and a guidebook, I know all about it. Does your house open onto the common garden?"

"Yes, it does."

"Perhaps you'll show me the garden to-morrow."

"Certainly," Stone replied, though he wasn't quite sure what she meant.

"How does one afford a house of one's own, what with property prices the way they are in New York these days?"

"Easy. One has a great-aunt who dies and wills him the house. Then one works one's ass off renovating it."

"I can't wait to see it."

"You don't have to wait, we're here." He opened the door, and she slid across the seat. She leaned back into the car. "You can go," she said to the driver.

Stone liked the sound of that. He led her up the steps, unlocked the front door, and hung their coats in the front hall closet. "I didn't know you had any friends in New York," he said.

"Business friends."

"Oh. And I suppose their front hall closet has a selection of cloaks and daggers."

"Quite," she said.

Stone switched on some lights from the master panel in the foyer.

Carpenter walked into the living room. "This is very handsome," she said. "Did you choose the furniture, or did you have a designer?"

"Most of the furniture came with the house. I had everything reupholstered. I chose the fabrics."

"Oh? I thought I detected a woman's touch."

Stone didn't want to go there. "My study is through here," he said, leading the way.

"Beautiful paneling and bookcases," Carpenter said.

"My father designed and built them."

"Your father the Communist?"

"Ex-Communist," Stone replied. "You pulled a few files on me, didn't you?"

"A few. Mother, a painter. Both parents disowned by their parents, who were textile tycoons in New England. Why?"

"My father, because of his politics; my mother, because she married my father. The only family member who spoke to them was my great-aunt. She bought this house and hired my father to do a lot of the interior. It kept them from starving to death, early in their marriage. What else did you learn about me?"

"Went to New York University, then the law school. Joined the NYPD afterwards, served fourteen years, including eleven as a detective. Retired for medical reasons, ostensibly. A bullet in the knee, wasn't it?"

"Yes, but there were other, more political reasons. The department was never very comfortable with me."

"You must tell me about it when we have more time," she said.

"Don't we have time now?"

"Not really. Where is your bedroom?"

He led her up a flight. "Right here."

She began unbuttoning her suit coat. "I think we'd better get to bed," she said. "I have an early meeting tomorrow morning."

Stone stood, stunned, his mouth open.

She reached over and closed it, then kissed him lightly. "You mustn't believe everything you hear about proper British girls," she said, working on his buttons.

"I must remember that," he said, helping her.

Stone woke with the gray light of dawn coming through the windows overlooking the garden. He could hear the shower running. He got up, found a robe, brushed his hair, and was about to go and find her when she came out of the bathroom, wearing his terrycloth robe, her face shiny with no makeup.

"Good morning," she said. "You were very good last night."

"Why, thank you," he said.

"It's interesting how you talk during sex," she said. "Englishmen never do that."

"No?"

"No, they always seem in such a hurry. You, on the other hand, took your time, and I liked that."

"You are a very big surprise, Felicity."

"Oh, I hope so," she replied. "If I hadn't been, my carefully composed professional mien would have been compromised."

He put his arms around her. "I assure you, it was not. As I said, you were a very big surprise."

22

She picked up her watch from his dresser top. "I think we may have time to do it again," she said. "Are you up for that?"

"I'm getting there," Stone said.

4

Stone stood at the door, his arms around Carpenter. "Can't I get you a cab?"

"It's only in the next block," she said.

"What is?"

"The, ah, home of my friends."

"What is it, a town house? An apartment building?"

"It's very comfortable," she said, "though I like it here better."

"Then why don't you move in for the remainder of your time in New York?"

"What a nice idea," she said, kissing him. "Let me see if I can arrange it."

"Dinner tonight?"

"Love it. I'll come here at, say, eight o'clock?"

"See you then." He watched her walk quickly down the street, then turn the corner. Then he went back inside and made himself some breakfast.

Herbie Fisher was forty minutes late for his appointment. He was small, ferret-like, sleekly dressed, and annoying. "Hey," he said, plopping down in a chair across the desk from Stone.

"You're late," Stone said.

Herbie shrugged. "Traffic."

"If I give you this job you can't be late," Stone said.

Herbie shrugged. "So get somebody else," he said, standing up.

Stone picked up the phone and punched a button for a line that didn't exist. "Joan," he said, "get me that guy I used last month for the photography work." He hung up and pretended to go through some papers, then he looked up. "You still here?"

"Okay, okay," Herbie said. "I get the picture. I'll do it your way, on time and everything. What does it pay?"

"Five hundred," Stone said. "It just went down from a thousand. You want to try for two-fifty?"

"Five hundred's fine," Herbie said contritely. "Gimme the pitch."

Stone handed him a sheet of paper. "The pitch is, you show up at this address at eight o'clock this evening. Can you pick a lock?"

"What kind of lock?"

"The street door of a town house with several apartments."

"No problem."

"If you can't pick the lock, you'll have to get somebody to buzz you in, or wait for somebody to leave the building so you can get in. If there's an elevator, take it to the top floor; if not, walk up the stairs."

"Carrying what?"

"At least two cameras, one wide lens, say a thirty-five-millimeter, one medium telephoto, a hundred-, a hundred-thirty-five-millimeter, in that range. Fast color negative film, no flash. This is strictly existing light. When you get to the top floor, get yourself onto the roof. The sixth-floor apartment has a skylight. There'll be a man and a woman in the apartment around nine o'clock. I want explicit photographs of whatever they do to each other. Is that clear?"

"Clear as gin."

"Then get out of there and process the film. Do it yourself; no labs. Got it?"

"Got it. Don't worry, I got all the equipment. Who are the people?"

"I don't know, and you don't want to. I want the negatives and two sets of eight-by-ten prints on my desk, here, no later than ten o'clock to-morrow morning."

"I got it," Herbie said. "I want to be paid now."

"Forget it. Five hundred, cash on delivery. If you do a clean job, no problems, and I like your work, I'll give you a thousand. Tell me right now if there's anything about this you can't handle; you get only one shot at it."

"I can handle it all, clean, no problems," Herbie said.

Stone gave him his cell phone number. "Call me when you're out of the building safely. Don't write the number down, memorize it."

"Got it," Herbie said.

"Then get this, Herbie: You screw up, and I never heard of you. Don't call me from a police station and ask me to make bail for you, understand?"

"I got it."

"You get yourself busted, you'll have to sit in jail until your uncle Bob gets back from the Virgin Islands."

"Yeah, yeah, yeah, I get the picture," Herbie said, picking up one of Stone's cards from a tray on his desk.

"Put that back," Stone said. "You and I have never met and have no connection whatever."

"Jesus, you're a hardass," Herbie said, returning the card.

"Now you're getting the picture," Stone replied. "But just in case you didn't, I'll spell it out for you: You get caught, you're looking at a Peeping Tom charge, and maybe attempted burglary, at the very least, and at worst, a blackmail rap. You could do time, and you'll do it with no weekly visits and freshly baked cookies from me. In short: Fuck up and you're on your own."

Herbie held up his hands defensively. "I told you, I got it. I'm a pro. I know the risks, and I'll take whatever, if things go wrong."

"If you're not back here with the goods at ten tomorrow morning, I'll know things went wrong, and I'll be joining your uncle Bob in Saint Thomas for a week or two. He'll testify that I was with him the whole time."

27

"You think Uncle Bobby would do that to me?"

"He's already told me he would. He doesn't like fuckups, either."

Nodding furiously, Herbie got up and fled the premises.

Stone hoped to God he'd made an impression on the kid.

He buzzed for Joan.

"Yes, Stone?"

"Book me a table for two at Café des Artistes at eight-thirty, please."

"Sure, and I promise not to tell Elaine."

"You'd better not. If I'm dead, you're out of a job."

"You have a point."

"And if a woman named Carpenter calls, give her my cell phone number. I don't want to miss her call."

"Somebody new, Stone?"

"Somebody old, but not all that old."

5

Carpenter showed up at Stone's house exactly on time, followed by a uniformed chauffeur carrying two large suitcases.

"I'm accepting your invitation," she said, kissing Stone lightly on the lips.

"And you're very welcome," Stone said. "Put the cases in the elevator," he said to the chauffeur. "I'll do the rest."

They rode up to his bedroom together, and he showed her where to put her clothes. "Make it quick," he said. "Our dinner table is in half an hour." He looked at his watch: Herbie Fisher should be in the building by now.

Stone employed a service that provided drivers, and his usual man had his Mercedes E55 waiting at the curb when they came out of the house.

"Very nice," Carpenter said, settling into the backseat beside Stone.

"And armored, too," Stone said. "Just in case anybody intends to do you harm."

"You're kidding."

"No. When I went car shopping a while back, they were wheeling it into the showroom. Some mob guy had ordered it and had got himself popped the day before it arrived."

"Bad timing."

"Good for me, though. I was being shot at, at the time, and I bought it from the widow at a nice discount. The armor is only good for small arms — no land mines or rockets."

"You get a lot of land mines and rockets on the streets of New York?" she asked.

"Not as many as we used to. Giuliani discouraged that sort of behavior, and Bloomberg seems to be following his lead."

They arrived at 1 West Sixty-seventh Street on time for their table at Café des Artistes, and they were seated immediately. Stone ordered two *champagnes fraise des bois.*

"What's that?" Carpenter asked.

"A glass of champagne with a dose of wild strawberry liqueur."

The drinks arrived. "I like the murals," Carpenter said, looking around at paintings of nude nymphs greeting conquistadores.

"They're a big reason this is one of my favorite restaurants," Stone said. "Notice that, while they have different faces, the nymphs all seem to have the same body. I think the artist, Howard Chandler Christy, must have had a favorite model."

"I hope we aren't here entirely for the nudes," Carpenter said.

"Fear not, the food is excellent." He glanced at his watch. Herbie should be in position on the roof by now.

Stone ordered them the charcuterie and the bourride, a seafood stew in a thick, garlicky sauce.

"Mmmmm," Carpenter said, tasting it. "Good thing we're both having this, what with all the garlic."

"Felicity," Stone said. "No kidding?"

"No kidding. It was my grandmother's name."

"And what is your last name?"

"I'm not sure I know you well enough to tell you," she said.

"After last night, I should think you'd know me well enough to tell me *anything*," Stone said.

She laughed. "All right, it's Devonshire."

"Like the county?"

"Exactly."

"Felicity Devonshire. Sounds like an actress on *Masterpiece Theatre*."

"What's *Masterpiece Theatre*?"

"It's a program on our Public Broadcasting System that features British television plays."

Stone checked his watch again: nine-thirty. Herbie should be calling any second.

"Why do you keep looking at your watch?" Carpenter asked.

"Sorry, something's going on tonight, and I should get a call saying it went well."

"Sounds like you're in my business."

"Not exactly," Stone said. "Though we probably use some of the same techniques."

"What's this evening's technique?"

"Candid photography," he replied.

"Keyhole stuff? You're joking."

"All's fair in love and divorce."

"I thought we British had a corner on that market, except for the French."

"Nope. New York is not a no-fault state."

"What's no-fault? Sounds like car insurance."

"It means the divorce is legally considered to be neither party's fault. Lots of states have that, but not New York. In New York one needs grounds for divorce — cruelty or, especially, adultery. Sometimes my clients ask me to substantiate grounds. In this particular case, the evidence is more important than the divorce itself, since the husband signed a prenuptial agreement stating that, if he fooled around, he'd get none of his wife's very considerable fortune."

"Poor bloke."

"I may have asked you this before, but why have you never married?" he asked.

"The job," she said. "My firm frowns on marriages, unless they're intramural. Marrying outside the profession almost guarantees divorce, often an ugly one, and the firm doesn't like that sort of publicity."

"None of the gentlemen of your trade ever appealed to you?"

"Oh, there was a time," she said. "A couple of years ago one of my colleagues and I got very serious, but not as serious as I thought. When he was offered a posting abroad, he accepted with alacrity, much to my annoyance. I broke it off immediately. He made the wrong choice."

"Maybe it wasn't so wrong after all, if he could leave you so readily."

"I entirely agree," she said, "and I got over it. You're my first, ah, liaison since then, which is why I was so eager to get you into bed last night. I hope I didn't put you off with my assertiveness."

"Did I seem put off?"

She laughed. "No, I don't think you did. You were . . . very interesting."

"And what, exactly, does that mean?"

"It means exactly that. Don't worry, it's a very considerable compliment."

They finished their main course and had dessert. When they were served coffee, Stone had entirely forgotten about Herbie Fisher. Then his cell phone vibrated. He looked at his watch: just after eleven o'clock. "Do you mind?" he asked, holding up the phone.

"Go ahead," she said.

Stone opened the phone. "Yes?"

"It wasn't my fault!" Herbie said, sounding very agitated.

"What?"

"The goddamned skylight must have been old or something."

"What the hell happened?" Stone demanded, trying to keep his voice down.

"It collapsed," Herbie said. "I fell right on top of both of them."

"You fell into . . ." Stone stopped and looked around. "Where are you?"

"It's not my fault the guy's dead," Herbie said.

"He's *what?*"

"You've got to come down here," Herbie said.

"Down where?"

"I'm being arraigned in night court."

"Listen to me very carefully," Stone said. "Don't say a word to anybody — not to a cop, not to an ADA, not to *anybody*. Do you understand?"

"Sure, I understand. Do you think I'm stupid?"

"I'll be there inside of an hour, and you keep your mouth shut," Stone said. He snapped the phone shut.

"Somebody get a thumb in his eye looking through a keyhole?" Carpenter asked.

"Something like that," Stone said, waving for the check.

"You don't look so good," Carpenter said.

"I'm not so good," Stone said, feeling as if he might toss his dinner back onto the table. "This is very, very bad."

He signed the check, grabbed Carpenter, and headed for the door.

"Where are we going?" Carpenter asked.

"I'm going to night court; you're going home."

"Oh, no I'm not. I want to see night court."

Stone hustled her into the car. "This may take a while," he said.

"I've got all night," she replied.

"This is very, very bad," Stone said, half to himself, as the car drove away.

6

Stone sat in one of the little rooms where attorneys met with their clients. Carpenter was upstairs in the big courtroom, taking in the American way of justice.

The opposite door to the cubicle opened, and Herbie Fisher walked in. He looked terrible — no belt or shoelaces, his hair mussed, and an expression of terror on his skinny face. He sat down on the stool opposite Stone and grasped the chain-link partition between them.

"You gotta get me out of here," he said, tears in his eyes.

"Take it easy, Herbie," Stone said. "Nobody's going to kill you."

"You haven't seen the guys I'm sharing a cell with," Herbie replied. "Now you gotta get me out of here."

"Herbie, do you remember the little chat we had yesterday?" Stone asked. "The one where I told you that if you fucked up, you were on your own?"

"It wasn't my fault!" Herbie cried.

"Keep your voice down. Now I want you to tell me exactly what happened."

"Get me out of here first," Herbie said. "Then I'll tell you."

"Herbie, unless you tell me what happened and tell me right now, I'm going to walk out of here and let you rot in jail."

"You can't do that! You gotta get me out! I can't be in jail."

"Herbie, listen to me very carefully," Stone said. "Take a few deep breaths and calm down."

Herbie sucked air.

"I'll tell you what's going to happen."

Herbie appeared to be a little calmer.

"Sometime tonight, you're going to be arraigned in night court. The charges could include manslaughter or negligent homicide, breaking and entering, and attempted burglary. Do you understand?"

"But I didn't kill anybody!" Herbie cried. "You gotta get me out of here!"

"Shut up and listen. At the arraignment, a lawyer will represent you, and you'll plead not guilty to all charges. Then bail will be set, and you'll get out. You'll be having breakfast at home."

"You're going to represent me?" Herbie asked plaintively.

"No, another lawyer will. You are not to mention my name to him or anyone else. Do you understand?"

"Yeah."

"Now I want you to tell me exactly what happened tonight. Start when you entered the building."

Herbie took a couple more breaths. "The downstairs door was open — like, ajar, you know? All I had to do was push it open."

"Good, that helps with the breaking-and-entering charge."

"Then I took the elevator to the sixth floor, like you said, and I found a door to the roof. When I went out onto the roof, it locked behind me and that scared me, because I was stuck up there. I was going to have to shinny down a drainpipe or something."

"Okay, you got onto the roof. Then what happened?"

"The apartment under the skylight was dark for a few minutes, then, a little before nine, a light came on, and I could see inside."

"What did you see?"

"A girl was in the room and she was setting up one of those portable massage tables, you know?"

"I know. Go on."

"Well, she set everything up, and she seemed to be real careful about everything in the room. She was turning lights on and off, until she got them the way she wanted them. Then she spread out sheets and stuff on the table."

"Okay, go on."

"Then, a little after nine, this guy arrived, and he took off his clothes. They both did, as a matter of fact."

"Did they kiss or embrace?"

38

"Just a peck on the cheek and a pat on the ass."

"Did you photograph that?"

"No, not yet. I was getting my gear ready."

Stone resisted the temptation to yell at him. "Go on, what happened next?"

"Then the guy got on the table, facedown, so I figured it wouldn't do any good to shoot him, if I couldn't see his face."

"So you still didn't take any photographs?"

"No, not yet. So, anyway, the girl was rubbing him all over, and he was kind of squirming. Then he turned over on his back and I could see his face."

"So you started photographing him?"

"No, not yet."

"Herbie, did you take any photographs at all?"

"Sure, yeah, I did."

"When?"

"I'm coming to that. Anyway, she starts to work on his thing, you know, and he's writhing around, but my angle wasn't so good, so I crawled out onto the skylight so I could get a better shot. It looked strong enough to hold me."

"So, when you got a better angle, did you start shooting?"

"Yeah. I took a couple of wide shots with the thirty-five-millimeter lens, then I heard — no, I guess I *felt* — this creaking under me, you know?"

"Go on, Herbie."

"So I stopped shooting and started thinking about getting off that skylight."

"You stopped shooting?"

"Well, yeah, the skylight was sounding like it was going to break, so I had to get off it."

"Did you get off it?"

"Not exactly."

"What do you mean, not exactly?"

"I was kind of backing up, and the skylight creaked again, and the girl looked up, right at me."

"Did you photograph her face?"

"I'm not sure. It all started happening very fast," Herbie said.

"Then what happened?"

"The guy was just lying there, like he was done and had fallen asleep, the way you do, you know? And the girl started backing away from the table."

"Yes, then what happened?"

"Then the skylight caved in and I started falling into the room."

"Then what?"

"I don't remember."

"What do you mean, you don't remember?"

"Well, I must have been out for a little while, and when I came to, I was lying on top of this guy, and he was dead."

"Wait a minute," Stone said. "How do you know he was dead?"

"Because he was just kind of staring up with these dead eyes. He wasn't blinking or anything."

"What did you do then?"

"Well, I got to my feet and brushed glass and stuff off me and kind of walked around to see if anything was broken. Anything of mine, I mean."

"But you were all right?"

"Yeah, but the guy was dead. I think I might have broken his leg, though."

"When you fell on him?"

"Yeah. I fell on his legs."

"That shouldn't have killed him."

"That's what I've been trying to tell you. I didn't kill the guy; I couldn't have."

"What happened then?"

"I heard all these guys coming," Herbie said. "It sounded like a lot of them coming up the stairs."

"They didn't use the elevator?"

"No."

"What happened next?"

"I figured it was the cops, so I looked around for someplace to hide my camera, and I saw this wood box by the fireplace. So I went over and opened it and took out a log, and I put my camera inside and put the log back on top of it. I was looking for another way out of the room when the door opened and all these guys came in."

"Were they cops?"

"I guess so."

"Were they in uniform?"

"No. They looked like detectives, in plain clothes."

"And what did they do?"

"A couple of them grabbed me and threw me up against the wall, and a couple more went over to see about the naked guy on the table. I heard one of them say his leg was broken, and another one said he was dead."

"And then what happened?"

"Then they left."

"They left? You mean they left the apartment and left you alone there?"

"Yeah. One of them said, 'You stay put.' So I did."

"And then what?"

"I tried to find another way out of the apartment, except by the door, but there wasn't one. So I sat down on a chair and looked at the dead guy for a minute. Then the cops arrived. This time they had uniforms. And guns. And they arrested me and took me to a police station, where they put me in a van with some really badass guys and brought me here."

"So the detectives just walked out, and a few minutes later the cops came?"

"Yeah, except I'm not so sure they were detectives."

"What do you mean?"

"Well, when they were talking to each other, they had funny accents."

"What kind of accents?"

"The kind you hear on PBS, on that show *Mystery.*"

"You mean English accents?"

"Yeah, like that. Like English cops."

Stone was stumped. "Now listen: I'm going to get you a lawyer and arrange bail. If your lawyer asks about your relationship with me, you tell him I'm a friend of your uncle Bob, who's out of town, and when you thought you needed a lawyer, you called me. Got that?"

"Yeah."

"And you say nothing about our meeting yesterday. If he wants to know what you were doing on that roof, tell him you're a freelance photographer, and you were trying to take a picture you could sell to the tabloids. Nobody hired you. Got that?"

"Yeah."

"When bail is set and you get out, go home and get some sleep. I'm going to be looking into this, and I'll call you when I find out something."

"Okay."

"Herbie, have you ever been arrested?"

"No, not until tonight."

"Never? Drunk driving? Burglary? Disturbing the peace? Anything? They'll find out if you have been, and it will make a difference."

"Never. I'm clean."

"Do you have a job?"

"Yeah, I run a one-hour photo processing machine at a drugstore in Brooklyn."

"How old are you?"

"Twenty-two."

"Do you live with anybody?"

"I got a little place near the drugstore."

"Tell all this to your lawyer."

"What's his name?"

"I haven't picked him out yet. I'm going to go and do that now."

"When will I get out of here?"

"When they call your case. It could be two or three hours, there's no way to tell right now. Your lawyer may be able to find out." Stone pressed the button to call the guard. "Now go back to your cell and keep your mouth shut. Don't talk to anybody about why you're here, and don't form any friendships with your cellmates. Any one of them will sell you out for a pack of cigarettes."

"Okay."

The guard came and took Herbie away, and Stone went upstairs to the courtroom.

7

Stone walked into the courtroom and looked around. He saw Carpenter sitting in the second row, apparently rapt, and he kept looking until he found his man, waiting with a prisoner in an orange jumpsuit who was about to be arraigned.

Tony Levy was short, stocky, and crafty. He earned his living as a lawyer by hanging around the courts, picking up cases on the fly. Stone had met him half a dozen times in the courthouse, and he was perfect for tonight's purpose. He reached across the railing and tapped Levy on the shoulder.

"Hey, Stone," Levy said, smiling and offering his hand. "I haven't seen you down here for a while."

"I try to stay uptown," Stone said. "I've got a case for you. Can you talk?"

Levy turned back to his client, who was sporting a full set of restraints. "Don't go any-where for a minute," he said, then he waved Stone to the side of the courtroom and led him through a door into a small conference room. "What's up?" he asked.

"Nephew of a friend of mine — you know Bob Cantor?"

"Ex-cop? Yeah, I had him on the witness stand a few times."

"His nephew, name of Herbert Fisher, is downstairs awaiting arraignment on charges of man two, B and E, and attempted burglary."

"Nice," Levy said.

"He was apparently taking some bedroom shots for a divorce case, and he fell through a skylight and onto a guy who was getting a very thorough massage from a young lady."

"Jesus!"

"Right. Trouble is, when Herbie came to, the guy was dead."

"And that's the man two?"

"Right, and it sounds wrong because Herbie fell on his legs. The cops came and took him away. I can work on reducing the charges later, but right now I just want him bailed. I'll call Irving Newman and arrange that, so his man in the court will be ready for you."

"Okay."

"Herbie is twenty-two, no priors, has a job and an apartment. I figure twenty-five grand for bail, but I'll be prepared for more, if necessary."

"Okay, seems straightforward. A grand will buy me."

"I'll send you cash by messenger tomorrow," Stone said. "I don't want my name on any paper connected with this. In fact, I don't want to be associated with it in any way. Understand?"

"I read you loud and clear, Stone. I guess the

46

partners at Woodman and Weld would frown on Herbie's sort of activity."

"They like me to stay out of night court, unless it's their client," Stone replied. "So I'm getting out of here now. Call me on my cell if there are any problems you can't deal with. The kid is scared silly, and he needs to sleep in his bed tonight."

"I'll do everything but tuck him in," Levy said.

Stone walked to where Carpenter was sitting, tapped her on the shoulder, and beckoned her to follow.

"Enjoy yourself?" he asked when they were outside the courtroom in the corridor.

"It's fascinating," she said. "When does your case come up?"

"It's not my case. I'm just doing a favor for a friend. Another lawyer will represent the guy." He dug out his cell phone and dialed a number. "Excuse me for a minute," he said.

"Hello?" The voice didn't sound sleepy. Irving Newman, Stone's favorite bail bondsman, was accustomed to being awakened in the night.

"Irving, it's Stone Barrington."

"Stone, you okay? What'd they charge you with?"

"Thanks, Irving, I'm fine, and it's not me," Stone said, chuckling. "I'm down at night court. You know Bob Cantor?"

"Ex-cop?"

"Yeah. His nephew, one Herbert Fisher, is

coming up tonight on man two, B and E, and attempted burglary. I figure bail will be twenty-five, but let's be ready with more, just in case."

"I'll call my guy in court," Irving said. "You putting up your house?" This was Irving's idea of a joke.

"Yeah, sure, Irving. Call my secretary in the morning, and she'll messenger you twenty-five hundred in cash. We never talked, okay?"

"Of course not. Who the hell is this, anyway?" Irving hung up.

Stone closed his phone and tucked it away. He took Carpenter's arm and led her from the courthouse to his waiting car.

"So, what's this all about, and why wouldn't you tell me on the way down?" Carpenter asked.

"It's strictly need-to-know," Stone said. "You know about that in your trade, right?"

"Well, I already know your client's name and the charges, don't I? And Irving is arranging bail."

"Herbie is not my client. I'm just doing a favor for a friend."

"Somehow, I think the favor extends back to earlier in the evening," Carpenter said. "You were looking at your watch all night, and you were clearly expecting that phone call, but not what you heard."

Stone pointed at the driver and put a finger to his lips.

"All right," she said. "When we get home. I'm not going to bed with you until I know all."

Carpenter stood at the foot of the bed, her robe dangling invitingly open, revealing a slim, well-buffed body. "So tell me the whole story."

Stone stared, and he was very ready for her. "Oh, come to bed," he groaned.

She tied the robe firmly. "Not until I hear it."

"This is blackmail," Stone said.

"No, it's extortion. As a lawyer, you should know the difference."

"Oh, all right," Stone said. "I arranged for a photographer to take dirty pictures of a married man and an unmarried lady in compromising positions. The photographer got too enthusiastic and fell through a skylight onto the man, who somehow died. The cops came and took the photographer away."

Carpenter looked very interested. "Who was the dead man?"

"You don't need to know that."

"It'll be in the papers tomorrow, Stone."

"Oh, all right. It was a compatriot of yours, one Lawrence Fortescue, married to a sometime client of mine."

Her face became expressionless. "How dead is he?"

"All the way," Stone replied. "Herbie couldn't understand it, because he fell on the guy's legs. No reason for him to be dead. Something else funny, a bunch of apparent cops in plain clothes showed up in no time at all, and at least one of them had a British accent, according to Herbie, who learned everything he knows about British accents watching Brit cop shows on TV."

"What happened to the woman involved?"

"Funny, I don't know," Stone said. "Herbie was out for a short time. She must have departed the premises, which, given the circumstances, was a wise move."

"I need to use the phone in the next room," Carpenter said. "And don't you dare listen in."

"Aren't you coming to bed?"

"In a minute," she replied, opening the door. "Don't fall asleep on me."

Stone watched the light on the phone come on and resisted the temptation to listen in. He was still watching the light ten minutes later, when he fell asleep.

8

A full bladder woke Stone early in the morning, and he had relieved himself and crawled back into bed before he realized he was alone. He raised his head from the pillow. "Carpenter?" he called. No answer.

Stone struggled from the bed and looked in the bathroom, then in his study. She was gone, but her bags were still there. He stumbled back to bed, but as he lay there, his unconscious began to reveal what it had come up with during the night. After a few minutes of communing with his psyche, Stone sat up in bed and looked at the clock. Ten past nine, and he had slept like — excuse the expression — a stone.

He picked up the phone and called Dino at his office.

"Bacchetti," Dino snapped into the phone.

"It's Stone."

"Don't say another word. Meet me at Clarke's for lunch." He hung up.

"What the hell?" Stone said aloud. He was wide awake now, and he got into a shower and shaved, dressed, and went down to his lower-level office. He could hear Joan Robertson's computer keyboard clicking away as he came into his office from the rear door. The clicking stopped.

"I'm in," Stone called out.

Joan appeared in the doorway. "Herbie Fisher has called three times in the past twenty minutes," she said, placing a call slip on his desk.

Stone groaned. "Get him for me. And I'm having lunch with Dino, so don't book me for anything before three."

Joan left, the light on Stone's phone went on, and she buzzed him.

Stone picked up the phone. "Shut up, Herbie," he said, before the kid could say anything.

"What have you gotten me into?" Herbie yelled.

"I told you to shut up, and if you don't do it right now, I'll hang up, and you can handle your own legal difficulties."

Herbie shut up.

"Now listen to me very carefully, because this is the last time you and I are going to speak, on the phone or in person. Do you understand?"

"Yeah," Herbie replied, sounding contrite.

"I'm going to work on getting the charges against you reduced —"

"*Reduced?* I'll still have to go to jail."

"Shut up, Herbie."

"Sorry."

"I'm going to work on getting the charges against you reduced to something that will get you probation instead of time."

"But I'll still have a record," Herbie protested.

"Shut up, Herbie."

"Sorry."

"You don't have any prior arrests or convictions, and you're gainfully employed, so we can probably get you unsupervised probation, so you won't have to report in every week."

"That would be nice."

"It would be *very* fucking nice, seeing that the alternative is probably five to seven for the manslaughter charge."

"When do I get paid?" Herbie asked.

"PAID!!!!????" Stone screamed down the phone. *"Paid for what?"*

"Well, I did the job, sort of," Herbie said.

"Yeah? Then where are the photographs of two people doing disgusting things to each other?"

"Well, my camera is still in the apartment," Herbie pointed out. "I could go back and —"

"Don't you go anywhere near that apartment!" Stone shouted.

"Could you stop yelling at me, please?" Herbie said, sounding wounded. "It's not very polite. And could I point out that my camera is brand-new, and the warranty is registered in my name, and if the cops find it, they can trace it back to me?"

Stone was momentarily taken aback by the appearance of a rational thought from Herbie, but not for long. "They've already arrested you for being in the apartment. What difference does it

53

make if they trace the camera back to you?"

"Oh," Herbie said. "Right."

"Leave the camera to me," Stone said. "Where do you work?"

"At Walgreens, in Brooklyn." Herbie gave him the address and phone number of the drugstore.

"Listen," Stone said. "If I can get that camera back, and if the pictures are worth anything, and if you never, ever call me again for any reason, then you'll get paid."

"I guess that's fair," Herbie said, seeming to sense it was the best deal he was going to get.

"Did Tony Levy give you his card?"

"Who?"

"The lawyer who got you bailed out last night."

"Oh, him. Yeah."

"If you have any further problems with the police, call Levy, not me. He'll deal with the situation."

"Okay."

"How much was your bail?"

"Two hundred and fifty thousand dollars."

"*What?*"

"That's what the judge said."

"Oh, shit," Stone muttered. "If you run, Herbie, I'll hunt you down and deal with you myself. You hear me?"

"I hear you."

"Did Levy explain the conditions of your bail?"

"Well, yeah."

"See that you follow those conditions to the letter."

"All right."

"Now, you sit tight and wait to hear about the charges. When I hear something, I'll call Levy, and he'll call you."

"I got it."

"And you understand never to call me again?"

"Right. And since I won't be talking to you anymore, Stone, I'd just like to say what a pleasure it's been working with you, and —"

Stone slammed down the phone, swearing. He buzzed Joan.

"Yes, boss?"

"Joan, please dip into the cash in the safe. Hand-deliver twenty-five thousand dollars to Irving Newman and a thousand to Tony Levy. Both addresses are in our book."

"Right now?"

"Take a long lunch and do it then. And make them count it, and get a receipt from both."

"Will do, but that will pretty much clean us out of cash."

"Okay." Stone hung up and listened to his stomach growl. He hadn't had any breakfast, and it was too early for lunch. He rested his forehead on the cool desktop and tried to empty his mind of everything.

Then Joan buzzed him. "Bill Eggers on line one," she said.

Stone groaned again and picked up the phone.

55

9

Eggers was not happy. "Have you seen this morning's *Daily News*?"

"No."

"Well, everybody else on the planet has. I don't know how you missed it."

"Bill . . ."

"Your guy killed Larry, you know."

"Bill . . ."

"Elena wanted him caught cold, but not *that* cold."

"Bill . . ."

"Explain to me how this could have occurred."

"Accidents happen?" Stone said hopefully.

"Accident? This was no accident! This was pure, unadulterated stupidity and ineptitude. Do you know that Elena Marks, along with her trust, is one of the largest and most profitable clients this firm has? And now I have to go and explain . . ."

Stone pressed the hold button and buzzed Joan.

"Yes, boss?"

"Please go and get me a copy of the *Daily News*, right now."

"Be back in a jiffy."

Stone pressed the line button again.

". . . and to every partner in the firm, too. You and I have a meeting with Elena Marks at three o'clock this afternoon at her apartment, and you'd better be ready to pull this out of the fire. And in the meantime, if the press gets wind of your association with this fiasco, you're going to be looking for a new career or a country that will let you practice law. And when you show up at Elena's, you'd better not forget those photographs!"

"Bill . . ." But Eggers had already hung up.

Stone buzzed Joan. "Please get me Tony Levy — try his cell." He sat staring at the wall, trying to figure out what to do.

"Levy's on one," Joan said.

Stone picked up the phone. "You bailed out Herbie for two hundred and fifty grand?" he said.

"Take it easy, Stone," Levy said soothingly.

"Easy? Twenty-five grand is easy. A quarter of a million is very, very hard."

"Judge Simpson got sick in court, and Judge Kaplan came in and subbed for him. You know what she's like: I was lucky to get Herbie bail at all. We're lucky she didn't order him executed."

"Kaplan came in?" Stone said. Tony was right. Kaplan wasn't just a hanging judge; she was a draw-'em-and-quarter-'em judge. "Did you explain to Herbie how important it is for him to adhere to the terms of his bail?"

"Don't worry, I scared the shit out of him," Levy said. "He's not going to run."

"If he does, I'm going to let you pick up half the bail," Stone said.

"In your fucking dreams," Levy replied evenly. "I did the best I could for him. You and Johnnie Cochran together couldn't have done better with Kaplan. Where's my money?"

"It'll be there at lunchtime," Stone said.

Joan laid a fresh copy of the *News* on Stone's desk.

"I see you've been talking to the press," Stone said, flipping from the page-one lead to the rest of the story inside.

"You don't see your name anywhere, do you?" Levy asked. "Let me have my little moment in the sun, Stone. It's all a little shyster like me can hope for. After all, we can't all do dirty work for Woodman and Weld."

"This has nothing to do with the firm," Stone said. "I told you, I was doing a favor for Bob Cantor."

"Yeah, sure, Stone. And I'll be representing the Bush girls the next time they get busted for ordering cosmopolitans at the college cafeteria. Don't worry, buddy, I'm not going to embarrass you or blackmail you. But you'd better have some more work for me soon, or I might weaken." He hung up, laughing maniacally.

Stone walked into P. J. Clarke's, waded through the lunchtime bar crowd, and found

Dino at a good table in the back room. "Good day, Lieutenant," Stone said.

"Sit down," Dino replied, "and shut up."

"What is it with you today?" Stone asked. "Why can't I talk anymore?"

"Because I already know everything you're going to say," Dino replied, sinking half a draft beer and waving at the waiter. "Two bacon cheeseburgers, medium, and two bowls of chili," he said, "and bring Clarence Darrow, here, a beer." The waiter vanished.

"About last night . . ." Stone began.

"I already know about last night," Dino said. "Everybody who can read at the sixth-grade level knows about it." He tapped his copy of the *News*, resting on the table.

"I do have a few questions," Stone said.

"And I'll answer them for you. One: The girl got away from my people across the roof. She apparently has the agility of a cat burglar, which is more than I can say for your boy, Herbie. Two: The four suits who got there first work for a foreign intelligence service, and their country of origin shall remain nameless. Three: They and the cops got there so fast because they were waiting on the landing below, laying for one or both of the people in the apartment. Four: No, I don't know where the photographs are that Herbie took. Any other questions?"

Stone shook his head. "Thank God Herbie kept my name out of it."

"Yeah? What makes you think that? He was

spilling his guts in the patrol car, up the front steps of the precinct, and into an interview room faster than anybody could write it down, and you were the star of his story." Dino swept a hand expressively across the table, nearly spilling his beer. "Above-the-title billing!"

The waiter set their food before them.

"I'm going to throw up," Stone said.

"Well, do it in your hat, pal. I'm eating, here."

"I can't eat this," Stone said, beginning to eat the chili.

"Don't worry, the detective knows we're friends; he'll keep it to himself, and I've already scrubbed the interview tape clean."

"Thank you, Dino."

"Is that all you can say? You ought to be offering me Carpenter's sweet body on a platter."

"Carpenter's in this, somehow," Stone said. "I have a feeling she knows the country of origin of the gentlemen present last night. When I told her what happened, she started making phone calls, and when I woke up, she hadn't slept in the bed."

"Poor you."

"I don't think Herbie's fall killed Larry Fortescue," Stone said.

"Well, neither do I," Dino replied, "but we'll probably never know."

"Why not? The medical examiner will figure it out."

"The ME was poised over the corpse this morning, scalpel raised, when two guys showed up with a federal court order and took the body away in a van."

"Holy shit."

"My sentiments, more or less."

"This whole business is completely out of control," Stone said.

"Well, completely out of *our* control," Dino agreed. "But *somebody* must know what's going on. Certainly, nobody in the NYPD does."

Stone finished his chili. "I do know something you don't," Stone said.

"What?"

"I know where the photographs are."

"I want them now," Dino said, pushing away from the table.

"Just a minute," Stone said. "You get one set of prints, I get the negatives and all the others."

"Deal," Dino said, standing up.

"And I need them processed by two-thirty, with nobody the wiser. You know somebody who can do that?"

"You bet your ass," Dino said. "Let's get out of here."

Stone threw some money on the table, took a quick swig of his beer, grabbed his burger, and ran after Dino.

10

Stone dove into the cab behind Dino, who sat staring at him.

"You going to tell the driver where to go?" Dino asked.

Stone gave him the address of the building with the skylight, then he took a huge bite of his burger.

"The camera is still in the building?" Dino asked.

"If we're lucky," Stone replied through the cheeseburger.

"Nobody from the precinct has been there today," Dino said. "I checked. The Feds were in on this. I hope to God they haven't turned it over."

"Me too," Stone replied.

The cab screeched to a halt in front of the building. Dino got out.

"Pay the guy," he called over his shoulder.

Stone paid the cabbie and followed along, still trying to eat his bacon cheeseburger.

Dino was on the stoop, ringing doorbells. The super appeared, chewing his own lunch.

"What d'ya want?" he said, in heavily accented English.

Dino showed him his badge. "Is the sixth-floor apartment locked?" he asked.

"You better believe," the man said. "FBI guy gave me instructions."

"Give me the key," Dino said.

"I'm not fucking with FBI," the man replied, swallowing food.

"Give me the key now, or I'll arrest you for obstruction of justice and send you back to whatever godforsaken country you came from."

The man dug into a pocket and gave Dino a key. "Don't tell nobody," he said, then went back into his apartment.

They took the elevator to the sixth floor. "There's the door to the roof," Dino said, as they got off. He opened the apartment door.

It was dark inside, and Stone found a light switch that turned on a lamp in a corner. The massage table, two of its legs broken, lay on its side in the middle of the floor.

"There's why it's dark," Dino said, pointing upward. The broken skylight had been replaced with sheets of plywood. "Cozy little pad," Dino said.

"Looks like it was rented furnished," Stone observed. "Nobody would buy those pictures, except a landlord."

"Okay, enough of the art lecture," Dino said. "Where's the film?"

Stone went to the fireplace and opened the wood box next to it. It was half full of logs made of compressed sawdust. He lifted one and extracted a 35mm camera with a zoom lens attached. Stone rewound the film, popped the case, and put the film cartridge in his pocket. He removed the lens from the camera and put the lens in one inside pocket of his raincoat and the camera body in the other. "Let's get out of here," he said.

"I want to see the roof," Dino said, striding toward the door. He opened the door and walked outside. Stone followed him. The door closed behind them.

Stone looked around. "I don't see how that girl got down from here," he said.

"Well, we'd better figure out how in a hurry," Dino said.

"How come?"

"Because the Feds will probably be here any minute, and you've closed the fucking door and locked us out."

Stone tried turning the knob. Nothing. "Shit," he said.

Dino peered over the edge of the roof. "There's a drainpipe," he said. "You go first. I want to see if it'll hold your weight."

Stone peered over the parapet. "I'm not shinnying down that," he said. "I'm wearing a good suit. You go down it, then take the elevator back up and open the door."

"You know, that's a terrific idea," Dino said. "Why should both of us have to shinny down the drainpipe?" He pulled out his gun and

64

pointed it at Stone. "Go down the drainpipe, or I'll shoot you."

Stone shook his head. "Go ahead and shoot me. It beats falling off a building."

They were standing there like that when the door opened, and the super stepped out. "The FBI just call," he said. "You guys got to get out or I get in trouble."

Dino put his gun away and stepped inside. "Lucky for you," he said. "I was going to shoot you."

"No, you weren't," Stone said, getting into the elevator.

"Oh, yes I was," Dino replied. "I wasn't about to shinny down that drainpipe."

"Neither was I," Stone pointed out.

"That's why I was going to shoot you."

Downstairs they got into another cab and got out in front of a photo shop on Third Avenue. Dino went inside and walked over to the one-hour processing machine, flashing his badge.

Stone handed him the film cartridge.

"I want this developed right now — two sets of five-by-seven prints, and don't you look at them," Dino said.

"Make it three sets," Stone said.

"Yes, sir," the kid behind the counter said. He took the film and went to work.

"How long is this going to take?" Stone asked.

The kid pointed at the one-hour sign. "An hour," he said.

"It better not," Dino said.

Ten minutes later, the kid was holding up a strip of film to the light. "There are only four frames exposed," he said.

"Stop looking at them and make the prints," Dino said.

Ten more minutes and they had the prints.

"Can I drop you?" Stone said, giving the cabbie Elena Marks's address.

"You betcha," Dino replied. "Gimme my prints."

Stone gave Dino a set, put a set in his raincoat pocket, along with the negatives, and looked at the third set.

"What a fucking mess," Dino said. "You couldn't nail anybody in a divorce with these. In this one, he's lying on his belly. In these three, he's got his arm over his face, and in all of them her head blocks his crotch. For all we can see, she might have been giving him a legit massage. Where'd this kid learn his photography, in juvenile hall?"

Stone looked at the fourth photograph. The woman was looking up at the skylight. It was the only shot that showed part of her face. She had long, dark hair and, from what he could see, was attractive. "Not bad," he said.

"Yeah," Dino agreed. "What you can see, anyway."

The cab stopped on Dino's corner, and he got out.

"What are you going to do with the photographs?" Stone asked through the window.

"I haven't decided yet."

"Don't give them to the Feds."

"I never give anything to the Feds without a court order and a gun at my head," Dino replied, walking away.

11

The cab took Stone to 1111 Fifth Avenue, near the Metropolitan Museum. Bill Eggers was waiting for him.

"Thank God you're on time," he said. "Now listen, when we get upstairs, I'll do the talking. You just keep your mouth shut and nod a lot."

"Whatever you say," Stone said, grateful that he would not have to explain the events of the night before.

The elevator opened directly into the foyer of Elena Marks's apartment. The foyer, Stone noted, was nearly as large as his bedroom. The floors were marble, and the walls were hung with good art. A flower arrangement the size of a big-screen TV rested on a Louis Quinze table. A man in a white jacket entered the foyer.

"Mr. Eggers? Mr. Barrington? Please follow me." He led them through a living room the size of a basketball court and into a library with a double-height ceiling. A spiral staircase in a corner led to the upper level. Every book in sight was leather-bound and matched several other books. Elena Marks was nowhere to be seen.

"Please have a seat," the butler said. "Mrs.

68

Fortescue will be with you shortly. May I get you some refreshment?"

"No, thank you," Eggers replied.

Stone wanted a beer; the cheeseburger still hadn't gone all the way down. "First time I ever heard her referred to as Mrs. Fortescue," he said.

"Well, she's a widow now, isn't she?" Eggers replied.

A section of the bookcases along one wall suddenly opened, and Elena Marks Fortescue entered the room. The bookcase/door closed silently behind her. She was a razor-thin woman with bright, blond hair, wearing a bright yellow, flowered dress, the sort of thing that would have been perfectly acceptable for a recent widow in, say, Palm Beach, Stone thought.

"Good afternoon, Elena," Eggers said smoothly. "Thank you for seeing us."

"Bill," she said, nodding. Then she turned a withering gaze on Stone. "Mr. Barrington," she said through clenched, beautifully capped teeth.

Stone tried smiling, but it didn't work. "Good afternoon, Ms. Mar . . . ah, Mrs. Fortescue."

She held her gaze a little longer, as if to punish him, before looking away.

Stone felt as if a hole had been burned through him.

"Sit," Elena said. "Speak," she said to Eggers. She appeared to be barely in control of her anger, but addressing them as dogs seemed to help.

"Elena," Eggers said plaintively, "please let me express my condolences, along with those of everyone at Woodman and Weld."

"Accepted," Elena said, her face like marble.

Stone realized that she had had so many Botox injections that she was probably incapable of any expression, short of baring her teeth.

"What happened," she said to Eggers, a command rather than a question.

"A terrible accident," Eggers replied. "Our investigation has determined that the skylight above the apartment had been fatally weakened by dry rot."

What investigation? Stone wondered. Nobody had asked him anything.

"And when Stone's operative put a little of his weight on it, in order to be able to photograph the scene below, it gave way."

"Who do we sue?" Elena asked.

That brought Eggers up short "Ah, well, I, ah . . . Stone? You want to answer that one?"

Stone, who had thought he was to keep his mouth shut, wasn't ready for the question. "Not really," he said, tossing the ball back to Eggers.

"Do you mean to tell me," Elena said, "that the people who are responsible for my husband's death should go unpunished?"

Stone found his voice. "Mrs. Fortescue," he said, "if I may be candid, you hired a man, through Bill and me, to climb onto the roof of a building and photograph your husband in compromising positions. The attorneys for the owner of the building would work hard to make a case that *you,* therefore, are responsible for your husband's death, and they might very well win with such a defense. Even if you won, the resulting publicity would be devastating to your reputation."

"Then perhaps I should sue you for hiring an incompetent," Elena said.

Eggers made a small choking noise.

"That would have the same result," Stone said. "At the moment, the story the press has is that a burglar or Peeping Tom fell through the skylight. It is being reported as nothing more than a freak accident, which, of course, it was. There has been no mention of the woman or the motives of the man who fell. To pursue this further would not react to the benefit of anyone involved."

Elena attempted to frown and failed. "What about your Peeping Tom? It seems to me that he might have a lawsuit against you, and eventually, me."

"You may rest assured that that will not happen," Eggers said.

Stone hoped he was right. The idea of Herbie Fisher suing had not occurred to him, and he hoped to God it hadn't occurred to Herbie.

"But *I'm* the injured party here," Elena cried, banging her bony fist against the arm of the sofa. "*Somebody* has to pay for that injury!"

Eggers turned white and said nothing.

"Mrs. Fortescue," Stone said, "may I be perfectly frank?"

"You'd fucking well better be," Elena snarled. Her marble skin had turned bright pink.

"These events, as unfortunate for everyone as they are, have inadvertently accomplished something that could not have been foreseen."

"And what is that?" Elena demanded.

"It's an ill wind that blows nobody good," Stone said, hoping that the cliché would find its mark.

It did not. "What the hell is that supposed to mean?" Elena cried, turning pinker.

"An act of God, for want of a better term, has rid you of a husband who was unfaithful to you, and whom you had already decided to be rid of, and it has done so in a way that avoids the inevitable, damaging publicity of divorcing him and enforcing your prenuptial agreement." Stone paused for effect. "Not to mention the very considerable expense of so doing."

There was a long silence, finally broken by Elena Marks Fortescue. "You have a point," she said. Then she got up and left the room the way she had entered it.

Eggers had been holding his breath, and he let it out in a rush.

Back on the street, looking for a cab, Eggers turned to Stone. "What about the photographs?" he asked.

Stone handed him a set, and Eggers looked at them briefly.

"And the negatives?" he asked.

Stone handed over an envelope containing the four frames. "You think we're out of the woods with Elena?" he asked.

"She didn't fire us, did she?" Eggers said cheerfully, waving down a cab and getting in. "Let's do lunch sometime." He drove away.

12

Stone felt lighter than air. This was all going to work out; everything had been taken care of. All he had to do now was to get something worked out with the DA's office about Herbie's charges — get them to drop the manslaughter charge, plead him down to a misdemeanor, and get him probation. It was a bright, cool day, and he felt like a walk.

He strolled down the west side of Fifth Avenue, occasionally glancing into the park, then farther downtown, turned left on East Fifty-seventh Street and walked to the Turnbull & Asser shop. He would treat himself.

He looked at the new sea island cotton swatches and ordered a dozen shirts. He didn't know what they cost; he didn't want to know. Joan would pay the bill when it arrived, and he had instructed her not to enlighten him; some things were best left unknown. He picked out a few ties and waited while they were wrapped; the shirts would take eight weeks, or so. Then he left the shop and turned down Park Avenue toward home in Turtle Bay.

In the upper Forties, as he turned to cross Park, a stretched Bentley glided to a momentary halt, then drove on, but not before Stone had seen, through the open rear window, Elena Marks, now clad in proper New York widow's weeds by Chanel, in earnest conversation with someone Stone knew. He pulled out his cell phone and speed-dialed Woodman & Weld and Bill Eggers.

"What is it, Stone?" Eggers asked, sounding rushed. It was a technique of his when he didn't want to talk to somebody.

"Bill, I was crossing Park Avenue a moment ago, when I saw Elena Marks in her car with Robert Teller, of Teller and Sparks."

"*What?*" Eggers cried.

"I kid you not."

"That buccaneer! That bastard! Poaching my clients!"

"I thought you'd want to know."

"What were they talking about?"

"Well, Bill, I couldn't hear them. I just saw them in that big Bentley of hers, talking."

"Well, I've already got our tax people working on something that might save her a few hundred grand. It's the kind of thing she likes."

"I'd tell her about it soon, Bill. Bye-bye." Stone punched off. He thought about calling T&A and canceling his shirt order, but he thought better of it.

Stone arrived home and went upstairs to leave his new ties, before returning to his office. As he approached his bedroom, he heard a snore. He pushed open the door and peered inside. Carpenter lay on her back, a breast exposed, sawing lightly away. He tiptoed across the room toward his dressing room, left the ties and tiptoed back into the bedroom. He was greeted by a wide-awake Carpenter, sitting up in bed, clutching a sheet to her bosom with one hand while using the other to point a small, semiautomatic pistol at him.

"You caught me hanging up neckties," he said, raising his hands in surrender.

"What are you doing here?" she asked, seeming confused.

"I live here," Stone explained. He pointed at the bed. "I sleep there. Is that my Walther you're pointing at me?"

"No, it's mine. My firm has issued them to everybody since the first James Bond novel."

"And why are you still pointing it at me?"

She lowered her hand. "Sorry," she said, dropping the sheet, to good effect, and running her fingers through her hair. "I didn't get any sleep last night."

"I remember," he said. "I was all curled up in bed, waiting anxiously for you. When I woke up, you were gone."

"Business," she said.

Stone sat down on the bed, removed the pistol from her hand, and set it on the night table. "Something to do with Herbie Fisher's big night?" he asked.

"Why do you ask?" she said warily.

"Well, as soon as I told you what happened, you were on the phone in the next room, and that's the last thing I remember."

"There was something I was supposed to ask you," she said, scratching her head.

"You don't seem quite awake yet."

"It's jet lag, I think."

"Why don't you go back to sleep. I'll wake you at dinnertime." He pushed her gently back onto the bed, pecked her lightly on each nipple, pulled the covers up and tucked her in.

"Mmmmm, thank you," she murmured, closing her eyes. She seemed instantly asleep.

Stone left her there and closed the door behind him. He was about to start downstairs when the bedroom door was flung open, and a very naked Carpenter stood there.

"The photographs!" she cried, pointing at Stone.

"What?"

"The photographs that Herbie Fisher took. Where are they?"

Stone walked her back into the bedroom and sat her on the bed. "Why do you want to know?"

"Business," she said. "Sort of."

"Those were some of your people who turned up at the flat after Herbie took his dive," Stone said.

"Maybe," she said warily.

"What were they doing there?"

"Stone, I need those photographs."

"Why?"

77

"They're important to something I'm working on."

"I don't understand," Stone said. "How could some bedroom divorce photographs be important to MI Five, or whatever number it is you work for?"

"I can't talk about that," she said.

"All right, then, I'll trade you."

"What do you mean, trade me? Isn't that a baseball term?"

"I'll trade the photographs for some information."

"What information?"

"I want to know how Larry Fortescue died."

"Your rabbit-brained photographer fell on him," Carpenter replied.

"Nah, that's not what killed him; Herbie fell on Larry's legs. He was already dead, wasn't he?"

"How would I know that?" she asked, looking out the window.

"Because somebody — somebody you're very likely associated with — arrived at the morgue this morning with a federal court order and took the corpse away."

"What makes you say that?"

"Okay," Stone said, standing up, "no photographs for you."

"Wait!"

Stone stopped.

"You can never tell anyone I told you this."

"Why would I want to do that?"

"Fortescue died from the application of some sort of poison to the base of his spine. We haven't figured out yet what it is."

"I'm going to need a letter to the DA from a credible authority, stating that Fortescue was already dead when Herbie tried to fly."

"I'll see what I can do," she said. "It may take a few days."

"As few as possible, please." Stone reached into his pocket and handed her the four photographs.

Carpenter looked at the first one, of Fortescue lying on his back, the woman hovering over him. "Oh, Lawrence," she murmured.

"Huh?" Stone said.

She looked at the other three photographs, then her mouth dropped open. "Jesus!" she said. She got up, found her handbag, took out a cell phone and dialed a number.

"It's Carpenter," she said into the phone. "I've got a photograph of her." She looked at the bedside clock. "Half an hour," she said, and punched off.

"What's going on?" Stone asked.

"Get out of here. I've got to get dressed," she said, rummaging through the closet for clothes.

"Are you going to be free for dinner?" he asked.

"I'll call you when I know," she replied, then she went into the bathroom and shut the door, taking the photographs with her.

He opened the door a little. "It's not even that good a photograph," he called out.

"It's the only one in existence," she called back.

13

Stone stayed at home the early part of the evening, waiting for Carpenter to call, until hunger got the better of him. What the hell, she had his cell phone number, so why wait?

He arrived at Elaine's only moments before she would have given away his table. It was a very busy night, and even regulars were waiting at the bar. They shot him evil glances as he sat down.

Elaine came over. "You know how much I could have gotten for your table?" she asked, nodding at the bar.

"Let them eat . . . cake," Stone replied. "You'll overcharge them anyway."

"You could get a fork in the chest, talking like that," she replied equably.

"I just want one in my hand, and something to eat." He grabbed a waiter and ordered a spinach salad and osso buco. "Tell Barry I want it with polenta instead of pasta," he said. "And I need a Wild Turkey on the rocks, and bad."

"Tough day?" Elaine asked.

"I had to face Elena Marks today," he replied.

"You mean, explain how you killed her husband?"

"I didn't kill her husband, and neither did the guy I sent. You been talking to Dino?"

"I'll never tell."

"Just between you and me and the nearest gossip columnist in this joint, Larry had already bought it when the kid took his dive."

"The cops don't seem to know that."

"They will soon," Stone said. "I've seen to it."

"So where's Felicity, the English doll?"

"Working. I was hoping she'd make it to dinner."

"What does she do?"

"You wouldn't believe me if I told you."

"Try me."

"If I did, she'd have to kill me, and believe me, she would."

"I don't think she would enjoy it," Elaine observed.

"Maybe not, but she'd do it just the same. She's already pointed a gun at me once today."

"I didn't know you were *that* bad in the sack."

Stone's cell phone vibrated. "Hello?"

"It's me," Carpenter said.

"Who's this?"

"Don't give me a hard time. I'm in a car on the way to Elaine's; that's where you are, isn't it?"

"Maybe."

"I'll be there shortly." She punched off.

"Was that Felicity?" Elaine asked.

"It was Carpenter," he replied.

"Her last name is Devonshire," Elaine said. "Why do you call her Carpenter?"

"It was how she introduced herself at our first encounter," Stone said.

"I don't get it."

"She had an associate named Mason and another named Plumber."

"What is she, an English cop?"

"Elaine, if I told you any more, she'd have to kill *you*."

"Enough said," Elaine said, throwing up her hands. "And here she is," she said, looking toward the door.

Carpenter walked in and came to the table. "Dino will be here in a minute," she said, pecking him on the cheek.

"How do you know that?" Stone asked.

"Because we came here in his car."

Dino came in, a newspaper tucked under his arm, and sat down. "Evening, all," he said.

Elaine reached over and patted his cheek affectionately.

"Wait a minute," Stone said. "What were you and Dino doing in the same car?"

Carpenter smiled. "You're beautiful when you're jealous."

"I'm not jealous."

"No?" she said, frowning.

After his session with Elena Marks, Stone was glad she could still frown. "I'm just curious."

"Should we tell him, Dino?" Carpenter asked.

"Nah," Dino said. "Let him sweat."

"I'm not sweating," Stone said.

"Sure you are," Dino replied.

"He's sweating," Carpenter agreed.

"Yeah," Elaine said.

"Okay, don't tell me," he said to Carpenter. "You want a drink and some dinner?"

"Yes, please. I'll start with one of those bourbon whiskies."

Stone flagged down a waiter. "Bring her what I'm having," he said.

"And what are you having?" Carpenter asked.

"Unborn calf," Stone replied. "With a very nice sauce."

"Sounds yummy," she replied. "Okay, Dino and I were in the same meeting."

"About what?" Stone asked, puzzled.

"If we told you, we'd have to kill you," Dino said.

Elaine roared with laughter, then she got up and hopped to another table.

"You know," Carpenter said, "your Herbie Fisher character wasn't entirely useless."

"That's right," Dino said, flipping idly through the *Post*.

"You mean, because of the picture he took?"

"Can you think of any other way he wasn't entirely useless?" Dino asked.

"Now that you mention it, no." He turned to Carpenter. "You said it was the only one in existence. What did you mean by that?"

"I meant it's the only one in existence."

"Thank you for the clarification. Why is it the only one in existence?"

84

"Because she has scrupulously avoided ever being photographed."

"In her entire life?"

"Since she was about twelve, in school."

"Why?"

"Because she doesn't want anybody to know what she looks like."

"All right," Stone said. "Who is she?"

"She's a woman who goes around assassinating people," Carpenter said. "And the luckiest thing in your life is that she doesn't know you're responsible for the only photograph ever taken of her."

"I wouldn't say that," Dino said, handing Carpenter the *Post* and tapping an item on Page Six.

Carpenter read aloud. " 'Rumor has it that the strange death of Lawrence Fortescue (Mr. Elena Marks), caused by a peeper photographer who fell through a skylight while taking candid snaps of Mr. M. and a certain young lady doing disgusting things to each other, was organized by a fairly sleazy Gotham "lawyer," with a very "hard" name, who hired the falling photog. Any guesses? We'll bet he's supping tonight at Elaine's.' "

Carpenter put the paper down. "Oh, shit," she said.

"Oh, yeah," Dino agreed.

14

Stone looked at Dino and Carpenter narrowly. "I hope this is some kind of joke."

"I'm afraid not," Carpenter said seriously. "My people are very interested in finding her, and they asked me to liaise with the NYPD. That's why Dino and I were in the same meeting. Since we were already acquainted, I picked him to liaise with."

"Who is this woman?" Stone asked.

"I'll tell you all we know about her, and believe me, it won't take long. She was born Marie-Thérèse du Bois, in Zurich, of a Swiss father and an Egyptian mother, but she doesn't use that name anymore, because if she did, she might get caught."

"Tell me all of it."

"Little Marie-Thérèse grew up in Switzerland and in Egypt, and she was something of a whiz with languages, being exposed to four — the usual Swiss three, plus her mother's Arabic — while growing up. Even as a girl, her hobby was studying languages. In addition to her native tongues, she picked up Farsi, Urdu, and some Hindi. Her father imported Middle Eastern products to Switzerland — rugs, olive oil, dates, pottery — whatever he could turn a profit on, and he was very prosperous, ended up rich, in fact. She traveled with him often around the Mediterranean basin, picking up Spanish and Greek along the way. She'd sit in hotel rooms, watching local television and conjugating verbs."

"Good God, how many languages does she speak?"

"Nobody knows, but I'd guess at least a dozen, and with perfect accents in various dialects."

"So, why does she go around killing people?"

"When she was twenty, my firm and the CIA were pursuing the members of a terrorist organization in Cairo who had been killing foreign tourists. We received a tip that half a dozen members of the group would be traveling in a white Renault van along a major boulevard, en route to planting some explosives. Cooperating with Egyptian intelligence, our people set up an elaborate trap for them at an intersection. There wasn't supposed to be any traffic to speak of. Unfortunately, Marie-Thérèse and her parents were driving home from a very late party in another white van, and someone fired a rocket launcher at the wrong vehicle. Her parents were both killed instantly, but Marie-Thérèse, who was asleep in the third seat, was blown clear and survived with only scratches.

"She retreated to her Cairo home and became reclusive, but she was bitter about her parents' death. She refused compensation from all three governments, but then she was a wealthy young woman, having inherited two large houses and her father's considerable fortune.

"She had a boyfriend, an Irani, whose politics extended to extreme violence, and we think she was recruited by the boy and sent to a terrorist training camp in Libya, where she made contacts among others of her kind from Ireland, Japan, Germany, and God knows where else.

"She was trained in firearms, explosives, and chemical weapons, but her handlers, when they learned of her language skills, thought her meant for better things. They taught her assassination skills, document forging, and just about anything else a budding terrorist could possibly want to know, keeping her interest by telling her they would help her find the people responsible for her parents' death so she could kill them. She also became very physically fit in the desert, and she's known to work out almost obsessively, wherever she goes.

"When she finished her schooling in Libya, she returned to Cairo, then Zurich, selling her two houses and secreting the money in accounts around the world. Some say her holdings ran to several tens of millions of dollars. She returned to Cairo and, in effect, ceased to exist. The little we know of her since then comes from rumors and a couple of very aggressive interrogations of people who knew her.

"She seems to have assassinated two Egyptian politicians who held views unpopular with her terrorist friends. She shot one in the head while he waited in his car at a traffic signal, then calmly boarded a bus and rode away. That evening, she dropped cyanide, or something like it, in the other's drink in a crowded restaurant, then climbed out the ladies'-room window while he was still in his death throes. We think she performed half a dozen other such jobs over the next couple of years. Her handlers realized that they had a very valuable commodity on their hands, and they strung her along by telling her they were making progress in learning the names and locations of her parents' killers. They were lying, of course.

"Finally, she became impatient. She kidnapped the head of our Cairo station and tortured him until he gave the names of everyone involved in the operation," Carpenter said calmly. "Then she cut his throat and watched him bleed to death. The body, naked and very damaged, was deposited on the steps of the British embassy."

"Then she started hunting them?" Stone asked.

"Yes. The Americans were the first and easiest target. They were husband and wife. Both worked in their embassy in Cairo, and she firebombed their apartment while they slept.

"The British contingent, four of them, took longer. She garotted one in a railway station men's room in Bonn. The other, she stabbed with a poisoned umbrella tip as he walked across Chelsea Bridge, in London." Carpenter started to continue, but stopped.

"Go on," Stone said.

"She murdered Lawrence Fortescue the night before last," Carpenter said quietly.

"Larry Fortescue was a member of your service?"

"He was the man I told you about, the one I had a relationship with who decided to work abroad. He came here two years ago, married Elena Marks, and resigned from the firm."

"So she got them all," Stone said. "One by one."

"No," Carpenter said, "not all. She hasn't gotten me yet."

"*You?*"

"It was my first assignment abroad," she said. "I went along merely as an observer."

Stone gulped. "Does she know you're in New York?"

"I don't know," Carpenter replied. "But I'm moving out of your house tonight, and into a hotel."

"But why? You're safe with me."

"Stone," Dino said, tapping the newspaper on the table, "if little Marie-Thérèse, or one of her friends, happens to read today's *Post*, she'll know that the taking of her picture was insti- gated by a certain lawyer with a 'hard' name."

"But that's not enough to identify me, surely."

"And," Dino said, "she knows where you're dining tonight."

Stone looked slowly around Elaine's. He saw half a dozen women who could have been the woman in the photograph.

"Do you think this Marie . . . what's her name . . ."

Carpenter spoke up. "She picked up a sobriquet in Paris, after murdering a member of the French cabinet. Interpol calls her 'La Biche.' And yes, she could be here tonight."

Stone pushed back his chair. "Let's get out of here," he said.

15

Dino's driver took them to Stone's house, where Carpenter packed her bags, then they were driven to the Lowell, a small, elegant hotel on East Sixty-third Street, off Madison Avenue.

They were met at the door by the night manager, who, without bothering to register Carpenter, took them directly to a suite on the top floor.

"Are you known here?" Stone asked when the manager had gone and the bellman had deposited her luggage in the bedroom.

"My firm is," she said. "We've used the hotel often. We missed out on dinner; should we order something?"

They dined in the room on Dover sole and a good bottle of California Chardonnay, and without much conversation.

"So Dino," Stone said when the dishes had been cleared, "I guess you've put out an APB for this woman."

"Pretty tough, putting out an APB without a description," Dino replied, looking at the dessert menu.

"Description? You've got a photograph of her!"

"Yeah, well," Dino replied.

Carpenter went to her purse and brought back a sheet of paper. "Here's what the CIA's photo people were able to come up with," she said, handing it to Stone.

He opened the paper to see a rather bland face, framed by long, dark hair — straight nose, big eyes.

"The photograph Herbie took was of her looking up, so only her hair, forehead, eyes and nose were visible, no jaw, and the hair was a wig."

"This could be nearly anybody," Stone said.

"Exactly. La Biche's stock-in-trade is looking like anybody. She can walk through the toughest airport security and pass herself off as an American businesswoman or a French fashion designer, an Italian countess or a Spanish nun."

"I thought, what with electronics, it was getting harder to use false passports. Every time I've used mine, it gets swiped through a reader, and my information pops up on a screen."

"All true, but over the years there have been numerous thefts of blank passports from embassies and consulates all over the world, which solves the problem of paper authenticity, and if such thefts can be concealed for a few days or weeks, the numbers don't come up as stolen when going through immigration. It's very, very tough to catch somebody when your suspect is using real paper."

"I would imagine," Stone said.

The phone rang, and Carpenter went to answer it. "Yes? No, absolutely not. It would attract the attention of anybody who knew what to look for. Are you trying to make me a marked woman?" She paused and listened. "Well, that makes sense, I suppose, though the thought doesn't really appeal. Oh, all right, send them over." She hung up and returned to the table.

"What was that?" Stone asked.

"First, they wanted to put a team on me, which I thought was a bad idea. Even if they're very good, they can be spotted."

"But you agreed to something," Stone pointed out.

"The CIA is sending somebody over to see me."

The doorbell rang.

"That was quick," Stone said.

"Too quick," Dino said, shoving his chair away from the table.

"Go into the bedroom," Stone said to Carpenter. He went to the door, while Dino took up a position beside it, gun drawn. He looked through the peephole and saw a young woman — light brown hair, medium height, slim. "It's a woman," he said. "Ready?"

Dino nodded.

Stone put the chain on the door and opened it. "Yes?" he said.

"Carpenter," the woman replied.

"I don't understand," Stone said. "If you need a carpenter, see the manager."

The woman produced an ID. "I'm here on official business."

"It's all right," Carpenter said from behind Stone. "I know her. Come on in, Arlene."

Stone unhooked the door and admitted the woman, who was carrying a small suitcase.

"Stone, Dino, this is Arlene," Carpenter said.

Arlene nodded. "Let's go into the bathroom," she said to Carpenter.

Stone and Dino watched CNN while water ran and a hair dryer made noise behind the door. Forty-five minutes later, Arlene emerged from the bathroom. "May I introduce my friend, Susan Kinsolving?"

Carpenter emerged, nearly unrecognizable. Her brown hair was now a pronounced auburn, and though she usually wore little makeup, she was now pretty much a painted woman.

"Hi, there," Carpenter said in a Midwestern American accent.

"Hate the accent," Stone said.

"Get used to it, buddy," Carpenter replied.

"Let's get you outfitted with some ID," Arlene said, opening her suitcase. "Have a seat."

Carpenter pulled up a chair.

"Okay, here's your American passport. It was issued three years ago and has a dozen stamps from Europe and the Caribbean. We've already changed the hair color. You're a marketing executive with a computer company in San Fran-

95

cisco. Here are your business cards and some stationery. The company knows your name, and if anyone calls there, you have a secretary and voice mail. You were born in Shaker Heights, a suburb of Cleveland, Ohio, thirty-four years ago, educated in the public schools there and at Mount Holyoke College, in western Massachusetts. You have, in your wallet, in addition to your California driver's license and credit cards — all valid — an alumni association membership card. You're registered at the hotel under the Kinsolving name." She pulled out half a dozen sheets of paper, stapled together. "Here's your legend. Memorize it."

Carpenter flipped through the sheets. "Very thorough." She turned to Stone. "What do you think?" she asked, tossing her hair.

"Very nice, Susan. You want to have dinner sometime?"

Stone and Dino sat in the back of Dino's car, rolling down Park Avenue.

"Dino, a favor?"

"What do you need?"

"Since Larry Fortescue's death has been established as murder, would you feel comfortable calling the DA's office and letting them know that? I'd like to get the charges dismissed, and then I can plead Herbie down to a misdemeanor and get him probation."

"Sure, I'll call down there first thing. You know who the ADA is?"

"Call the deputy DA and do it through him. It'll be faster."

"Okay."

They pulled into Stone's block.

"Slow down," Dino said, checking both sides of the street. "Stop here." The car rolled to a stop in front of Stone's house. Dino got out and looked around. "Okay," he said, waving Stone out of the car.

"Come on, Dino," Stone said, "you're creeping me out."

But Dino stood by the car, his gun in his hand, until Stone was inside.

16

Florence Tyler left the brownstone on West Tenth Street and strolled slowly through Greenwich Village, looking into bars and restaurants and, occasionally, checking a menu posted in a window. It was nearly six o'clock, and she was dressed in a business suit and carried a Fendi purse. Then she saw what she was looking for.

The bar was called Lilith, and a peek through the window showed it to be quite stylish. The after-work crowd was building, and all the customers were women.

She walked in and took a stool at the end of the bar. The bartender, dressed and coiffed to look as much as possible like a man, came over. "Good evening," she said in a smooth baritone. "Can I get you something?"

Another woman, butch, but still pretty, slid onto the next stool. "Let me get it," she said.

"Thanks, I'll stay on my own," Florence said, not unkindly, meeting the woman's gaze.

The woman hesitated, then vacated the stool. "As you wish, sweetheart," she said, as she sauntered off.

"Dewar's, rocks," she said to the bartender,

and the drink arrived. She was halfway through it when she saw what she was looking for. A woman in her late twenties had entered the bar and stopped just inside the door, looking hesitantly around her. She was dressed very much as Florence was, in a pin-striped suit, and she was carrying one of those purses that was half briefcase. She was about Florence's height and weight and had the same streaked blond hair. She crossed the room, took a stool three down from Florence, and ordered a cosmopolitan.

"Those are too sweet for me," Florence said, smiling.

"Well, they are sweet, but they're addictive," the young woman said, smiling back.

"Put that on my tab," Florence said to the bartender.

"Thank you," the girl said.

"Why don't you slide over here and join me?"

The girl fumbled with her briefcase and her drink, but she made it to the stool.

"I'm Brett," Florence said, offering her hand.

"I'm Ginger," the girl replied.

Brett didn't let go of her hand immediately. "Are you a New Yorker?" she asked, finally releasing it.

"I'm from Indianapolis originally, but I've been here for six years. I'm a paralegal in a downtown law firm. Do you live in New York, too?"

"No, I'm in from San Francisco for a few days. I'm an art dealer, and I'm in town to bid on some things for a client. There's an auction at Sotheby's the day after tomorrow."

"Oh, I love art," Ginger said, sipping her drink. "What sort of things are you bidding on?"

"Late-nineteenth-century representational paintings mostly; one piece of sculpture, too. They're not the most expensive things in the world; you can find quite nice pictures in the thirty- to fifty-thousand-dollar range."

"Well, that's certainly out of *my* range," Ginger replied.

"Have you ever been to an art auction?" Brett asked.

"No, but I'd love to go sometime."

"If you can take the time off from work, why don't you join me at Sotheby's the day after tomorrow?"

"Gosh, I'd love to do that, but I only get an hour for lunch, and the workload is fierce. My boss specializes in divorce work, and the clients are very demanding."

"Maybe another time?"

"That would be great."

"Do you live in the neighborhood?"

"No, I'm on the Upper East Side — Eighty-first and Lexington Avenue. Where are you staying?"

"At the Carlyle — Seventy-sixth and Madison. What's your favorite restaurant, Ginger?"

"Oh, I guess Orsay, at Seventy-fifth and Lex, just down from my building."

"Will you have dinner with me there tonight?" Brett pulled out a small cell phone. "I'll bet we can get a table if we go early."

"Well, sure, I'd like that."

Brett called the restaurant and secured a table. "Finish your drink, and we're off," she said.

At Orsay, they had another drink, then ate a three-course dinner and shared an expensive bottle of French wine. They kept up a steady stream of conversation, mostly about Ginger's family and background and the sort of work she was doing.

"You're not going to believe this," Ginger said, but we're representing a woman who is demanding two million dollars a year in alimony, and half a million in child support, plus five million for an apartment on Fifth Avenue. *And* she wants a limousine and security guards."

"No doubt to protect her from her husband," Brett said, laughing. She waved at a waiter for the check.

"Why don't we share this?" Ginger asked, reaching for her briefcase.

"Oh, no, this one is on me — or my gallery," Brett said. "You're . . . Let's see, you're representing a client who has a very nice Magritte for sale."

"Oh, all right, but can I give you a nightcap at my place?"

"You bet," Brett said, handing the waiter one of Florence Tyler's credit cards.

Ginger lived in a ground-floor rear apartment in a town house, with a little garden out back.

"It's lovely," Brett said, when Ginger switched on the garden lights.

"It's just a year's sublet," Ginger said. "It belongs to a friend of the family who's in Europe."

"What's that low, shed-like thing?" Brett asked, pointing.

"Oh, that's a hotbox. It's like a tiny greenhouse, where you can get things growing early in the season, then plant them when it gets warm enough. At least, that's what I saw on Martha Stewart. I'm not really a gardener."

"Me either," Brett said, stroking Ginger's cheek with the back of her fingers. She kissed the woman lightly, and got a warm reception. A moment later, they were working on each other's buttons.

When they reached the bedroom, Brett lay back and let Ginger have her way with her. Brett wasn't a lesbian, strictly speaking, but she liked this. When she had had a couple of orgasms, she rolled Ginger onto her stomach. "Now it's your turn," she said. She reached down and picked up a Hermès scarf where Ginger had dropped it on the floor, and quickly bound Ginger's hands behind her.

"I've never done it like this," Ginger said.

"You just leave everything to me, sweetheart," Brett replied. She rolled the girl over on her back. "Now the feet," she said, grabbing a belt from the pile of clothing beside the bed.

"What are you going to do to me?" Ginger asked, half anxiously, half eagerly.

Brett picked up a pad and a pencil from the bedside table. "Well, first, I'm going to need your office number."

"What?"

"Your office number, and I'll bet you have one of those voice mail systems. I'm going to want your boss's extension number, too."

"I don't understand," Ginger said.

Brett placed a pillow over her face and pinched her hard in a tender place. When the scream was over, she removed the pillow. "Ginger, you do exactly as I tell you. Do you understand?"

Ginger gave her the phone and extension numbers, and Brett wrote them down. Then she found her handbag and removed a straight razor from it.

Ginger was attempting to squirm off the bed now, and Brett grabbed her by the hair and dragged her back. She held her hand over Ginger's mouth, then placed the razor against her throat and drew it lightly across her skin, raising a hairline of red. "When I take my hand away," Brett said, "don't scream, or I'll hurt you badly." She took her hand away.

Ginger was crying now.

"That's very good," Brett said. "You keep that

up. Now here's what we're going to do, Ginger: I'm going to dial your office number and your boss's extension, and when his voice mail answers, here's what I want you to say. What's his name?"

"Mr. Arnold," Ginger sobbed.

"You say these words exactly. 'Mr. Arnold' — you're sobbing — 'this is Ginger. I'm afraid there's been a death in my family, and I have to fly back to Indianapolis tonight. I'm going to be away for at least a week, and I'll call you when I know when I'll be back. I'm awfully sorry about the short notice.' Did you get that?" Brett pressed the razor against her throat again, eliciting another paroxysm of sobbing.

Brett began dialing the number.

"I'm not going to say that!" Ginger said, suddenly collecting herself.

Brett hung up the phone and held the razor to Ginger's left breast. "You'll do it exactly that way, or I'll slice your nipples off, Ginger."

Ginger began sobbing again, but she nodded.

Brett dialed the number, waited, then dialed the extension number. She held the phone to Ginger's lips and the razor to her nipple.

Ginger performed admirably, Brett thought.

Brett waited a full minute after Ginger stopped struggling before removing the pillow from her face. She checked for a pulse, then listened at her chest for a heartbeat. Nothing. She untied Ginger's hands and released the belt from her feet. She went into the kitchen and found a pair of kitchen gloves, a bottle of spray cleaner and a cloth, then she rubbed down the body, carefully removing any possible trace of a fingerprint or her own body fluids. She got a clean bedspread from a linen closet and rolled Ginger's body in it, leaving her on one side of the king-sized bed. She pulled her panties on, then got into a pair of Ginger's jeans, a sweatshirt, and sneakers, then she switched off the garden lights, went outside, and looked around. She couldn't see any neighbors at their windows. She opened the hotbox, which was empty, and noted two large bags of potting soil leaning against the fence. She went back inside, hoisted Ginger's body over her shoulder, looked around outside, then went into the garden and dumped the body into the hotbox. She emptied both bags of potting soil over the body, covering it completely, then tossed in a few flowerpots that were lined up against the garden fence.

Having worked up a sweat, Brett went back inside, stripped off her clothes, and took a hot shower, never removing the rubber gloves. When she had dried herself and her hair, she cleaned the hair from the shower drain and saved it, then walked around the apartment, naked, selecting things. She found a good suitcase and packed some of Ginger's clothes. She found her passport in a desk drawer — Ginger Harvey, her full name was — then emptied her briefcase on the bed and took the wallet and credit cards, putting them into her own bag.

When everything was packed and in order, she got into bed, set the alarm clock for five A.M., and went immediately to sleep.

When the alarm went off, she rolled up Florence Tyler's clothing and effects, then stripped the bedcovers, put them into the over-and-under washing machine in the kitchen, added detergent and a generous amount of bleach and switched it on. She ate a breakfast of juice, fruit, yogurt, and coffee while the things washed, then she put them into the dryer. While they tumbled dry, she put fresh sheets and a new duvet cover on the bed, then dressed in Ginger's best suit.

Finally, she folded the laundered bedcovers and put the contents of the lint filter and her hair from the shower drain into a plastic bag, rolled it into Florence Tyler's things. She went around the apartment with the spray cleaner again, obliterating any possible trace of herself. Satisfied, she tucked Florence Tyler's clothes under her arm, picked up Ginger's suitcase, let herself out of the apartment and the building, and began walking down Lexington Avenue. After a block, she stuffed Florence's things into a street-corner wastebasket and caught the next bus downtown.

When she got off, she was Ginger Harvey.

17

Stone settled at his desk the following morning and sipped the single cup of coffee he allowed himself after breakfast, an Italian espresso roast, made very strong in a drip coffeemaker. He buzzed Joan.

"Good morning. Please get me Herbie Fisher at his place of work. It's a Walgreens in Brooklyn. You have his numbers, don't you?"

"Got them on his first visit. I'll buzz you back."

Stone read the front page of the *Times* and washed it down with his black coffee.

Joan buzzed back. "He didn't show up for work. You want to talk to his boss?"

"Yes." Stone picked up the phone. "Good morning," he said, "is this Herbert Fisher's supervisor?"

"Yes, this is Mr. Wirtz, the manager."

"I understand that Herbie didn't show up for work this morning?"

"That's right."

"Do you know why?"

"Nope. He didn't show up yesterday, either."

"Is this unusual?"

"Well, he's come in late and hungover before, but at least he always showed up."

"Thank you," Stone said. He buzzed Joan. "Try his home number."

Joan buzzed back a moment later. "His mother answered the phone. I've got her on the line."

Stone pressed the button. "Mrs. Fisher?"

"Mrs. Bernstein," she replied curtly. "Mr. Fisher took a hike a long time ago."

"I'm sorry. Mrs. Bernstein, this is Stone Barrington. I'm Herbie's lawyer, and it's important that I speak to him. Where can I reach him?"

"You're *who?* I thought his lawyer was Mr. Levy."

"Mr. Levy works for me on Herbie's case. It really is very important that I reach him."

"You're a cop, aren't you?"

"No, ma'am, I'm not. You can look me up in the phone book, if you want to be sure."

"Hang on." She put the phone down.

Stone waited, drumming his fingers on the desktop. Why was she taking so long?

She came back on the line. "Yeah, all right, I got you in the book."

"Where's Herbie, Mrs. Bernstein?"

"He's on a boat somewhere or other."

"A boat? Where would somewhere or other be?"

"Down in some islands, you know? His uncle Bobby is down there, too."

Stone was having trouble breathing. "In Saint Thomas?"

"Saint something or other," she said.

"And did he say when he'd be back?"

"He said when things cooled down, and the judge forgot about him."

Stone was having trouble speaking now. "And did he say when he thought that would be?"

"A year, maybe. He took a lot of clothes."

"Mrs. Bernstein, did he leave a phone number or the name of his hotel?"

"He said he'd send me a postcard," the woman said, then she hung up.

Stone was left listening to a dead phone. He wondered, in passing, what his blood pressure might be at this moment. When he recovered himself enough to speak, he buzzed Joan.

"Any joy?" she asked.

"Anything but," Stone replied. "Get me Bob Cantor on his cell phone."

"Okay." She went off the line, then came back. "I'm getting a recording saying that the person's phone is out of the calling area. What next?"

"First of all, if Irving Newman, the bail bondsman, calls or sends anybody over, I'm out of the country, can't be reached, and you don't know when I'll be back. Got that?"

"Got it."

"Now get me Tony Levy. He's probably on his cell phone, too."

Levy came on the line. "Yeah?"

"Tony, it's Stone Barrington."

"Yeah, Stone, you got something for me?"

"Just the opposite," Stone replied. "When is

Herbie Fisher's next court appearance?"

Levy let out a short laugh. "He jumped bail, didn't he?"

"There are some things it's better for you not to know, Tony. When's his next appearance?"

"The day after tomorrow."

"Oh, shit. Is Judge Simpson back yet?"

"No, out for at least another week. Kaplan's still sitting."

Stone tried to think how things could be worse and failed. "Tony, I want you to get a postponement."

"On what grounds, and for how long?"

"On any credible grounds you can dream up and until Judge Simpson is back on the bench and in a really good mood."

"I'll see what I can do. If I can't get the postponement, any chance Herbie will show?"

"If he doesn't, it'll be because he's dead."

"Whatever you say, Stone. What are you going to tell Irving Newman?"

"I'm not going to tell him anything, and don't you, either."

"He'll hear about the postponement, you know. He's got a guy in court every day."

"He'll hear whatever you tell Judge Kaplan, and it better be good."

"Stone, this is going to cost you."

"Cost me what?"

"Five grand. That's my price for lying to a judge."

"Tony . . ."

"Come on, Stone. We both know it's a bargain."

"All right. Joan will send you a check today."

"Cash, like before. I don't want to share it with Uncle Sam."

"All right, Tony. You may be able to reach me on my cell phone, if it's absolutely necessary." Stone gave him the number.

"It's a pleasure doing you, Stone."

Stone hung up and called Dino.

"Bacchetti."

"Dino, can you take a few days off?"

"For what purpose?"

"To spend a little time on a tropical island, feeling the warm breeze waft across your bald spot."

"I don't have a bald spot; I'm Italian."

"So's Rudy Giuliani."

"On whose nickel am I traveling?"

"Mine, but you've got to get me an extradition warrant without logging it in."

"For who?"

"For Herbie Fisher. He's jumped bail, and I'm on the hook to Irving Newman for two hundred and twenty-five thousand dollars."

"Oh, boy. The warrant can't be done; new procedures."

"Then get me a blank warrant and I'll fill it in."

"That, I can manage. When do we leave?"

"Go home now and pack, and you might start working on what you're going to tell Mary Ann."

111

"I'll blame it on you, the way I always do."

"I'll call you when I've got a flight booked." Stone hung up and buzzed Joan. "Please get Dino and me on the next flight to Saint Thomas, and I'm going to need an open, one-way ticket back for Herbie Fisher. And find us a decent hotel there."

"I stayed at Harborview the year before last," Joan said. "You'll like it."

"That will be fine," Stone said.

Joan came back a few minutes later. "Your flight leaves in an hour and a half, change in San Juan. You'll be there for dinner."

"Thank you," Stone said. He called Dino's cell phone.

"Bacchetti."

"We fly in an hour and a half," Stone said. "Your driver is taking us to the airport, with the siren on."

"I hope you got first-class seats," Dino said.

Stone gave him the flight number. "Get on the phone to the airline's station chief at Kennedy, sound official, and tell them not to let the flight leave without us," Stone replied. "And for Christ's sake, don't forget your badge."

"I never leave home without it," Dino said.

18

They sat at the end of the runway in San Juan, the engines of the DC-3 roaring, while the pilot did his runup.

Stone was enchanted. He hadn't been on a DC-3 since he was a boy, and he loved the deep rumble of the radial engines. "This is great, isn't it?" he said to Dino.

Dino, who was holding tight to the armrests, his knuckles white, did not reply.

"Isn't it great, being on a DC-3?" Stone asked, elbowing him.

"It has propellers," Dino said.

"Of course it has propellers."

"It's not a jet."

"You're very observant."

"Why is the tail on the ground and the nose in the air? We'll never get off the ground."

"It's a tail dragger," Stone explained. "It doesn't have a nosewheel, just a little one at the back. It's the way all airplanes used to work."

"They used to crash a lot, too." Dino let go of an armrest long enough to grab the wrist of a flight attendant, who was walking down the short aisle. "I need a drink," he said.

"I'm sorry, sir, but our flight is too short to

offer drink service. We'll be in Saint Thomas in half an hour."

"I'm a cop. Does that make any difference?"

"We don't even have liquor aboard, sir. Please relax, it's going to be a very short flight."

Dino let go of her wrist and resumed his death grip on the armrest. The airplane rolled onto the runway and kept going, while Dino helped by keeping his eyes tightly shut. After an interminable roll, the airplane lifted off and began to climb.

"See," Stone said, "it flies."

They crossed the coastline and entered clouds. The airplane began to shake. The pilot came on the intercom. "Ladies and gentlemen," he said, "this is the captain speaking. We apologize for the turbulence, but I'm afraid we'll be dodging thunderstorms along our route today, so please keep your seat belts fastened."

Dino let go of an armrest long enough to yank his seat belt tight enough to cut off circulation to his legs.

"This is going to be great," Stone said, as the airplane leveled off.

Dino looked out the window. "We're flying awful low."

"It's a short flight, Dino. There's no point in climbing higher; we'll be there in twenty minutes."

The airplane suddenly dropped a couple of hundred feet.

"Jeeesus!" Dino said through clenched teeth.

"Nothing to worry about," Stone said, sounding unconvinced. He was feeling a little queasy himself.

The airplane banked sharply to the right, kept that course for ten minutes, then banked sharply to the left. Items were falling out of the overhead racks.

Then, unexpectedly, they were on the ground, just as a rain squall struck the airplane. It did some weaving as it braked, but then they were at the terminal.

"I want a drink," Dino said.

"When we get to the hotel," Stone replied.

The rain continued as they got into a taxi, and what little they could see of the town of Charlotte Amalie through the rain-streaked windows seemed drab. The taxi climbed steeply for a few minutes, then deposited them on the doorstep of a small hotel. Shortly, they were in their adjoining rooms.

"You want a drink now?" Stone called.

"I want a blood transfusion," Dino called back. "Leave me alone."

"Our dinner table is in twenty minutes," Stone shouted. "Get changed."

Twenty minutes later, they walked out onto a broad terrace overlooking the twinkling lights of the town. The rain had passed, and the night was filled with stars. A pair of cruise ships anchored in the big harbor far below were bathed in their own lights, while the anchor lights of sailing vessels bobbed around them. They found a couple of comfortable chairs, accepted menus from the waiter, and Stone ordered two piña coladas.

"I want a double Scotch," Dino complained.

"Shut up, you're in the tropics," Stone explained.

The drinks were icy cold and delicious. Stone flipped open his cell phone to see if he could get a signal. He did, and he dialed Bob Cantor's number and got the out-of-range recording. "Either Bob's on a boat somewhere or he's turned his phone off," Stone said.

Dino looked out at the view. "Can you blame him? I'd do the same in this place."

They listened to the piano player as the bar filled with arriving customers.

"Did you call the DA's office this morning, about getting Herbie's charges dropped?" Stone asked.

"Who had time?" Dino replied. "You yanked me out of my office before I had time to do anything."

"Call him in the morning," Stone said. "It'll be easier to convince Herbie to go back to New York if the manslaughter charge has disappeared."

"Yeah, okay," Dino said. "Now can I drink this ridiculous drink and enjoy the view?"

"Be my guest."

"You'd better believe it."

The waiter came and took their orders. "It'll

be twenty minutes or so," he said. "Would you like another piña colada?"

"You betcha," Dino replied.

"What, no Scotch?" Stone asked.

"We're in the tropics, dummy."

Stone laughed. "I'm sorry we couldn't bring Mary Ann along."

Dino looked at him as if he were mad. "You bachelors," he said, "don't understand anything. The duty-free shopping alone would break you."

"Break *me?*"

"We're on your nickel, remember?"

"My nickel doesn't extend to duty-free shopping. It won't support a camera or a Rolex, you remember that. Besides, you're not going to have time to shop. We have to find Herbie."

"And how do you figure to go about doing that?" Dino asked.

"If Bob Cantor won't answer his phone, then I don't have a clue," Stone said.

Then a flashbulb went off in their faces.

"Good evening, gentlemen," somebody with a New York accent said. "Here's my card. Can I print that great shot for you? Only twenty bucks."

As his eyes readjusted to the available light, Stone looked up into the smiling face of Herbie Fisher.

19

Herbie's smile collapsed. "I, ah . . ." He couldn't seem to get it out.

Stone was too stunned to speak for a moment. Finally, he said, "Hi, Herbie."

Herbie turned and sprinted across the terrace like a terrified rabbit, then out through a door.

"Come on!" Stone said. He and Dino struggled out of the deep soft chairs, around the table, and ran after Herbie. Stone got a glimpse of him fleeing the parking lot, and he turned on the speed, losing a loafer in the process. "Get him!" he yelled at Dino, then went back for his shoe. By the time he caught up, Dino was standing in the street, looking around.

"Which way did he go?" Dino asked.

"I don't know. I had to stop for my shoe."

"You're a big fucking help, Stone."

From behind a little stand of trees beside the street, they heard a car start, then the sound of tires spinning on gravel. Stone ran around the trees in time to see a yellow jeep disappear around a curve. "Well," Stone said, "at least we know what he's driving."

"A jeep?" Dino said, laughing. "Haven't you noticed that half the tourists on this island are driving rented jeeps?"

"It's a *yellow* jeep," Stone pointed out. "They're not all yellow."

"I'm hungry," Dino said.

They walked back into the hotel and out onto the terrace, where two new piña coladas were melting.

"Your table is ready, gentlemen," the waiter said. "Right this way."

They settled into a banquette near the door, where they could still see some of the view, and accepted a glass of wine.

"How the hell are we going to find him?" Dino asked, as he dug into his first course.

"He'll call his uncle Bob as soon as he can, but he's having the same problem contacting him that I am. As soon as Bob gets within range, I can explain things to him, and he'll explain them to Herbie."

"And how long do you figure that will take?" Dino asked.

"Well, Bob's been down here for at least four days. Maybe he's ready to go home."

"What if he's on a three-week vacation?"

"Don't say that."

"When does Herbie have to appear in court?"

"The day after tomorrow."

"Oh, swell."

"I called Tony Levy and told him to get a postponement, no matter what."

"Who's the judge?"

"Kaplan."

"You're fucked," Dino said, chuckling. "You're out of a quarter of a mil, and by the time you get home, Irving Newman is going to own your house."

"Dino, you're ruining my appetite."

"Have you called Irving?"

"No. I'm hoping he hasn't heard that Herbie jumped. How could he know?"

"Well, when Herbie doesn't show the day after tomorrow, and Tony Levy is standing in front of Kaplan with his dick in his hand, Irving is going to suspect something. He's got a guy in every courtroom, you know."

"I know. Can we just drop it?"

"And Irving is not the kind of guy to just trust you for a quarter of a mil."

"It's not a quarter of a million, it's two twenty-five."

"Oh, that'll make all the difference," Dino said.

"Really, Dino, you're ruining my dinner."

"Of course, you've got some bucks in the bank. You could write Irving a check."

"I'd have to sell stock, and my portfolio is way down. I have hopes of it bouncing back, but it would cost me dearly to write that check right now."

"Didn't you have to make a margin call last week?"

"Dino, if you keep talking about this I'm

going to go back to the room, find your gun, and shoot you."

"I didn't bring a gun."

"Let's change the subject, all right?"

"Okay." Dino chewed for a moment and sipped his wine. "Does Carpenter know you left town?"

Stone groaned. "I didn't have time to call her." He dug out his cell phone and called the Lowell. "What's the name she's registered under?"

Dino looked thoughtful. "I don't remember," he said. "She's got too many names."

The hotel answered.

"Just a moment," Stone said, covering the phone. "Come on, Dino, help me out here."

"I swear, I can't remember it."

"Neither can I." Stone slapped his forehead. "Susan!" he said.

"That's right!"

He put the phone to his ear. "May I speak to Susan Kinsolving, please?"

The phone rang and rang, then the operator came back on. "I'm sorry, sir, but there's no answer. Would you like voice mail?"

"Yes, please." Stone listened to the message and heard the beep. "It's Stone. I've had to leave town on business. Please call me on my cell phone." He repeated the number, in case she had lost it. "I'll be back in a day or two." He punched off.

Dino laughed. "A day or two? That's funny."

"We might get lucky."

"We already got lucky, and you blew it."

"*I* blew it?"

"It wasn't me," Dino pointed out.

"You were closer to him than I was. You could have just grabbed him."

"Who could see after the flash went off?"

"Well, I couldn't see either."

A woman at the next table leaned over. "Excuse me," she said, "but are you two married to each other?"

"I'm very sorry," Stone said.

"You sure sound married," she said, then went back to her dinner.

"You're embarrassing me," Stone whispered.

"*I'm* embarrassing *you?*" Dino asked, astounded.

"I asked you to change the subject."

"And I did," Dino replied.

"Gentlemen, *please*," the woman at the next table said.

"I'm very sorry," Stone said again.

"I did change the subject," Dino whispered.

"Shut up," Stone said.

20

Carpenter picked up the phone, dialed Stone's home number, and got an answering machine. She hung up without leaving a message. She tried his cell phone number and got a recording saying he was out of the calling area.

She was sitting in a barely furnished office kept for visitors in the New York headquarters shared by MI5 and MI6, neither of which was supposed to have a presence in New York. She was tired, out of sorts, and hungry, and she wanted Stone to take her to dinner, and he wasn't cooperating. She grabbed her coat, signed out at the front door, and was buzzed out of the building. P. J. Clarke's was only a couple of blocks away, and she headed there. She didn't give a thought to the notion that she might be followed.

It was nearly eight o'clock, and the dining room was busy. "We're not going to have anything for forty-five minutes," a waiter told her, "but if you're really hungry, you can order at the bar."

She went back to the bar and looked it over. At one end were two construction workers, still in their hard hats, who apparently didn't want to go home. In the middle was a clutch of admen who seemed to be ordering a fourth drink, and at the other end was a woman alone, taking off her coat. She took a seat two stools down from her and ordered a Wild Turkey, remembering to use her American accent.

"A bourbon drinker?" the woman next to her asked. "You must be from the South." She was dressed in business clothes, and a combination briefcase and handbag rested on the bar beside her. She was reading Page Six of the *New York Post*.

"Nope, Midwesterner," Carpenter said, not unhappy to have somebody to try her legend on.

"Been in New York long?"

"Actually, I live in San Francisco. I'm just here on business."

"One of my favorite cities," the woman said.

"One of everybody's," Carpenter replied, smiling. "What do you do in the city?"

"I'm a lawyer."

"What firm?"

"I left a job last week, and I'm just starting the search."

"Any luck so far?"

"I had two interviews today. One looked fairly promising. You know a firm called Woodman and Weld?"

"I know about them. I have a friend who does some work for them." Carpenter sipped her bourbon and asked the bartender for a menu.

"Join me?" she said to the woman. "I'm eating here, since there's not a table available."

"Sure," the woman said, looking at the menu. "I think I'll have the strip steak, medium rare, with home fries. I'm hungry."

"Me too," Carpenter said. "Two strip steaks, medium-rare, home fries," she said to the bartender. "And a bottle of a decent Cabernet. You choose."

The bartender nodded and went away to place the order.

"I never thought I'd hear a Californian let a bartender choose a wine for her," the woman said, laughing. "Every left-coaster I know has a mental list of boutique wines that nobody east of Las Vegas ever heard of."

"Actually, I'm not all that interested in wine, though I'm happy to drink it. I let the guys order."

"What's your favorite restaurant out there?" the woman asked.

"Postrio," Carpenter replied.

"Oh? I thought that was closed."

"Nope. They've redone it, and they have a new chef. It's wonderful." Carpenter made a mental note to find out if the restaurant was really closed. She couldn't go around making obvious mistakes, even if she was just practicing the legend.

"Where are you staying in New York?" the woman asked.

"At the Carlyle."

"Pretty expensive for business travel, isn't it?"

"I'm a senior vice-president of the company, so I rate the good hotels and first-class air travel," Carpenter replied.

"That's great."

"It ain't bad," Carpenter said, wondering if she was stretching the Americanisms too far. "What part of town do you live in?"

"Uptown, East Eighties."

"I like the Upper East Side," Carpenter said.

Their steaks arrived, and both dug into their dinners.

"Not a bad wine," the woman said, turning the bottle to see the label.

"Jordan Cabernet."

"Yes, it's a nice one."

"Maybe asking the bartender to choose isn't such a bad idea."

"See? I told you. Have you lived in the city long?"

"Four years," the woman replied.

"Is it easy to meet men here?"

She shook her head. "So many, yet so few."

"That's how I feel about San Francisco," Carpenter said. "All the good ones are married, or gay — or both."

The woman laughed. "It's the same here."

They finished their steaks.

"Dessert?" the bartender asked, taking away their plates.

"What do you recommend?" Carpenter asked.

"I like the walnut apple pie, with a big scoop of vanilla ice cream."

"Sold!"

"Make it two," the woman said, "though I'll regret it tomorrow when I weigh myself."

"Never weigh yourself," Carpenter said.

They finished their apple pie, and Carpenter asked for the check. She paid it with one of her Susan credit cards. "This one's on me," she said.

"What's your name?"

"Susan Kinsolving," Carpenter said, offering her hand.

"I'm Ginger Harvey," the woman said. "Can I buy you a cup of coffee somewhere?"

"Thanks, but I've had a long day, and I'm really tired. Maybe I'll see you in here again sometime." Carpenter waved goodbye, walked outside, and found a cab. "The Carlyle hotel," she said. "Seventy-sixth and Madison."

"Right," the cabbie said.

"Do me a favor, will you? Check your rearview mirror and see if there's a woman getting into a cab behind us."

"Coming out of Clarke's?" the man asked. "Yeah."

"Take your time going uptown," she said. "Don't jump any lights." Carpenter got out her cell phone and speed-dialed a number. "It's Carpenter," she said. "I think I've been made, and I think it's our friend. I'm in a cab, heading up Third Avenue at Fifty-seventh Street, and she's right behind me. I'm going to the Carlyle hotel. Call the manager there and set me up quickly, get me registered. I don't suppose you can get anybody there in ten minutes? I didn't think so. No, don't call the cops. We're going to have to handle this the best way we can, and all by ourselves." She hung up.

"That's funny," the driver said.

"What's funny?"

"You didn't have an English accent when you got into the cab."

Carpenter handed him a fifty. "Forget you heard it," she said. "Drop me at the hotel, leave your meter running, and don't pick up a fare until you're at least twenty blocks away, all right?"

The driver looked at the fifty. "Yes, *ma'am!*"

Carpenter got out of the cab at the Seventy-sixth Street entrance to the Carlyle and walked briskly to the front desk. "My name is Carpenter. May I have my key, please?"

The man at the desk looked at her for a moment, then opened a drawer and handed her a key. "High floor, interior suite, as requested," he said.

"Anybody asks for me, call the number you were given," she said. "There'll be somebody here soon."

"Sleep well," the clerk said.

Carpenter got onto an elevator before she looked at the number taped to the key. She gave the operator the floor number. Her cell phone

128

vibrated as soon as the elevator began to move. "Yes?"

"It'll be twenty minutes before we can get a team into place," the voice said.

"So long?"

"We're scattered. Don't answer the door until you get a call first."

"Right." She snapped the phone shut and got off the elevator. She found the door and let herself into a small suite, chaining the door behind her. The view was of an air shaft, but she closed the curtains anyway before turning on lights. She picked up the phone and dialed a number.

"All right," she said, "check this: Name Ginger Harvey, lawyer, lives in the East Eighties."

"Hold, please."

She could hear the tapping of computer keys.

"East Eighty-first, near Lexington," he said.

"Get somebody over there now. If no one answers, go in and call me back." She hung up, shucked off her shoes, and paced the floor. It worried her that Ginger Harvey was real.

21

They finished their dinner quickly, and Stone went to the front desk. "The photographer who was here earlier," he said to the woman. "Do you know where I can find him?"

"Why?" the woman asked. "Did he annoy you? He only started coming here last night, and I told him not to bug the guests unnecessarily."

"No, nothing like that," Stone said. "I just want to talk to him."

"All I've got is a phone number," she said, digging into a drawer and handing over a card. It was crudely printed and read "Herbie the Eye, Great Photography Quick."

"Thanks," Stone said. "Do you have a rental car available?"

"I've got a jeep," she said, handing him the keys. "I'll charge it to your room, Mr. Barrington."

"Thanks so much." Stone and Dino hurried to the car park, where they found a red jeep waiting.

"Your job is to remember how to get back here," Stone said, starting the vehicle.

"Sure," Dino said. "We're just going to cruise?"

"We're going to cruise hotels," Stone replied. "Having lost us, I don't think Herbie is going to pass up a buck, do you?"

"He doesn't seem like the type."

They drove through the warm night, stopped at every hotel they passed and cruised the parking lot. They found two yellow jeeps, but no Herbie. Stone tried Bob Cantor's cell phone again.

"Yeah?" Cantor said.

"Bob? Where the hell have you been?"

"Who's this?"

"It's Stone. I've been trying to reach you."

"I've been on a boat. We just got into Red Hook this evening."

"Where's Red Hook?"

"Out at the eastern end of the island. What's up? Why have you been trying to reach me?"

"Have you heard from Herbie Fisher?"

"No, you're my first call since I switched on my phone. Why would I hear from Herbie?"

"He's jumped bail."

"Jumped bail for what? Did you get the kid arrested? My sister will kill me when I get home."

"I didn't get him arrested. Herbie got himself arrested, and I'm trying to get him out of it. I bailed him out through Irving Newman, and he jumped a quarter-of-a-mil bail."

"A quarter of a mil! What did the kid do?"

"I'll tell you when I see you," Stone said. "Where are you staying?"

131

"It's my last night on the charter boat. I was planning to go home tomorrow."

"How do I get to Red Hook?"

Cantor gave him directions and the name of his boat. "It'll take you half an hour, forty-five minutes."

"All right," Stone said. "Herbie is going to call you. Count on it. When he does, tell him to come to Red Hook, and don't tell him you've talked to me. I think he thinks that if I find him, I'll take him back to jail."

"Is that what you want to do?"

"No! I want to get the charges reduced to a misdemeanor and get him probation. He's got a court appearance in about thirty-six hours, and if he misses it, it's going to cost me a hell of a lot of money."

"Okay, I'll talk to the kid, Stone."

"Don't talk to him, let me do that. If he somehow gets there before I do, play dumb and sit on him."

"Whatever you say," Cantor replied.

Stone hung up. "We're going to Red Hook."

"I want to go to bed," Dino said. "It's midnight."

"Later." Stone began picking his way toward Red Hook.

Carpenter jumped. There had been a noise outside her door. She grabbed her handbag, extracted the little Walther, and screwed in a silencer. The Carlyle would not appreciate gunfire in their hallways. She ran across the room in her bare feet and checked the peephole. Nobody visible. She flattened herself against the wall and waited.

The doorbell rang, and she jumped again. She didn't open it.

"Carpenter!" somebody said from the hall.

She checked the peephole again. "Who are you?" she asked.

"Mason," he replied.

He wouldn't use that handle if he were at gunpoint. She unchained the door and opened it, stepping back, the pistol ready, just in case.

Mason walked in. "It's all right, I'm alone."

"Why the hell are you alone?" she demanded. "Don't you know who we're dealing with?"

"Of course I know who we're dealing with," he said in his upper-class drawl.

"And why didn't you call before you came up? I could have shot you."

"I was supposed to call?"

"Oh, never mind. Where is everybody?"

"I sent two men to the Harvey apartment. We're waking up more."

"She's around this hotel somewhere," Carpenter said, "I can feel it."

"Give me a description, and I'll circulate it."

"Early thirties, five-five, a little under nine stone, medium brown hair, shoulder length, black eyes . . ."

"Black eyes? Nobody has black eyes."

"All right, very dark brown. She's dressed in a

business suit, carrying a handbag that looks like a briefcase. God knows what's in there."

Mason produced a cell phone and made a call. "Why don't you want to call the police?"

"I'd like it if we could bag her on our own," Carpenter replied. "Wouldn't you like that?"

Mason shrugged. "Why share victory with the NYPD or the FBI?"

The telephone rang, and Carpenter waited for Mason to get to an extension before answering. They picked up simultaneously. "Yes?"

"We're in the Harvey flat," a man said. "It's clean as a whistle."

"It would be, wouldn't it?" Carpenter said.

"Hang on, we're checking the garden."

Carpenter hung on for a very long time before the man came back.

"We've got a corpse — female, might be thirty, medium height and weight."

"Got her where?"

"Got her in a hotbox in the garden."

"A gardening hotbox?"

"Exactly."

"How long dead?"

"No rigor present, she doesn't stink. That's all I can tell you."

"Get out of there, and clean up after yourself. Tell me you didn't jimmy the door."

"I picked the lock."

"Then stake out the place in case La Biche returns, and be very, very careful."

"All right."

"Tell me you didn't make this call on Harvey's phone."

There was a brief silence. "Ah, we're getting out."

Carpenter punched off. "Dunces! They called here on Harvey's phone!"

Mason groaned. "Now we'll have to talk to the NYPD. They'll surely check her phone records."

"You let me do the talking," Carpenter said. She looked up Dino Bacchetti's cell phone number in her book and dialed it.

22

The jeep ground to a halt in the parking lot of a marina. "This way," Stone said, pointing.

Dino jumped. "Hang on, it's my cell phone," he said, groping for it. "This time of night, somebody's gotta be dead." He opened the phone. "Bacchetti."

"Dino? It's Carpenter."

"Oh, hi," Dino said. He held his hand over the phone. "It's Carpenter."

"Why the hell is she calling *you?*" Stone asked, reaching for the phone.

Dino held it away. "She's calling me, I'm talking to her. What's up, Carpenter?"

"I have a little problem for you, Dino."

"For me? What kind of problem?"

"A couple of my people stumbled into a murder on your patch."

"Who did they murder, Carpenter?"

"Nobody. La Biche took care of that."

"Who'd she murder, one of yours?"

"A civilian, a woman named Ginger Harvey, and La Biche has taken her identity, at least for the time being."

"Tell me about it."

Carpenter gave him the address. "It's a

ground floor, rear apartment with a garden. The body's in a hotbox in the garden."

"What's a hotbox?"

"It's a gardening thing, like a small green-house without glass."

"I'll send some people over there."

"They're not going to find much, except for the body. This woman is very smart, and she will have eliminated all trace of her presence there."

"Yeah, but we've gotta go through the motions."

"A favor, Dino: Can you wait until, say, mid-morning tomorrow before going in there? I've got the place staked out in case La Biche returns, and she'll run like the wind if she spots anything resembling a policeman."

"Okay. I'll wait to call it in."

"I appreciate that, Dino. I know it's not proper procedure, but we've got at least a chance of bagging her."

"Don't worry about it. Keep in touch."

"Let me give you my cell phone number."

Dino fished for a pen. "Shoot."

"I want to talk to her," Stone said.

Dino nodded, writing down the number. "Hang on, Stone wants to talk to you."

Stone took the phone. "Hi. You all right?"

"Right now, I'm running. La Biche has made me, and I'm holed up at the Carlyle."

"Oh, shit. How'd she find you?"

"I think when she kidnapped our man in

Cairo, he must have given up our New York office address. She probably waited outside for me to leave the building and followed me to P. J. Clarke's, where we had a nice little chat at the bar."

"Are you going to stay at the Carlyle?"

"No, I'll get out of here in the morning. I can't go back to the Lowell, either."

"Go to my house."

"She may know who you are."

"She may not."

"I'll think about it. Why don't you come around to the Carlyle a little later, when I've sorted this out?"

"A little problem there. I'm in Saint Thomas."

"A church?"

"An island."

"What on earth are you doing there?"

"Bringing back Herbie Fisher, who jumped bail, leaving me holding a great big bag."

"When are you coming home?"

"Tomorrow, I hope."

"Dino has my cell phone number. Call me when you get back."

"You watch your ass."

"I wish you were here to watch it for me."

"Me too. I'll call you tomorrow." Stone hung up and handed Dino his phone. "Let's find the boat. She's called *Tenderly*."

They walked down the main pontoon slowly, checking boat names, until they came to one, a sailboat, with a light burning.

"Here we are," Stone said, stepping aboard. He rapped on the hatch. "Bob?"

"Come on down, Stone," Cantor replied.

Stone and Dino clambered down the companionway steps. Bob was sitting at the saloon table, and Herbie Fisher was sitting beside him, looking like a small animal caught in a spotlight.

"Well, hi, Herbie," Stone said. "You're a tough guy to catch up with."

"He called right after you did, Stone," Cantor said. "He just got here."

"I'm not going back," Herbie said.

"Yes, you are," Stone replied, taking a seat on the banquette opposite the saloon table. "Let me tell you why."

"Shut up and listen to this, Herbie," Cantor said.

"You didn't kill the guy," Stone said.

"Don't hand me that shit," Herbie said. "You think I don't know when a guy's dead? I grew up in Brooklyn."

Stone let the non sequitur pass. "He was dead, Herbie, but you didn't kill him. There was an autopsy. The girl killed him. He was already dead when you fell on him."

"I don't believe you," Herbie replied.

"Let me introduce Lieutenant Dino Bacchetti, chief of the detective squad at the Nineteenth Precinct. Show him your badge, Dino."

Dino gave a little wave and showed Herbie his badge.

"Dino," Stone said, "am I lying to Herbie?"

"Nope," Dino replied. "The guy was poisoned."

Herbie looked at them, back and forth.

"He's not lying to you, Herbie," Cantor said to his nephew.

"I'm still not going back," Herbie said.

"What?" Stone asked, confused.

"I like it here. I've already got five hotels lined up. It's going to be a sweet deal."

"Herbie, you have a court appearance in thirty-six hours. We'll get the manslaughter charge dropped, plead the other stuff down to a single misdemeanor, and get you non-reporting probation. Then you can come back here and take pictures at hotels."

"But I'll have a record," Herbie said plaintively.

"Herbie," Stone replied, "if you don't show up for your court appearance, a fugitive warrant will be issued, and cops everywhere, including here, will be looking for you. Would you prefer that to probation?"

"I don't know," Herbie said.

Bob Cantor reached behind Herbie and brought the flat of his hand hard across the top of his nephew's head. "Putz!"

"Ow," Herbie said, flinching.

"Go home with Stone and fix this, or I'll tell your mother," Cantor said.

"Okay," Herbie said sheepishly.

23

Carpenter was jarred awake by the slamming of the door. Her hand was immediately on the Walther. She was in bed, naked, and she could hear somebody whistling in the sitting room of the Carlyle suite. It was only Mason. She got out of bed, brushed her teeth with the hotel's toothbrush, found a robe hanging on the back of the bathroom door, and walked into the sitting room, running her hands through her hair. She hadn't borrowed a hairbrush.

"Good morning," Mason said cheerfully. His jacket and Eton tie were draped across a chair, and his shirt was open at the collar.

"Good morning," she said, not meaning it. She had never seen him, in any circumstances, without his Eton tie.

Mason waved a hand at the rolling table. "We've got eggs, kippers, and sausage, and that wonderful fresh orange juice they get from Florida."

She was surprised to find that she was hungry, and she sat down and began lifting dish covers, dropping them on the floor.

"Sleep well?"

"Yes, but not long enough," Carpenter replied. "You?"

"Like a top. The sofa was quite comfortable."

"Mason, have you *ever* been uncomfortable in your entire life?" she asked. Wherever they went, Mason always seemed to bring along his father's campaign furniture, or a down sleeping bag, or a portable bar.

"Not since the Army," Mason replied thoughtfully.

She knew he had served in the SAS, the Special Air Services, Britain's toughest commando outfit. "Describe to me a single occasion when the Army managed to make you uncomfortable."

"Northern Ireland," he said after a moment's thought. "I was in Londonderry, keeping an eye on a house where we thought one of those Real IRA chaps might turn up. It was raining, and my Land Rover had a leaky canvas top, and the rain kept dribbling down my neck. Oddly enough, I was more comfy after the bomb went off. I was upside down, but the canvas top was more comfortable if you were lying on top of it, with the vehicle over you. It didn't leak that way."

"Oh," she said. She took a big bite of eggs with a little kipper. "Had any overnight reports?"

Mason paused for a moment, then assumed a more somber mien. "Tinker is dead," he said, "and Thatcher is in hospital, a couple of blocks from here, at Lenox Hill."

Carpenter swallowed hard and put down her fork. "She got *both* of them?"

"Well, she got Tinker. She didn't quite *get* Thatcher, if you see what I mean. He's still alive."

"How did she do it?"

"Ice pick, apparently. You can still buy them at ironmongers' here. Did you know that?"

"I did not." She thanked God that her firm did not require that she write letters to the families of those killed on duty. "So La Biche went back to the Harvey flat after all?"

"It would seem so." Mason sat down and began to eat. "Funny thing," he said, "I'm ravenous, in spite of the news."

"It's a psychological thing," she said. "Relief to be alive when others are dead instills a feeling of well-being, increasing the appetite. It's why people bring food to the families of the deceased. I feel a little hungry, myself." She began eating again.

"You're out of the Lowell," Mason said. "Where do you want your things sent?"

She gave him Stone's address.

"Think that's a good idea?"

"I haven't got a better one at the moment. How am I getting out of here?"

"We've got hold of a fishmonger's van. It will pull into the garage downstairs in . . ." He consulted his wristwatch. ". . . fifty minutes. The fish will come out, and you'll go in, and the van will proceed to the Waldorf, where you and more fish will be delivered. You'll change to a taxi there, to go . . . wherever you want to go."

"All right," she said.

"I hope you don't mind the smell of fish."

"I can stand it as far as the Waldorf. Has anybody talked to Thatcher?"

"Oh, yes. He remembers very little, just the pain. He never saw her coming. Are we going to tell our policemen friends about the Harvey woman?"

"I have already done so," Carpenter replied. "Lieutenant Bacchetti's people will swarm over her flat at mid-morning."

"They're going to find fuck-all," Mason said, stabbing at a sausage.

"I've already told Dino that, but they have to go through the motions. I wouldn't be shocked if they found signs of Tinker and Thatcher's being there. They were obviously not up to this one."

"I wouldn't be too hard on them," Mason said. "This woman is quite . . . *extraordinary*. What were your impressions of her when you met her at Clarke's?"

"I'll tell you, if you won't tell anybody else."

"All right."

"She was good — so good that I didn't twig until she invited me for coffee somewhere else, which would have been the Harvey flat, I think. I wasn't actually sure until she got into a cab and followed me here."

"Then she is very good, indeed."

"She was so *ordinary*."

"That's what's extraordinary about her, I suppose," Mason observed. "Someone who can hunt people down as coldly as that, while seeming so ordinary. You think she has an organization here?"

"I'd bet she has a name or two to ring up if she needs something, or if things go sour," Carpenter said. "She's too good not to have some sort of backup. Did we flag the Harvey passport?"

Mason stopped eating. "I'm not sure," he said, sounding guilty.

"That means you didn't do it."

"Well . . ."

"Do it now."

Mason got up and went to the phone, but it rang before he reached it. He listened for a moment, then held out the phone to Carpenter. "It's for you." He rolled his eyes upward, as if to God.

Carpenter got up and went to the phone. "Yes?"

"It's Architect." Her boss, in London.

"Yes, sir?"

"A flight landed at Heathrow this morning with one Virginia Harvey listed on the manifest. "I believe she's called Ginger?"

"Yes, sir."

"She got onto the airplane, but she didn't get off — at least, she didn't make it to immigration. Her body was found in a ladies' room off the corridor leading from the gate to baggage claim. Her passport was in her handbag, but the photographs didn't match the corpse."

"They wouldn't, since they were of a different woman."

"Of course, but you're missing the point."

Carpenter sucked in a breath. "I think I just got it," she said.

"We're tracking two other single women who were on the flight," Architect said. "Both cleared customs and immigration. One has turned up at her London hotel, the other hasn't been found."

"That makes sense."

"So it seems we've taken her off your hands, for the present, at least."

"It would seem so. I'll be on the next flight."

"I think you're better off in New York at the moment. You and Mason take a few days. I'm sorry about Tinker. I take it Thatcher will be all right in a few days."

"Yes, sir."

"I'll be in touch if there's news." He hung up.

Carpenter replaced the phone in its cradle.

"What?" Mason asked.

"La Biche apparently went from killing Tinker and wounding Thatcher straight to Kennedy Airport, took a flight to London, and after leaving it but before reaching baggage claim, murdered another woman, took her purse, and left Ginger Harvey's in its place. She's loose in London."

"Mmmm," Mason said. "I suppose I should

have flagged the Harvey passport last night."

"She thought we wouldn't move that fast," Carpenter said. "And she was right."

24

Stone, Dino, Bob Cantor, and Herbie Fisher got off the airplane at Kennedy. Dino flashed his badge at customs, and the moment they were through, Stone felt a handcuff close on his wrist. He looked at it and found Herbie on the other end.

"I'm not taking any chances," Dino said.

"I have to go to the john," Herbie said.

"There's one," Dino said, pointing. "You two guys have a nice time."

"Come on, Dino," Stone said. "Unlock them."

"I'm not taking them off," Dino said, "unless I cuff both Herbie's hands behind him, then you can help him in the john. That okay?"

Stone went into the men's room with Herbie and waited impatiently while he used the urinal, then they found Dino's car waiting for them outside and got in. Stone got out his cell phone. Dino got out his own.

Dino dialed. "Gimme the deputy DA's office," he said.

Stone dialed. "Tony," he said, "are you in court? In ten minutes? I've got Herbie, but we're twenty minutes, half an hour out. Can you stall Judge Kaplan? Do your best. Tell her the subway broke down." Stone hung up.

"George?" Dino said, "Dino Bacchetti. . . . Yeah, you too. Listen, I'm going to save you some time: One of your people is dealing with a Herbert Fisher, charged with manslaughter in the Larry Fortescue case. . . . Right, his appearance is in about ten minutes. Thing is, I've been reliably informed that Fisher's fall through the skylight didn't cause Fortescue's death. . . . No, he was poisoned, and by a pro, so he was already dead when Fisher hit him. . . . No, I'm not kidding you, I've had a look at the autopsy report. . . . From an intelligence source. This thing is real cloak-and-dagger. Also, these people tell me that Fisher actually did them some good, because he took a photograph of the woman who killed Fortescue. . . . Come on, George, could I make this up? . . . What do I want? George, manslaughter sure isn't going to stick, and, given the help Fisher was to these people, I'd kick the other charges, if I were you. I think it's better if this just goes away. . . . My interest in this? My interest is keeping egg off my face, and that oughta be your interest, too. . . . Okay, kiddo. Talk to you later."

Dino hung up and turned to Stone, who was occupying the backseat with Herbie. "George is going to talk to the ADA on the case. He's on his way to the courtroom now."

"You mean this is all going to go away?" Herbie asked.

"Shut up, Herbie," Dino said. "You're not out

of the woods yet. We've still got to get you to court before Kaplan realizes you're not there."

"Turn on the siren, Dino," Stone said.

Dino turned on the siren. "Not that it makes a hell of a lot of difference at this hour."

Twenty minutes later, as the bailiff was calling the *State of New York v. Herbert Fisher*, Stone walked into the courtroom with Herbie in tow. He turned over Herbie to Tony Levy.

"What's happening?" Levy whispered.

"Keep your mouth shut and let the ADA do the talking," Stone said.

"Mr. Levy," Judge Kaplan said, "I guess you want bail continued?"

Levy was about to open his mouth when the ADA, a short woman in a bad suit, spoke up. "Your Honor, this office is dropping all charges against Mr. Fisher at this time."

Kaplan looked at the young woman askance. "You're dropping murder two? What's going on here?"

"This office has learned that the victim died of other causes before Mr. Fisher, ah, intruded on the scene."

"Well, I never," Kaplan said.

"Neither did I, Judge," the ADA replied, "but our information is from a reliable source."

"Okay, Mr. Fisher, you're off the hook. Bail will be refunded."

"Thank you, Your Honor," Levy said. He walked Herbie back to the rear of the courtroom

150

where Stone was waiting. "How did you pull that one off, Stone?" he asked.

"You don't want to know," Stone replied.

Levy pulled Stone aside. "I believe you owe me five big ones," he said.

"No, five is your fee for lying to a judge. You didn't have to do that. I'll send you a grand today." He grabbed Herbie and walked him out of the courtroom, leaving Levy to wonder what had just happened.

"Well," Herbie said, "I'm outta here."

"Yes, you are," Stone said. "And if you breathe a word of what Dino told the DA to anybody at all, including your mother, you're going to find yourself back in this courtroom."

"Jesus, I love this cloak-and-dagger stuff," Herbie said. "Tell me what happened in that apartment that night."

"Herbie," Stone said, "if I told you, I'd have to kill you."

"You gonna have some more work for me soon?" Herbie asked.

"No, Herbie, I'm not."

"Why not? This one worked out okay, didn't it?"

"No, Herbie, it didn't. You nearly went to prison, and you nearly cost me a quarter of a million dollars."

"But it worked out okay. Nobody got hurt."

"That's not what I call working out okay," Stone said, "and you'll never know how close you came to getting hurt by me."

"I'll give you a ring next week and see what you've got for me," Herbie said hopefully.

"Herbie, if I ever see or hear from you again, I'm going to have a word with the people who dealt with what happened in that apartment, and they're going to make sure that you never give anybody a ring again."

Herbie gulped. "You mean . . ."

Stone nodded gravely. "If I were you, I'd be on the next flight to Saint Thomas, and I'd *never* come back to New York."

Herbie backed away from him, nodding, then he turned and ran.

Stone hoped the kid could get to the airport without his help.

25

Marie-Thérèse was awakened at three in the afternoon by the housekeeper. She was in a safe house for a Middle Eastern intelligence service, in Hampstead, a north London suburb.

"He's here," the woman said.

"I'll be down in five minutes," M-T said. She took a quick shower and, her hair still wet, dressed in Ginger Harvey's good suit and went down to the dining room, which had been turned into an operations center. Abdul, as he was code-named, sat at a desk, reading his e-mail on a laptop computer. There were three other computers in the room, along with a high-frequency radio and two satellite phones. There was also equipment for encoding messages, plus a special recording device for creating short-burst transmissions that could be transmitted, then expanded by anyone who had the codes and proper equipment.

Abdul looked up from the laptop. "I take it you had to leave New York in a hurry?"

"I had to go before they called in the local authorities. There would have been too many people looking for me. I made sure they knew I left the country."

"And now?"

"And now I want to go back, preferably today. I need very good cover, and I hope you can help."

"You're in luck," Abdul said, "but you can't leave until tomorrow."

"How will I do it?"

"We are infiltrating a young couple into the States. They're married and have a young child." He went into a briefcase beside him and took out two passports, handing her one.

"We don't look at all alike," she said.

"I'll put your photograph into her passport now. She'll travel on the same flight with another passport. You'll carry the child and sit with the husband."

"I like it," M-T said, smiling. "They won't expect me back so soon, especially not with a child."

"Are you sure you want to go back now?"

M-T nodded. "Yes, I have unfinished business, and they won't be looking for me since they know I've left the country."

"You're very bold," Abdul said, smiling.

"Sometimes boldness works best."

Abdul handed her a package. "You'll need to dye your hair black before I take your new passport photo. Better get started. You'll find some women's clothes in a cupboard upstairs. Find something suitable."

"What time is my flight tomorrow?"

"Eleven A.M., British Airways. You'll arrive in New York around two, what with the time change. What else will you need? Weapons?"

M-T shook her head. "I couldn't carry them onto an airplane these days."

"It can be done," Abdul said, "but we prefer to save that for special occasions."

"I have sufficient resources in New York, but I could use a couple of passports."

"All right, but we'll have to send them via diplomatic pouch to our UN embassy. I'll give you a contact there."

"Good."

"How many people did you kill in New York?" Abdul asked.

"Three," she said. "Two of them were British intelligence. The other was merely for convenience."

Marie-Thérèse was back downstairs in half an hour to have her hair done by the woman of the house, then she was photographed for the new passports, two of them in wigs.

"It's good," she said when she saw the Polaroids.

Abdul went to work on the passport, deftly removing the old photograph and replacing it with that of M-T. When he was happy with his work he gave her the passport and a few sheets of paper. "This is the woman's background," he said. "It's completely legitimate. She was born in Cairo, studied economics in Paris and London. She's never been suspected of any involvement with us."

"What am I going to owe you for this, Abdul?" M-T asked.

Abdul smiled. "We have a man in our UN embassy in New York who has been talking to the CIA, taking their money. We'd like him eliminated in an obvious sort of way, then we'll blame the CIA for his murder. We'll furnish you with the sort of weapon the agency would use."

"Very good," M-T said.

"I'll have the other passports done before you leave. That should square us," Abdul said.

Stone arrived back at his house and entered through his outside office door. Joan was working at her desk.

"Welcome back, boss," she said. "What did you think of Harborview?"

"It was wonderful, what little I saw of it. I never slept in my bed, as it happened. The only sleep I got was on a small boat, and it wasn't comfortable."

"Did you get Herbie back?"

"I did. Herbie's off the hook, and so am I. Send Tony Levy another thousand dollars today, and send Bill Eggers a bill for my services and for the twenty-five thousand I paid to Irving Newman for Herbie's bail."

"Will do. By the way, your friend Felicity is upstairs, sacked out in your bed. She got here a couple of hours ago, with company: There's a man in your study and another in the garden, pretending to read a book."

"Swell. I need some sack time, myself, so hang on to my phone messages." He took the elevator upstairs, and as he stepped out of it he felt cold steel on the back of his neck. "I'm Barrington," he said.

"ID?"

Stone showed the man his driver's license. "I'll take over your duty up here. Why don't you make yourself comfortable in the library, downstairs?"

"All right," the man replied, then headed for the stairs.

Stone went into the bedroom as quietly as possible. Carpenter lay on her belly, breathing softly. Stone undressed, got into bed, and lay down beside her.

"Welcome home, sailor," Carpenter said sleepily. "I suppose you want a sailor's welcome?"

Stone lay on his side and cupped a buttock in his hand. "Nothing too strenuous," he said. "I am, after all, home from the sea." He moved his fingers up and down between her cheeks, and she made an appreciative noise. He explored a little further and found her already wet.

She rolled over on her side and pressed her buttocks into his crotch, reaching between her legs for him.

A moment later he was inside her, feeling her

cheeks pushing against his belly as they moved together. He reached around and found her clitoris, then, while kissing her on the back of the neck, continued moving in and out of her while letting his fingers do the walking.

Carpenter began moving faster, and a moment later, came in little whimpers, while he joined her. They lay still for a minute or two, then she rolled over and nestled in his arms. "An Englishman would never have started that way," she said. "It would have been the missionary position or nothing, not that I have anything against the evangelical. How did your trip go?"

"Later," Stone breathed. "Don't you know that sex renders men unconscious?" He took a deep breath, and by the time he had exhaled, he was asleep.

26

Her traveling companions arrived at the Hampstead safe house six hours before their departure time. Marie-Thérèse met the husband and baby, but not the wife, who was taken to another room. She played with the nine-month-old baby girl, whose name was Jasmine, talking to her in Arabic, making her feel comfortable with her temporary mother. Marie-Thérèse had always liked children, and she got on very well with the baby.

She went through her legend with the young man, whose name was, rather unfortunately, Saddam, discussing details of his wife's background. Saddam seemed very pleased to be in her company.

Three hours before their flight a taxi arrived to take the baby's mother to the airport, followed a few minutes later by another cab to take M-T, Saddam, and the baby. It would take a long time to get through security, but they wanted to be in the thick of a crowd, not too early or too late, which might call attention to them.

After checking their baggage the "family" approached the outgoing emigration control booth, and they could see the child's mother only a few people ahead of them. M-T stepped out of line and took the baby into the ladies' room for an unnecessary diaper change, and when she returned, the mother had passed through the control point, apparently with no problem.

M-T stepped up to the window and handed over her borrowed passport, which included details of the baby, and that of Saddam. She gave the inspector a little smile, which was not returned, and he stamped their passports.

The child behaved well in the departure lounge but offered real cause for another diaper change, which M-T accomplished expertly. After an interminable wait, they were herded onto the airplane, passing the child's mother a few rows ahead of their seats. She ignored them, as she had been told to do. M-T had been afraid she would pay too much attention to the baby.

The transatlantic crossing was routine, marked only by an attempt by Saddam to grope his new wife, which got him a hard pinch that nearly drew blood. He behaved himself after that.

Then they were at Kennedy Airport, lined up for customs and immigration. M-T and Saddam presented properly issued visas for a thirty-day visit to family in Dearborn, Michigan. The immigration officer, a woman, was distracted by the happy baby and passed them through after a routine check of their documents.

Then, as they were about to leave customs, a man in a dark suit approached them. "Will you come with me, please?"

M-T began looking for escape routes from the terminal. There were none. He led them into a small room containing four chairs and a steel table and indicated that they should sit down.

M-T was concerned, now. This man was no fifteen-dollar-an-hour security guard. He was intelligent, efficient, and knew his business. M-T, in the role of a good Muslim wife, let Saddam do the talking, and since he was accurately describing the background of himself and his wife, he did well. Then the man turned to Marie-Thérèse.

"Your date and place of birth," he said.

M-T told him and continued to answer as he picked his way through her life history. She was perfect, but not too perfect, but the man was unsatisfied. Clearly, his instincts were telling him that there was more to this couple than met the eye. Then little Jasmine did a wonderful thing.

The officer suddenly wrinkled his nose and pushed back from the table. "What the hell is that smell?" he asked. He was clearly not a parent.

Marie-Thérèse became embarrassed and flustered and started removing the soiled diaper. Before she was finished cleaning and rediapering the baby, the officer had his back against the wall and a hand over his nose and mouth.

"What shall I do with this?" Marie-Thérèse asked, extending a hand with the soiled diaper.

"Take it with you," the man said curtly. He pointed at the door, and the little family left. They stood in a long line for a taxi, and Jasmine, once again, came through, beginning to cry. They were pushed to the front of the line and got the next cab.

"Well," Saddam said in English, "I'm glad to be through that security gauntlet."

M-T elbowed him sharply in the ribs. "Shut up," she said.

They checked into a reserved room at the Roger Smith Hotel on Lexington Avenue and waited for the child's mother to arrive. She knocked on the door a few minutes later. The two women silently exchanged clothes, M-T wished them luck and left them in the room.

She changed taxis twice going uptown. Finally, she got out at a corner and walked down the block to a storage company. Once inside and satisfied that she had not been followed, she opened the combination lock on her rented storage closet, switched on the light, and stepped inside, locking the door behind her. She changed clothes again, put her hair up and chose a blond wig, then she checked the available weapons. She decided on a tiny .22-caliber semiautomatic pistol with a silencer. She unscrewed the silencer and placed it in a pocket in a large handbag, along with an extra magazine.

She also put an ice pick into the handbag, then she packed a few items of clothing into the bag, locked up, and left.

Stone woke up before Carpenter did, but by the time he returned from the shower, she was awake, sitting up in bed, her breasts exposed. "If that is supposed to interest me, it's working," he said.

"You smell all soapy and clean," she said.

He made a grab for her, but she eluded him and ran for the shower. "Fix me some breakfast," she called.

"What would you like?"

"Fruit, yogurt, and coffee."

"That's way too healthy for my kitchen," he called back. "You'll take fresh croissants and like it."

"If I have to," she said, closing the shower door.

"What do you have to do for the next few days?" Stone asked, munching a croissant.

"I've been given time off," she said.

"Oh? Why?"

She told him about the events of the day before.

"So she's in London now?"

"Apparently," Carpenter replied. "But I'm not taking any chances. I'm still in hiding."

"I think I have a better place to hide you than here," Stone said.

"And where would that be?"

"I have a cottage in Connecticut, in a lovely colonial village called Washington, and if you're willing to ditch your bodyguards, I'll take you up there."

"To the country? Now, that sounds wonderful."

"I have some catching up to do in my office," he said, "but I'll be ready to go by mid-afternoon. Put some things in a bag."

"Will do."

It was closer to four before Stone got free of work. The two bodyguards worked both sides of the street before calling Carpenter on her cell phone to report the coast clear. By that time, she and Stone were sitting in his car, waiting for the word to move. When it came, Stone opened the garage door with the remote and drove away from the house, closing the door behind them. They turned up Third Avenue, and as they made a left on Fifty-seventh Street, they nearly ran down a young woman, a well-dressed blonde.

The black Mercedes E55 with the darkened windows meant nothing to Marie-Thérèse, except that it had nearly killed her. The young woman meant nothing to Stone and Carpenter either.

Stone drove to the West Side Highway and turned north, toward Connecticut.

"How long a drive?" Carpenter asked.

"An hour and forty minutes from this spot," Stone said.

"Can I cook you dinner tonight?"

"I was going to take you out, but if you *really* know how to cook, well . . ."

"You'll just have to wait and see, won't you?" she said.

27

Marie-Thérèse showed one of her passports at the front door of the embassy on the Upper East Side and was let in. She approached a window in a thick glass wall.

"May I help you?" the woman at the window asked in Arabic.

"Yes," Marie-Thérèse replied. "I would like to speak to the vice-consul in charge of tourism."

The woman blinked and paused for a moment. "We do not have a vice-consul for tourism," she replied.

"Please tell him that Abdul suggested I speak with him."

Again, the woman said, "We do not have a vice-consul for tourism."

"He is expecting me," M-T replied.

"One moment, please." The woman left the window and went to a telephone. She spoke a few words, listened, then returned to the window, filled out a pass, and pushed it through the narrow opening. "Take the elevator to the fourth floor. You will be met."

"Thank you," M-T replied. She turned and walked to the elevator, then rode it to the fourth floor. As she stepped out of the car two men in civilian clothes approached her.

"Your handbag, please," the shorter of the two said. He was thickly built, with thick, black hair. Though clean-shaven, his beard showed through the skin.

She handed it over, then raised her arms for the search.

The shorter man emptied the handbag onto a small table in the hallway and quickly found the pistol and the ice pick. He picked them up in one hand and the handbag in the other. "Follow me, please." He led her down a hallway to the rear of the building, stopping at a steel doorway. He tapped a code into a keypad beside the door, then opened it and motioned for her to follow. He climbed a flight of stairs, entered another code beside another steel door, then took her down a hallway to a comfortably furnished office, where a rather handsome man sat at a desk, writing on a pad. The shorter man set M-T's handbag and weapons on the desk and left.

Without looking up, the man motioned for her to sit down. He kept her waiting while he finished writing, then closed the folder before him and set it aside.

"You have come to see us sooner than I expected," he said.

"I had a little time on my hands," she replied.

The man took a pair of latex gloves from a desk drawer, then picked up her little pistol. "Crude but effective, no doubt," he said.

"It does very nicely at short ranges. I wouldn't like to try to hit a target across a street."

He stood up, took a clump of keys from his pocket, and unlocked a steel cabinet. From it he removed a black cardboard box and set it on his desk.

"I'm told that you are proficient with firearms," he said.

"I am."

He handed her a pair of latex gloves, then opened the box, removed a pistol from it, and laid it on the desk. "Have you ever seen one of these?"

M-T donned the gloves, picked up the weapon, and examined it. It was a .22-caliber semiautomatic with a slightly thicker barrel than she would have expected. She ejected the magazine and examined that, too. "I've never seen one like this. It has no markings of any kind."

"We took it from a CIA agent in Beirut late last year," the man said. He took a silencer from the box and handed her that, too. She installed it with a simple half turn. "Very nice," she said. "An assassin's weapon — light, easily concealed, and, I've no doubt, very accurate, especially with the silencer."

"It was custom-manufactured for the CIA. Only a couple of hundred were made, according to the man we took it from in Beirut. While it has no manufacturer's markings and there are no identifying marks on any of its parts, we have discovered that the barrel's rifling leaves a very distinctive pattern on the bullets fired from it. Part of the inside of the barrel is a freely rotating cylinder, so every time the weapon is fired, a different ballistic pattern is etched onto the bullet."

"I've never heard of that," she said admiringly. "It's ingenious."

"We have also learned that if any American police department runs a ballistics check on one of its bullets, the FBI comparison program will flag it as being very special and highly classified."

"So, when the police remove the bullet from your traitorous colleague, it will be known that he was killed with a CIA weapon?"

"Exactly. But if you fire more than once, each bullet will appear to have come from a different weapon."

"And who is the gentleman? Do you have a photograph?"

"He is the man who brought you to this office," the man said. "The shorter of the two who greeted you at the elevator. Do you remember him well enough, or do you still want a photograph?"

"I remember him very well," M-T replied.

"He lives six blocks north of the embassy," the man said, "and he always walks home after work, leaving at around five-thirty. He walks up the east side of Park Avenue, where the sidewalks are wide and not crowded, even at rush hour."

"Will today be soon enough?" M-T asked.

"Today will be very satisfactory. What assistance do you require?"

"I will need an untraceable escape vehicle — a motorcycle, preferably — and someone to drive it. Can you do that in the time available?"

"We can manage that."

She looked at her watch. "I have a little over an hour. I'll reconnoiter and phone you with a location."

He wrote a number on a piece of paper and showed it to her. "Memorize it," he said.

She did so, then put the weapon into her handbag and stood up. "If there's nothing else?"

He took an envelope from his desk and handed it to her. "Some walking-around money, as the Americans say."

"I assume that, since the ballistics will identify the bullet as CIA, you will not need me to dump the weapon where it can be found?"

"Please keep it, with my compliments," he replied, standing up.

They shook hands, in spite of the latex gloves, and she left.

Downstairs, she walked to Park Avenue, then uptown. Four blocks along, she found a recessed, wrought-iron gate leading to a narrow alleyway beside a large apartment building. She stood in the recess and looked up and down Park. This would do nicely. She used her cell phone to call the number.

"Yes?"

She gave him the address of the building she stood next to. "Please have the vehicle follow your friend from a little distance. When the driver sees him fall, he is to pull up near the body. I will hop on, and he can drop me a few blocks away."

"It will be done."

"I won't shoot unless I see the motorcycle there. If the driver tries to go past me, I'll shoot him, so please instruct him carefully."

"I understand."

"Goodbye."

"You may call this number if you ever need assistance. I am called Ali."

"Thank you." She punched off. She walked over to Madison Avenue and window-shopped for half an hour, then walked back to her chosen spot. She stood in the little recess, leaning against the building, and looked downtown, from whence her quarry would be coming. Ten minutes passed before she saw him, a block away. She did not see the motorcycle.

"Right on time," she said aloud to herself. "Let's hope my transportation arrives as promptly." She watched the man approach, now half a block away, waiting to cross the street. As he stepped off the curb, she saw the motorcycle. She knelt beside her handbag and checked the weapon, then she stood up and slung the bag over her shoulder and put her hand inside. She turned to look uptown, then down again. He was walking quickly, and the nearest pedestrian was half a block from him. The motorcycle stopped at the corner, idling.

She pressed her back against the downtown side of the recess, so that he couldn't see her. Then he appeared. She stepped out of the alcove with a last look around, took the weapon from the bag, and fired once at the back of his head from a distance of six feet. He fell like a butchered animal. She stepped closer and fired two more rounds into his head, then returned the pistol to her bag.

The motorcycle came to a stop a few feet away. She hopped onto the pillion seat, sidesaddle. "Drive to Seventy-second Street and turn left," she said.

The driver followed instructions.

"Now, straight ahead, and into the park."

He drove into the park.

"Stop here," she said, "and thank you."

He stopped, she hopped off, and he drove away without a word. From his size, and in spite of the helmet, she thought he was Ali, the man who had given her the pistol.

She strolled south in Central Park, found a bench, and waited, her hand in her bag, on the pistol, to see if anyone pursued her. No one did.

28

Stone left the interstate north of Danbury and turned onto narrower country roads.

"It's beautiful up here," Carpenter said as they crossed a bridge over a long lake. "Like England, but with a great many more trees."

"It's not called New England for nothing," Stone said.

"England would have looked like this in the eighteenth century," she said, "before we denuded the country of forests."

They drove alongside a creek and passed an old mill. "Now *that's* my idea of New England," she said, "taken mostly from picture postcards."

They drove through Bridgewater. "Another twenty minutes," he said.

"Take as long as you like," she replied. "I'm enjoying it."

They came to Washington, and Stone turned left, then, after a short distance, left again. A couple of hundred yards along, he turned into his driveway.

"Oh, it's lovely!" They got out of the car, and Stone took their luggage from the trunk.

"It was originally the gatehouse for the big place next door," he said.

"Who lives there?" she asked, looking over at the large Shingle-style house.

"A writer, until recently, but he moved to the city. A movie producer bought it, but he hasn't moved in yet."

"Still, you have a lot of privacy," she said, "with the trees and the hedge. And I love the turret."

Stone unlocked the door, entered the alarm code, and adjusted the thermostat. "Can I get you a drink?"

"I'd love one of your bourbon whiskies," she replied, walking around the house, inspecting the new kitchen, the mahogany floors, and the comfortable furniture. She chose a sofa and sat down.

Stone brought in their drinks and sat down beside her. "We'll need to go to the grocery store soon. It closes at six-thirty."

Dino was clearing his desk, getting ready to go home for the day, still tired from lack of sleep the night before, when a message generated by a 911 call popped onto his computer screen. A shooting on Park Avenue? That hardly ever happened. Through the glass wall of his office, he saw two detectives rise from their desks. They were next on the rotation, and they would take the call. He would tag along, just to see what people were doing to each other on Park Avenue these days. Anyway, it was on his way home.

The block had been closed off, creating a

huge, rush-hour traffic jam. Dino got out of his car, ducked under the crime-scene tape, and found a uniformed officer. "What happened?" he asked.

The officer pointed at the body of a man, lying facedown on the sidewalk, leaking blood. Two EMTs were just turning him over.

"As soon as they pronounce him, throw a sheet over the body and open the street," Dino said to a sergeant as he approached the body. "Whataya got?" he asked an EMT.

"Looks like two, maybe three, to the back of the head," the EMT replied.

"You calling it?"

The EMT nodded.

"Okay," he said to the sergeant. "Run it down for me." His two detectives had arrived and were ready to take notes.

"The building doorman saw the guy fall," the sergeant said, "but he didn't hear anything. A woman — a blonde, medium height and weight, thirties — walked away from him, hopped onto the back of a light motorcycle, and was driven north on Park. That's about it."

"Two or three gunshots, and he didn't hear anything?"

"That's what he says. We haven't found anybody else who saw what happened."

"It's an execution," Dino said, "using a silencer. The lady was a pro. Who's the dead guy?"

"Mohammed Salaam, works at one of the UN

embassies, about four blocks down, between Park and Lex. He was carrying a diplomatic passport." He showed it to Dino.

"Sounds political," Dino said. He turned to the detectives. "Report it to the FBI after the scene has been milked dry. Tell the techs to hurry it along, and get the body off the street as soon as you can. We've got traffic backed up to Forty-second Street, and even opening Park isn't helping because of all the rubbernecking. I do not want to hear from the commissioner, or worse, the mayor, about this. Do you understand?"

"Yes, boss," the senior detective said.

Dino got into his car. "Take me home," he said. "Use the siren, if you have to." He dialed his captain's cell phone.

"Grady," the captain said.

"It's Bacchetti, Cap. We've got what looks like a political assassination on Park Avenue, diplomat from one of the UN embassies, Arab."

"Aw, shit," the captain said.

"My sentiments exactly. I told my guys to call the Feds after they've worked the scene. I'd appreciate a call to the ME to get the autopsy done before they yank the body out of our hands."

"Will do. You need any help?"

"I think we've got it covered. I've told the team to clear the scene as soon as possible. We've already got traffic moving on Park again, should anybody ask."

"You got any theories yet?"

"Could have something to do with this lady assassin the Brits are all hot about," Dino replied. "I'll look into that."

"Good man. Call me if you need me."

"Thanks, Cap."

Dino's car drew up in front of his building, and he went upstairs. His son, Ben, was lying on his belly in Dino's study in front of the TV, apparently making a stab at his homework. "Hey, kiddo," Dino said, ruffling his hair. "Whatcha doin'?"

"Math," Ben said.

"Do it in your room, okay? I gotta make some calls."

Mary Ann came into the room wearing an apron dotted with red sauce. She kissed him firmly on the lips. "You're home for dinner? Good God!"

"Don't gimme a hard time," he said, kissing her again.

"How was Saint Thomas?"

"Awful. I had to sleep on a goddamned boat last night, got about two hours. I'm beat."

"Have a drink, that'll help. Dinner's in an hour."

Dino poured himself a stiff Scotch and sat down in his favorite chair. He picked up the phone and called Stone, got an answering machine. "Call me," he said, and hung up. He tried Stone's cell phone and got a recorded message. "What the fuck?" he muttered to himself. He found his phone book and looked up the Connecticut number.

"Hello?" Stone said.

"What are you doing up there?" Dino asked.

"Hiding Carpenter."

"What's the latest on La Biche?"

"She got a late flight to London last night, and this morning murdered another passenger and took her ID. The Brits lost her."

"So she's not in the city?"

"Who knows? Carpenter says she wouldn't be surprised if she doubled back. Why do you ask?"

"An Arab guy got himself popped on Park Avenue an hour ago," Dino said. "Two or three in the head, no noise."

"Uh-oh."

"Could be our girl."

"Let's not jump to that conclusion. Could have been an irritated Israeli. That situation is hot right now."

"We'll look at that, too. Tell Carpenter to call me if she wants to talk, and I'd like to hear anything she has about what her people think."

"Okay. She's cooking dinner right now, and I'm sure as hell not going to disturb her."

"Time you had a home-cooked meal," Dino said.

"I won't argue with that." Stone hung up.

Dino hung up, took a big swallow of his Scotch, put his head back, and fell immediately asleep.

29

Stone walked back into the kitchen where Carpenter was doing something to a sauce. "Smells good," he said, pouring them both another drink. "What is it?"

"Chicken breast with tarragon sauce."

"A red wine okay?"

"That's fine. Who was on the phone? Who knows you're here?"

Stone went to the wine cooler and found a bottle of the Far Niente Cabernet. "Dino tracked me down. An Arab diplomat has been murdered on Park Avenue. Looks like a hit. That give you any ideas?"

"You mean, La Biche?"

"That's what Dino's wondering."

"I wouldn't be surprised if she's already back in the city, but why shoot somebody else when she's looking for me?"

"I don't know, maybe she doesn't want to get rusty."

"You get the guy's name?"

"No. You want me to call Dino back?"

"Tomorrow will be soon enough."

"Dino wants you to call him if you have anything to contribute. He wants to know what your people come up with."

"Tomorrow will be soon enough." She popped a pair of boned chicken breasts into some hot, clarified butter.

Stone liked the sizzle and the smell. "La Biche isn't going to get tired of looking for you, is she?"

"No, I don't think so."

"You know anything about her you haven't told me?" Stone asked.

"Well, let's see. She's unclassifiable as to type of killing. She's used everything from pistols to ice picks to garrotes. A favorite means of avoiding arrests is what she's just done in New York: She picks up a girl in a bar, usually a lesbian, goes home with her, murders her, takes her clothes and ID, then disappears. She did this three times in three days in Paris last year."

"Makes her awfully hard to track, doesn't it?"

"It certainly does. We don't know who to look for until the victim's body turns up, and that can take days. By then, she's somebody else."

"You've seen her face-to-face, now. Can you improve on the CIA-generated portrait?"

"I'm afraid not," Carpenter replied, stirring her sauce and dropping some French green beans into boiling water and adding salt. "The drawing is accurate, as far as it goes, but her looks are so unremarkable that, with some hair dye and a little makeup, she could be anybody. If we had a good mug shot, that might help, but not much. The girl is a chameleon."

"You think she's a lesbian?"

"I don't know. Maybe she hates lesbians."

"I'll set the table," Stone said. He got some dishes, napkins, and silver, and spread everything out. "Time to light the candles?" he asked.

She dumped the beans into a colander, then put them into a skillet with some butter and garlic. "May as well," she said. "It'll be ready in a minute."

Stone found a couple of Baccarat wineglasses and lit the candles. I do lovely work, he thought, gazing at the table.

"Bring me the plates," Carpenter called. "I'll serve us in here."

Stone took the plates into the kitchen and watched as she quickly arranged the food on them, looking very professional. He took them into the dining room, placed them on the table, held a chair for Carpenter, and poured the wine.

"*Bon appétit,*" she said, raising her glass.

"Looks wonderful," he said. He tasted his chicken. "You may cook all my meals," he said, eating hungrily.

"Don't count on it," she replied, taking a bite.

"What's your feeling about this Park Avenue shooting?"

"It doesn't feel good, does it?"

"Maybe we should just stay in Connecticut," he said. "She'd never find us here."

Marie-Thérèse walked into Elaine's and looked around. She'd read about this place, most recently on Page Six, and she was surprised that it wasn't fancier. What lay before her was a homey-looking neighborhood restaurant with a dining room stretching to the back of the building, checkered tablecloths, and a long bar on her left. The headwaiter was looking at her, but she pointed at the bar and took an empty stool at the end, her back to the window. She was wearing a sleek, black cocktail dress from Armani and some very nice pearls that she had stolen from a victim some time ago. The bartender came over.

"Johnnie Walker Black, on the rocks," she said, in her best American accent.

He brought the drink. "You having dinner?" he asked.

"Can I eat at the bar?"

"Sure. I'll get you a menu."

She sipped her Scotch and surveyed the crowd. She recognized two or three faces from the movies or the celebrity magazines, which she read voraciously. She liked the place. The bartender brought the menu, and she ordered a Caesar salad and a steak. "Have a drink on me," she said to the bartender.

He poured himself a small Scotch, raised his glass to her, and sipped it.

She wanted him friendly.

She fended off a couple of passes from guys at the bar, and when her dinner came, she ate it and ignored them. When she was finished, she ordered a cognac.

The bartender brought it. "Haven't seen you in here before, have I?"

"Nope. I'm from San Francisco. It's my first time in New York."

"Maybe you need somebody to show you the sights," he said.

"Maybe I do, at that," she replied, smiling. "Say, tell me something."

"Anything at all," he said.

She dug into her handbag and came out with a clipping. "I saw this on Page Six a few days ago." She handed him the clipping.

He chuckled and handed it back. "Yeah, Elaine gets mentioned like that all the time."

"Who's the lawyer with the 'hard' name?"

"Oh, that's Stone," the bartender said. "Stone Barrington."

"Who is he?"

"Used to be a cop, now he's a lawyer. He's in here two or three nights a week."

"Is he here now?" she asked, looking around.

"Not tonight," the bartender said. "You want to meet him, is that it?"

"Not really. I was just intrigued by the story about the guy falling through the skylight." She smiled. "I think I'd rather be shown the sights." She liked the bartender; he was cute.

Stone lay in bed, wide awake. They had made love half an hour ago.

"You awake?" Carpenter asked.

"Oddly enough, yes."

"I thought sex rendered men unconscious."

"Usually it does," he said.

"Stop thinking about La Biche. We'll get her, eventually."

"Before she gets you?"

She rolled over and put her head on his shoulder. "You wouldn't let that happen, would you?"

"Of course not."

She put her hand on his belly and stroked. "You want another shot at unconsciousness?"

"You betcha," Stone said, turning toward her.

30

Dino had finished dinner and was back in his chair with the TV going, but he was having trouble staying awake.

"Why don't you go to bed?" Mary Ann asked.

"It's too early," Dino replied. "I'd just wake up at four o'clock in the morning. Stimulate me. Talk to me."

She left the sofa, crossed the room, and sat in his lap. "I'll stimulate you," she said, moving around on his crotch.

The phone rang.

"Ignore it," she said. "Let the machine pick up." She kissed him.

Dino kissed her back. He seemed to be waking up.

The machine clicked on. "Dino, it's Elaine," she said. "I need to talk to you now. Pick up."

"Fuck her," Mary Ann said.

"Right," Dino replied, unbuttoning her blouse and reaching for a breast.

His cell phone rang. "That's gotta be the precinct," he said. "Let me get rid of them."

"Oh, all right," Mary Ann replied, running her tongue around his ear.

Dino fumbled under Mary Ann for the phone

and got it open. "This better be good," he said.

"It's Elaine. Get over here."

"What?"

"You remember that conversation about this woman finding Stone by reading Page Six?"

"Yeah."

"There's a woman at the bar with the clipping, asking about Stone."

"Describe her."

"Well dressed, thirties, medium everything."

"Do what you can to keep her there, but don't piss her off. I'm on my way." He shut the phone and kissed Mary Ann. "Sorry, baby, but something hot has come up."

"Is she hotter than me?" Mary Ann asked, pushing him back into the chair.

"She's committed four murders that we know of, and she's at the bar, at Elaine's."

"I give up," Mary Ann said, getting up and buttoning her blouse. "I'm never gonna get laid."

"Don't you believe it," Dino said, grabbing his coat and heading for the door, the cell phone in his hand.

He grabbed a cab in front of his building. "Eighty-eighth and Second," he said to the driver, then began dialing the precinct. "Gimme the duty commander," he said. "This is Bacchetti. We got a rumble on a suspect in this afternoon's shooting on Park Avenue. She's at Elaine's restaurant, Second between Eighty-eighth and Eighty-ninth, west side of the street, sitting at the bar, her back to the window. I'm on my way there now. I want a SWAT team . . . Scrub that, I want eight people in plain clothes, no visible weapons, no sirens on the way — shit, they can run all the way, it's that close. Nobody parks out front, nobody enters the restaurant but me."

The cab drew to a halt at the corner of Eighty-eighth and Second. Dino gave the driver a five and got out, still talking on the cell phone.

"I'm going into the restaurant now. I want two people on either side of the door, not visible from inside, and four across the street. Suspect is a white female, thirties, medium height and weight, alone, probably armed and very dangerous. Any questions?"

"No, Lieutenant," the detective answered.

"Call me on my cell phone when everybody is in position."

"Got it."

Dino hung up and called Elaine's, got her on the phone. "I'm coming in alone in just a minute. Is there an empty table by the bar?"

"No, but Sid Zion is at number four with two other guys. He's got a couple of empty chairs. I'll tell him you're coming."

"That's good. Pay no attention to the woman at the bar. Don't even look at her. Has she moved?"

"No."

"I'm coming in now." Dino checked his weapon, returned it to his holster, and walked into Elaine's.

★ ★ ★

Suddenly, Marie-Thérèse was nervous. The bartender had said something to the restaurant's owner, and she had made a phone call. Now she was on the phone again, and she had glanced at where she was sitting at the bar.

The front door opened and a man walked in: not too tall, Mediterranean-looking.

Dino walked toward table number four, where Sidney Zion, a journalist and writer, was sitting. "Hey, Sid," Dino said, pumping his hand. "Mind if I join you?"

"Sit down, Dino," Zion replied.

Dino took a seat with a good view of a woman at the bar he thought was probably Marie-Thérèse.

The man was a cop, she could feel it. "Where's the ladies' room?" she asked the bartender.

"Back that way, take a right, second door on the left."

Marie-Thérèse left her coat on the bar stool, picked up her bag, and began walking toward the rear of the restaurant. Straight ahead, all the way to the back, was a door, but two large men were sitting at a table squarely in front of it. She turned right, toward the ladies' room, first looking into the kitchen: no visible way out. She went into the ladies' room; no one there. She tried the window. It was small, but she could fit through it. She got it open, but it was covered with burglar bars.

She opened her handbag and began removing things. She took the top off the toilet tank, wiped the CIA pistol and the ice pick with a towel, dropped them into the tank, and replaced the cover. She ripped up her false passport, dropped it into the toilet, and flushed. Then she got out her cell phone and started dialing.

Dino's cell phone vibrated. "Bacchetti."

"Lieutenant, everybody's in place."

"Tell them to sit tight. We're going to wait until she's ready to leave. I'll follow her out the front door, then everybody converge."

"Got it."

Dino put the cell phone away and looked around. Still in the ladies' room.

"Hello?"

"Ali?"

"Yes. Is this my appointment from this afternoon?"

"Yes. I think I'm about to be arrested, and I'm going to need a lawyer."

"Where are you?"

"At a restaurant called Elaine's, on Second Avenue, between Eighty-eighth and Eighty-ninth streets."

"You're quite near the Nineteenth Precinct. They'll take you there, unless they're federal."

"My guess is local police."

"Your lawyer's name is Sol Kaminsky. I'll call him, and he'll be there in half an hour. Say nothing to the police."

"I'm going to talk to them, play it innocent," she said.

"That's your judgment to make. Are you dirty?"

"I've just cleaned up. I have a good passport."

"Good. I'll tell Kaminsky. Call his number from the police station and leave a message on his answering machine. Memorize the number." He recited it to her.

"You're sending me a Jewish lawyer?"

"We retain him. He's good. What will your name be?"

"Marie-Thérèse du Bois."

"Your *real* name?"

"Trust me."

"What will you give for an address?"

"I don't know."

"We keep room one-oh-oh-three at the Hotel Kirwan, on Park Avenue South at Thirty-seventh Street. Use that address. I'll get some women's clothes and a suitcase over there, too."

"Thank you." She closed the phone, returned it to her handbag, checked her makeup, and left the ladies' room. Maybe she was just paranoid. She hoped so. She returned to her bar stool. "Can I have the check, please?" she asked the bartender.

He brought her the check. "What's your name, and how can I get in touch?" he asked.

She took a pen and a small pad from her purse and wrote down her name and cell phone number. "Call me tomorrow," she said. She put some cash on the bar, including a big tip, got into her coat, and started for the door. Out of the corner of her eye, she saw the cop get up from his table and reach for his coat.

She walked outside and stood at the curb, her hand held up for a taxi. Then he was behind her.

"Freeze, police!" Dino said, his weapon stretched out before him. He kept a good six feet between them.

Marie-Thérèse looked over her shoulder, feigning surprise. "What?" she said.

Then they were all over her, cuffing her wrists, going through her handbag. "No weapons," a detective said.

"Search the ladies' room," Dino replied, as they hustled her into a squad car.

31

Stone snapped out of a deep sleep. The phone was ringing. He was momentarily disoriented, looking around the dark bedroom, trying to figure out where he was.

"Are you going to answer that?" Carpenter asked.

Stone fumbled for the phone. "Hello?"

"Gee, I hope I didn't interrupt any screwing," Dino said.

"Dino, what's going on? What time is it?"

"Not all that late. Let me speak to Carpenter."

"She's asleep."

"No, I'm not," Carpenter said, snatching the phone from Stone. "Hello, Dino?"

"Sorry to wake you up, but I thought you'd want to be brought up to date on developments."

"What's happened?"

"I arrested a young woman — early thirties, medium height, medium build — at Elaine's tonight."

"You mean you've *got* her?"

"Looks that way."

"How did you identify her?"

192

"She's carrying a Swiss passport in the name of Marie-Thérèse du Bois, and she matches the picture."

"I'm on my way," Carpenter said. "Don't you *dare* let her get away."

"She's locked in an interrogation room. She's not going anywhere."

"I'll be there in an hour and a half. You can use the time to good effect by photographing her repeatedly and fingerprinting her. Get DNA samples, too."

"She's called a lawyer, but I don't know how that's going to help her. I've got the deputy DA on the way, too. Hurry up!" He hung up.

"Dino's got La Biche?" Stone asked incredulously.

Carpenter was already digging clothes out of her bag. "Yes, and she's admitted who she is. I'm having trouble believing this myself! Get dressed, for Christ's sake!"

Stone started grabbing at clothes.

Dino walked down the hall to Interrogation One and checked out the woman through the one-way mirror. She was sitting, looking worried and baffled. "Yeah, sugar," Dino said aloud. "I'd be worried, too, because I've got your ass!"

His boss, Captain Grady, walked in. "Okay, so who is this woman?"

"Her name is Marie-Thérèse du Bois. She's the suspect in the diplomatic killing on Park Avenue."

"Is that all you know about her?"

"According to our friends across the sea in British intelligence, she's a big-time assassin who's murdered people all over Europe. By the way, she's killed at least three other people since she arrived in New York." He handed Grady her passport.

Grady flipped through it and stopped. "This says she arrived in the U.S. from Canada yesterday," he said, pointing at a stamp.

Dino looked at it. "Gotta be a fake," he said.

"Run it past the Feds."

"Not yet, Cap. I don't want them in on this. I've got a lady from British intelligence on the way here now."

"When's she coming?"

"She's driving down from Connecticut with a friend of mine; maybe an hour."

"Is this friend of yours Barrington?"

"Ah, yeah, Cap. Why do you ask?"

"Because you don't have any other friends. What's he got to do with this?"

"Well, he and the Brit lady are sort of an item. We both met her in London last year."

"Have you talked to your suspect yet?"

"I was just about to when you got here. I was waiting for the deputy DA to get here, too."

"You got him out of bed?" Grady asked, chortling. "I want to see that."

"You're looking at it, Captain," a voice behind them said.

Dino and the captain turned to find George

194

Mellon, the deputy DA, standing behind them.

"She doesn't look all that dangerous," he said, peering through the glass.

"I'm going to go in and feel her out," Dino said.

"Get her signature on a Miranda waiver before you ask her a fucking thing," Mellon said.

Dino opened the door and went into the room.

Stone was driving down the nearly deserted I-684 at 140 miles per hour.

"Won't this thing go any faster?" Carpenter demanded.

"Yes, it will, but *I* won't go any faster. I've never driven this fast in my life."

"Chicken," she muttered.

Stone eased the accelerator to the floor, and the speed climbed another fifteen mph. "I forgot, the speed is electronically limited to one-fifty-five."

"Shit," Carpenter said. "Why didn't you buy something fast?"

Stone began thinking about what he might say to a New York State trooper, and about the roadblock that might have already been set up ahead of him somewhere. He checked the sky for helicopters.

"Good evening," Dino said. "I am Lieutenant Dino Bacchetti."

She offered her hand without getting up, like a lady. "How do you do?" she said.

"I do very well," Dino replied, shaking her hand.

"Why on earth was I brought here?" she demanded, half angry, half frightened.

"Before we go any further, I have to advise you of your rights under the United States Constitution." He recited the Miranda mantra. "Do you understand these rights?"

"Of course. So you think I have never watched television?"

Dino handed her a sheet of paper and a pen. "Then please sign this statement to that effect."

She read it and signed it.

Dino placed her passport on the table. "This says you are Marie-Thérèse du Bois, of a Zurich, Switzerland, address. Is that correct?"

"Yes, it's correct."

"I'd like to ask you a few questions," Dino said.

"About what?"

"When did you arrive in the United States?"

"It's in my passport." She had put the stamp there herself.

"And where do you reside?"

"At the Hotel Kirwan, on Park Avenue at Thirty-seventh Street, room one-oh-oh-three."

"When did you check in?"

"Today . . ." She glanced at her watch. "Rather, yesterday. Do I need a lawyer?"

"I don't know, do you?"

"I am happy to answer your questions, but I would like a lawyer present, please."

196

Dino sighed. "I'll get you a phone." He went out of the room, got a cordless phone, and brought it back. "Would you like some privacy?"

"I doubt if I will get any," she said, nodding at the one-way mirror. She dialed a number. "Hello, this is Marie-Thérèse du Bois. I am being held at a police station. . . . One moment." She covered the receiver with her hand. "Where am I?"

"At the Nineteenth Precinct."

"At the Nineteenth Precinct, and I require legal representation at once. Please come here right away, ask for a Lieutenant . . ."

"Bacchetti."

"Lieutenant Bacchetti. Thank you." She handed the phone back to Dino.

"Now, will you please tell me why I am here?"

"You are here, Miss du Bois, because you are a suspect in four murders in New York City."

She laughed. "Good God! And when am I supposed to have committed these murders?"

"In the last couple of days."

"I have spent the last couple of days driving down here from Canada with a friend."

"What is your friend's name?" Dino asked, taking out his notebook. "I'd like to corroborate that."

"His name is Michel Robert. He is Canadian."

"And where might I find him?"

"Frankly, I don't know," she said. "We had a *petit contretemps*. He left me in New York and

197

went away, I don't know where. May I ask on what evidence you suspect me of these preposterous charges?"

"We'll get to that later," Dino said. "Excuse me a moment." He got up and went outside to speak to Mellon.

"She asked a good question, Dino," Mellon said. "On what evidence do you suspect her of these murders?"

"There's a British intelligence agent on the way here now who can identify her and tell you about her background," Dino said.

"Was she carrying anything that we can use?"

"No," Dino said, "but before I arrested her at Elaine's she went to the ladies' room. That's being searched now."

Two detectives walked in, and one was holding a large Ziploc bag containing a black pistol and a silencer, as well as an ice pick.

"Am I glad to see *that*," Dino said. "Go dust it for prints, fire it for ballistics, and check it against the slugs from the guy on Park Avenue, and be quick about it." He turned back to Mellon. "Feeling better now?"

"A little," Mellon said. "Can you tie her to the murder?"

"You just heard me tell my guys to go do that, didn't you?"

"Have you printed her?"

"Not yet. We can do that now."

A small, plump man bustled into the room. "Where is my client?" he demanded.

"Hello, Sol," Mellon said. "Who brought you into this?"

"She did," Mellon said, pointing through the glass. "I want to talk to her now, and I want everybody out of here while I do it."

"How long do you need?"

"I'll let you know, George. Now get out of here and let me do my work."

Dino, the captain, and the deputy DA filed out of the room and went to Dino's office. "Who is that guy, George?"

"His name is Sol Kaminsky, and he's a very smart lawyer. But unless you can tie this woman to that weapon and the weapon to one of these murders, he's not going to have to be very smart."

32

Stone crossed the Harlem River Bridge, slowing down only for E-ZPass to let him through. He looked at his watch: He never would have believed he could have gotten to Manhattan this fast.

"What's taking us so long?" Carpenter demanded.

"We've just broken the world record for a trip from Washington, Connecticut, to Manhattan," Stone said, "and by half an hour."

She sniffed. "So *you* say."

Dino, the captain, and the deputy DA had been chatting uneasily for forty minutes, while Sol Kaminsky talked to his client. The two detectives walked into Dino's office and placed the pistol, silencer, and ice pick on his desk.

"What?" Dino asked.

"No prints on any of these."

"What about the ballistics test?"

"Two of the bullets were too deformed to get a match," one of the detectives said, "but one of them was whole."

"And?"

"No match. Not even close. This is not the

piece that killed the diplomat."

"Shit!" Dino said.

"But this is a very interesting pistol."

"How so?"

"It has no manufacturer's markings anywhere on it. We ran the ballistics against the FBI database, and it came up federal, probably CIA or Defense Intelligence Agency, something like that."

Dino looked up to see Stone and Carpenter coming into the outer office. "Here's our Brit spy," he said. "Now we'll get somewhere." Dino introduced the two to the captain.

"Hello, Stone," George Mellon said, not offering his hand.

"Hi, George." Stone had once beaten him in court in a very embarrassing way.

"Where is she?" Carpenter asked.

Sol Kaminsky walked into Dino's office. "You and I can meet with my client now," he said. "Come on."

Everybody followed Kaminsky back to the interrogation room, and Dino went inside with him, while the others stood behind the one-way mirror.

Stone elbowed Carpenter. "Well, is that La Biche?"

"God," Carpenter said, "she looks so different. I'm not sure I could swear to it."

"Nothing like an eyewitness," the deputy DA muttered.

"All right, Lieutenant Bacchetti," Sol Kaminsky said, "my client has identified herself with her valid passport and answered your questions. What evidence do you have to connect her to any crime?"

Dino placed the pistol, silencer, and ice pick on the table without saying anything. He wanted to see her reaction.

Marie-Thérèse looked at her lawyer uncomprehendingly. "I don't understand," she said.

"The lieutenant, my dear, thinks these weapons belong to you," Kaminsky said.

"I have never seen any of them," she replied. "I have no need for weapons."

Kaminsky turned to Dino. "What evidence do you have connecting these weapons to my client?"

"She put them in the toilet tank in the ladies' room at Elaine's," Dino said with a sinking heart.

"How do you know this? Did you find her fingerprints on any of them?"

Dino gulped.

"Have you connected any of these weapons with any of the murders with a ballistic or other scientific test?"

"Not yet," Dino temporized.

"Do you have any witnesses who can place Ms. du Bois at the scene of any crime?"

"I'll be right back," Dino said. He left the

room and joined the others behind the one-way mirror. "What about it, Carpenter?"

Carpenter winced.

"She can't make the ID," Stone said.

George Mellon spoke. "This is not looking worth getting me out of bed for, Dino."

"Just hang on a minute," Dino said. "This woman is a professional assassin well known to the European authorities. Right, Carpenter? I can run her name against the Interpol database and find charges against her, can't I?"

Carpenter looked at the floor. "No," she said.

"*No?* And why the hell not?"

"She's in our files, but we've never shared them with any law enforcement agency. We'd hoped to pick her up ourselves."

Mellon spoke up again. "Am I to understand that there is no open charge against this woman anywhere in the world?"

"Not that I'm aware of," Carpenter replied.

"And there were no fingerprints on the weapons, and the ballistics test was negative?"

"That's about the size of it," Dino replied.

"Well, then, book her on a weapons charge until we've got something concrete."

Nobody said anything.

Mellon looked at Dino. "Am I to understand that you can't connect the woman with the weapons?"

"She was in the ladies' room at Elaine's. We found the weapons in the toilet tank immediately after she left," Dino said defensively.

"But you can't prove that she put them there," Mellon said. "Fifty women a night use the ladies' room, and any one of them could have deposited the weapons in the toilet tank at any time for months past, right?"

"Yes," Dino replied.

Mellon looked at all of them. "Anybody have any charge I can hang on this woman, even to hold her? Did she resist arrest, maybe? Assault a police officer?"

Nobody said anything.

Mellon began putting on his coat. "Then I'm out of here. Cut her loose." He walked out of the room.

Carpenter was on her cell phone. "Mason? La Biche is about to be released from the Nineteenth Precinct. Get a tail on her *now*."

Dino turned to the two detectives. "Grab anybody you can find and get out front. When she leaves, don't lose her. Keep her in sight until she gets to her hotel, then put two men in the hallway outside her room and tail her if she leaves the hotel."

"I'm sorry, Dino," Carpenter said.

Dino went back into the interrogation room. "Mr. Kaminsky, your client is free to go just as soon as I've photographed and fingerprinted her."

"In your dreams," Kaminsky replied. "My client is not under arrest and there is no probable cause to believe she has committed a crime. Good night, Lieutenant."

Dino led them out of the interrogation room. "My apologies for the inconvenience, Ms. du Bois," he said.

"Think nothing of it, Lieutenant," she replied.

Dino watched them leave, then led Carpenter and Stone into his office. "All we can do is tail her and hope she tries to kill somebody else."

"Probably me," Carpenter said.

A detective knocked on the door. "Lieutenant, I need to log that pistol and the ice pick. You got them?"

"They're on the table in Interrogation One," Dino said.

"No, sir, they're not."

"Oh, shit," Dino said.

Marie-Thérèse and Sol Kaminsky were riding down Second Avenue in a cab.

"You want me to drop you at your hotel?" Kaminsky asked.

"No, thank you, Mr. Kaminsky. I'll be getting out before then."

Their cab stopped at a traffic light. Marie-Thérèse looked out her window to find a large truck next to them. "Mr. Kaminsky, please get out of the cab," she said, "and walk away."

He looked at her. "In the middle of the street?"

"Yes, please."

Kaminsky opened the left rear door and stepped out of the cab. As he did so, Marie-

Thérèse handed the driver a twenty. "Keep your meter running until Thirty-fourth Street, and don't pick up anybody," she said. She opened her door as little as possible, fell out of the taxi onto the street, and began rolling her way under the truck. She had just cleared it when the light changed, and the truck drove away. She rolled under a parked car and waited.

A block behind her cab, a detective radioed the precinct. "Tell Bacchetti the lawyer got out of the cab at Seventy-seventh Street," he said. "We're still following." The light changed, and he drove on down Second Avenue.

Marie-Thérèse waited for the next change of the traffic light before she rolled from under the parked car, dusted off her clothes, and disappeared into the night.

33

Stone got Carpenter into a cab.

"I'm exhausted," Carpenter said.

"Let the cops and your people do their work," Stone said. "You can get some sleep at my house."

"That was a humiliating experience," Carpenter sighed, as they rode downtown.

"You might have mentioned to Dino earlier the fact that there were no charges against her in Europe."

"We didn't want Interpol or the various police agencies to interfere," she said.

"You just wanted to find her and quietly kill her. Is that it?"

Carpenter didn't reply.

"If there were no charges against her, how did you gather all this information about her — the people she's killed, and her methods?"

"From people we've . . . interrogated," Carpenter replied.

"Can't the testimony of those people be used to file charges against her, so Dino can make an arrest?"

"Those people are . . . no longer available to testify," Carpenter said.

Stone took a deep breath. "Oh," he said.

The detective following La Biche's taxi radioed in. "Tell Bacchetti the cab didn't go to the hotel. It's continuing downtown."

"This is Bacchetti," Dino said. "Where is the cab now?"

"At Second and Thirty-fourth, stopped at a light," the detective replied. "Wait a minute. The cab's light is on and a guy is getting in."

"Stop the cab," Dino said. "Arrest her for tampering with evidence. She stole the pistol."

The detective switched on his flashing light and drove up next to the cab. His partner got out and shone a light into the rear seat, then got back in. "Lieutenant," he said into the radio, "she's not in the cab anymore."

"*What?*"

"She's not there. We saw the lawyer get out, but not the woman. We thought she was still inside."

"Oh, swell," Dino said. He hung up and called Stone's house.

"Hello?" Stone said. Carpenter picked up the other bedside extension.

"We've lost her," he said.

"How?" Stone asked.

"My guys saw Kaminsky get out of the cab at Seventy-seventh Street, but not La Biche. Now she's not in the cab anymore. What's more, she stole back the pistol and the ice pick, took them right off the table in the interrogation room when I went to the door. Didn't any of you behind the mirror see that?"

"We were talking to each other," Stone said.

"It's not your fault, Dino," Carpenter said. "It's ours."

"Sorry, babe," Dino said. "I can put an APB out for her for stealing the pistol, if you like."

"Can you prove she stole it?"

"I can, if I can catch her with it."

"And what do you think the chances of that are?"

Dino was quiet.

"Good night, Dino." Carpenter hung up.

So did Stone. "What now?"

Carpenter dialed a number. "Mason," she said.

Stone picked up the extension.

"Mason," a man's voice said.

"Tell me you're still on her," Carpenter said.

"We're not, I'm afraid," Mason replied. "There was no way we could get to the precinct before she left."

"I was afraid of that. The NYPD lost her. They've been chasing an empty cab since Seventy-seventh Street."

"Good God. Why didn't they hold her?"

"That one is our fault, I'm afraid. We never filed any charges against her, and the NYPD had nothing on her. They found a pistol in the ladies' room at Elaine's, but the ballistics didn't match the slug from the diplomatic killing, and she didn't use a gun on the others."

"I'm very sorry to hear it," Mason said.

"On top of everything else, she stole the pistol back from the police, walked right out of the precinct with it in her handbag."

"So where we are now sounds very much like square one."

"Very much."

"Architect will not be amused."

"Well, no. Get some sleep, Mason. We'll speak in the morning."

"Where are you?"

"At Barrington's house."

"I'll send some people over."

"Don't bother. I think we're safe for tonight."

"Good night, then."

"Good night."

Stone and Carpenter hung up.

"I loved your house in Connecticut," she said.

Marie-Thérèse let herself into the twenty-four-hour-a-day storage facility, went to her closet, and unlocked the door, closing it behind her. The space was about eight by ten feet, much like a prison cell, she thought. She stripped down to the skin, took a fur coat from a rack of clothes, and spread it on the floor. She found another coat and wrapped herself in it, then lay down on the fur coat.

Now she had used her most valuable, most hoarded resource: her own identity. She would not be able to use it again. Not, she thought, un-less they were so stupid as not to enter it into their computers and send it to Interpol.

She fell asleep thinking of the baby she had held in her lap all the way across the Atlantic.

34

Five men and four women got off a Concorde flight at JFK and got into two waiting vans. The driver of one handed one of the men a cell phone. "Just hold down the number one, sir."

He held down the number one, then put the phone to his ear.

"Trading Partners," a woman's voice said.

"Do you know who this is?"

"Yes, sir."

"We're en route. I want a meeting in one hour, with everybody, and I mean *everybody*."

"I understand, sir. I've been holding the conference room."

"Good." He snapped the phone shut and handed it back to the driver.

"It's yours, sir, while you're here," the driver said.

Architect put the phone in his pocket and turned his attention to the *New York Times*.

The phone rang in Stone's bedroom. "Hello?" he said sleepily, glancing at the clock.

"Miss Carpenter, please," a woman's voice said.

Stone shook Carpenter awake. "Call for you," he said.

"What time is it?" Carpenter asked, rolling over and picking up the extension.

Stone hung up his phone. "A little after two P.M. We slept pretty good."

"Hello?"

"Architect has arrived. There's a meeting here at three," the woman said. "Attendance is mandatory."

"Right," Carpenter said. She hung up. "I've got to get into a shower," she said to Stone. "My boss is in from London." She tossed off the covers and ran for the bathroom. "Any chance of some lunch?"

Stone went down to the kitchen and made a couple of ham sandwiches and brought them back upstairs. Carpenter came out of the shower, toweling her hair dry around the edges.

"That looks good," she said, grabbing a sandwich and taking a huge bite.

"So, what's this meeting going to be about?" Stone asked.

"I think you can guess."

"How the hell are you ever going to find her?" he asked.

"We'll find her, and we'll deal with her," Carpenter replied, her mouth full. She went back into the bathroom, taking her sandwich with her.

Stone picked up the phone and called Dino.

"Bacchetti."

"You had lunch?"

"I missed it," Dino said.

213

"Clarke's in half an hour?"

"You buying?"

"Yes."

"Then let's make it the Four Seasons." Dino hung up.

Stone went to his own bathroom and got into the shower. Twenty minutes later, he stood on his doorstep with Carpenter.

"Dinner?" he asked.

"I'll have to call you," she replied, kissing him. She ran down the steps and turned toward Third Avenue.

Stone turned toward Park.

The last of the lunch crowd lingered over their espressos in the Grill Room of the Four Seasons. Getting a table was easy, since half the crowd had gone back to their offices. Stone and Dino ordered salads and omelettes and a couple of glasses of wine.

"How'd La Biche come to be in Elaine's at exactly the time you were?" Stone asked.

"She came in looking for you."

"*What?*"

"I kid you not. She came in, took a seat at the bar, ordered dinner, and whipped out that Page Six clipping about you representing Herbie Fisher. Asked the bartender who you were."

"Did he tell her?"

"I don't know. I was pretty busy. Elaine called me at home and told me somebody was asking about you, so I disappointed my wife, who was snuggled up to me at the time, and got my ass over there in a hurry. There she was, sipping a brandy."

Stone thought about this.

"So why'd you want to have lunch? I had the feeling you had something on your mind."

"Something's brewing with our British friends," Stone said.

"Oh, yeah?"

"The big cheese arrived from London and has called a meeting of his people."

"Why do I care about this?" Dino asked.

"Because I think there's about to be a rumble on your turf."

"What kind of rumble?" Dino asked.

"Think about it."

"What, I have to guess?"

"That's what *I'm* doing. Anybody call you this afternoon? Any Brits, I mean?"

"Nope. Should I expect to hear from them?"

"I don't think so," Stone replied.

"Come on, Stone, what has Carpenter told you?"

"Only that there's a meeting."

"And what do you think is going to be the subject of that meeting?"

"Don't be obtuse, Dino."

"Okay, I know the subject. What are they going to do?"

"I think they're going to hunt her down and kill her," Stone said.

"Right here in New York City?"

"Yes. Of course, they may only want to kidnap and torture her, but I think the chances of taking the lady alive are nil."

Dino chewed his salad and thought about it. "Okay," he said finally.

"What do you mean, okay?"

"I mean, it's okay with me if they hunt her down and kill her, or just kidnap and torture her."

"Jesus, Dino, you're a New York City police lieutenant. Are you going to let that happen?"

"Yep," Dino said, sipping his wine.

"We're talking about murder, Dino. You're supposed to take a dim view of that."

"You're such a wuss, Stone," Dino said.

"No, I'm not. I'm just opposed to murder in the streets of my hometown."

"Well, I'm sure that when the murderers hear about that, there'll be a dramatic drop in the homicide rate," Dino replied.

"Dino, you've got to do something."

"What am I going to do?" Dino asked. "These people are not visiting policemen. They're fucking spies. They do things in secret. You think they're going to let me in on their plans?"

"Maybe I can find out something."

"I don't want to know," Dino said. "And if you want to keep rolling around in the hay with Miss Felicity Devonshire, you'd better not want to know, either."

"You want to know why there are no charges against La Biche in Europe?" Stone said.

"No, but I have a feeling you're going to tell me."

"Because the Brits got their information on her by torturing and killing her friends, so there's nobody left to give evidence against her."

"I didn't want to know that," Dino said.

"It's how they work. These people don't arrest criminals and try them. They put them in cellars while they extract information from them with tools, and when they're done, their captives are done, too. They're outside the law. They're *above* the law."

"Well then, if I were you, I wouldn't piss off Carpenter."

"When you and I were cops together, we had a common view of the law," Stone said. "We believed in doing it by the book."

"Well, not always *strictly* by the book," Dino said.

"All right, we slapped around a few people, frightened a few guys, but we didn't murder anybody."

"And I'm not going to start now," Dino said.

"But you're going to turn a blind eye to what these people are planning?"

"Stone, in this case, a blind eye is all I got."

"You don't *want* to see it."

"You're right, because, unlike you, I understand that there are two whole different worlds existing right alongside each other: There's your world and mine, then there's their world, where a crazy woman holds a grudge against their people and goes around killing them, plus a few other people along the way. How do we prosecute that? There's never any evidence. And suppose I could, somehow, stop them from killing La Biche? What would I do with her? Pat her on the head and send her back to Europe to kill a few more people? I don't have any evidence against her. Jesus, *somebody's* got to stop her, and it ain't going to be me."

"This is depressing," Stone said.

"It's not depressing if you don't think about it," Dino replied.

35

Carpenter rushed into the building, went to her temporary office, deposited her coat, and picked up her notes. She made it to the conference room just as Architect took his seat.

His name, as everyone who worked for him knew, was Sir Edward Fieldstone, but when he had chosen a code name, his bent for carpentry and building came to the fore. He had a huge workshop at his country home in Berkshire, and his large estate was dotted with barns, sheds, workmen's houses, and other structures that he had either built himself or supervised. He had come to the intelligence services by way of the Army and the SAS, and he was known to be partial to officers who had served in that unit, especially in Northern Ireland, where he had commanded it. His reputation from that time was one of being soft-spoken and completely ruthless.

Carpenter sometimes felt at a disadvantage for not having served in the Army. Her credentials in the service were, at the outset, hereditary, since her paternal grandfather and her father had both been intelligence officers — the former, during World War II, when he had been repeatedly parachuted into France to arm and train Resistance fighters, and the latter, who had been a specialist in dealing with Irish terrorists in mainland Britain. Those were considered historic credentials in the service, and Carpenter had worked hard to live up to them.

"Good morning," Architect said softly, causing an immediate hush to fall on the room. He gazed around the table at the two dozen faces, a third of them women. "Ladies and gentlemen," he said finally.

"The subject — the only subject — of this meeting is one Marie-Thérèse du Bois, known also as La Biche, an aptly assigned sobriquet, if I may say so." A tiny smile twitched at a corner of his mouth.

"I am sure that you have all read the dossier compiled on this woman, a dossier appalling in its nature and, especially, in its bearing on the members of this service. I need hardly tell you that she must be stopped."

There was a murmur of assent around the table.

"Carpenter," he said.

All eyes turned to her, and she felt her ears burning.

"Yes, sir?"

"Give us a little recap of her activities in this city over the past few days."

Carpenter did not need notes for this. "She has murdered a former officer of this service, a serving officer, an Arab diplomat known to be an intelligence officer, and an innocent female civilian. She has also seriously wounded a serving officer of this firm."

"And how is Thatcher?" Architect asked.

"He has suffered partial paralysis of both legs as a result of an ice pick wound to his spinal cord, but he is out of danger and is responding to treatment and showing signs of improvement. The prognosis is for a complete or nearly complete recovery."

"Good, good. Is he being well taken care of?"

"He is, sir."

"Good. Now, Carpenter, please give me your assessment of the current situation regarding La Biche. I'd especially like to know about her detention and release by the New York City Police Department. How were both these things accomplished?"

"An item appeared in a gossip column in the *New York Post* regarding the attorney who had arranged for an operative to photograph Lawrence Fortescue, formerly of this firm, during a tryst with a woman, who turned out to be La Biche. It was mentioned in the article that the attorney frequented a restaurant called Elaine's, on the Upper East Side, and La Biche turned up at the restaurant to inquire about the lawyer, whose name was not mentioned in the article. The restaurant's eponymous owner telephoned a police officer of her acquaintance to report the incident. He immediately organized an arrest, and La Biche was taken to the

Nineteenth Precinct and questioned."

"That covers her arrest. What about her release?" Architect asked.

"La Biche had dumped two weapons in the ladies' room of the restaurant, after wiping them clean. Although they were recovered, they yielded no fingerprints and could not be connected to her, since, in theory, anyone could have left them there. One weapon, a pistol, underwent a ballistics test, in the hope of connecting it to the murder of the Arab diplomat. The results were negative." She took a deep breath. "The police were also hampered by the fact that this service has declined to report her activities to any police force or to Interpol, so there were no outstanding charges under which she could be detained."

The room went very quiet, since everyone knew that the decision not to alert police had been Architect's.

"Quite," he said calmly, betraying no annoyance. "Go on."

"Finally, she presented a valid passport in her true name with a valid entry stamp, or at least a forgery so good that the police were unable to detect it. She was represented by a New York attorney named Sol Kaminsky, who has, in the past, been known to represent Arab terrorists in court. He was prominent in the unsuccessful defense of the men who placed a bomb in the basement car park of the World Trade Center some years ago."

"I am acquainted with Mr. Kaminsky's reputation," Architect said. "Who made the decision to release La Biche?"

"The deputy district attorney of New York County was personally present during her interrogation, and when no probable cause could be found to hold her, or even to photograph and fingerprint her, he ordered her release."

Architect nodded. "And how would you assess our current situation, Carpenter?"

"We don't know where she is or who may be helping her. We have no credible evidence against her, so that even if we were able to apprehend her, we could not bring her to trial — and, if we were somehow able to do so, she would be acquitted, in either a British or American court. I should point out that, due to her very average appearance, which changes constantly, and the absence of a fingerprint record, we would find it very difficult even to identify her. In short, we haven't laid a glove on her, nor are we likely to do so."

Architect fixed her with a steely gaze. "In your desire to be realistic, you are being too pessimistic, Carpenter. Do you have a plan for proceeding?"

"We know that she has, in the past, frequented lesbian bars, where she has picked up women, murdered them, and used their residences and identities for short periods. I suggest that, since we have a number of women present, we stake out as many such bars as we can, in the hope of spotting her. Every such officer should be wired and under constant electronic surveillance."

"You will note that I brought four female officers with me," Architect said. "Any other recommendations?"

"We should tap the telephones of Mr. Kaminsky's law offices and his home, and keep him under surveillance. He is the only person we know her to have contacted in New York."

Architect's voice became even softer. "Is that all? Surely you have a further recommendation."

Carpenter met his gaze and held it. When the inquiry into this situation came, as it surely would, she wanted to be on record. "I have no further recommendation, sir." It is bloody well going to have to come from you, you silky bastard, she thought.

"You disappoint me, Carpenter."

"I'm very sorry, sir."

"Quite." Architect looked around the table. "All right, here is how we will proceed: Mason, you will undertake the staking out and electronic surveillance of the lesbian bars. Incidentally, how will we find them?" He looked around the table for an answer.

Carpenter spoke up. "I would suggest that we begin by walking the streets of Greenwich Village and Soho. Once some such establishments have been located, our people can inquire among the customers present about the location of others."

"Well," Architect said, permitting himself another hint of a smile, "I feel some small relief in learning that none of my people has any personal acquaintance with such places. See to it, Mason."

"Yes, sir," Mason replied.

"Sparks," Architect said, singling out another male officer, "I will leave the electronic surveillance of Mr. Kaminsky in your hands. See that our presence does not become known to the local authorities."

"Yes, sir," the man replied. "Will we seek FBI approval?"

"Not exactly," Architect replied, "but I am having dinner this evening with the director of that agency, who is in New York, and I will see that he is appropriately apprised of our activities."

"Thank you, sir," Sparks replied.

"Well," Architect said, closing his briefcase, "I believe we're finished."

"Excuse me, sir," Carpenter said. "Do you have an assignment for me?"

Architect gazed at her. "Well, obviously, since La Biche has seen you up close, we can't send you around to these bars . . . however much you might wish to go. . . ."

Carpenter's ears got hot again.

". . . But I believe you are personally acquainted with this lawyer — Barrington? Is that his name?"

Carpenter looked over at Mason, who had assumed a studious attitude with some papers before him.

"Yes, Barrington. Since La Biche apparently has an interest in him, your assignment, Carpenter, will be to see that the twain do not meet. If she keeps killing civilians . . ." He left that thought unfinished.

"Yes, sir," she said.

"And further, Carpenter, you are directed to take whatever measures are necessary to remain alive. You're no good to me dead."

"Excuse me, sir," Mason said.

"Yes, Mason?"

"May we have instructions on what to do about La Biche, once we've found her?"

Good for you, Mason, Carpenter thought. Get him on the record.

"You are not — repeat, *not* — to attempt to detain her," Architect said. "She is far too dangerous, and I don't want to lose any more people." Architect closed his briefcase. "Dispose of her," he said, "by whatever means are available."

"Sir," Mason pressed on, "any such opportunities that arise are likely to be in public places."

"I am aware of that, Mason," Architect said. "Try to avoid collateral damage." He picked up his briefcase and walked out of the room.

As the group filed out, Carpenter fell into step with Mason. "Are you prepared to follow that order?" she asked quietly.

"I am unaccustomed," Mason said, "to not following his orders."

36

Stone was getting hungrier and hungrier, and Carpenter had not called. The phone finally rang.

"Hello?"

"It's me," she said.

"How did your meeting go?"

"I'll tell you about it later."

"How much later?"

"I'm afraid I'm going to have to work through the evening. Why don't you go to Elaine's, and I'll meet you there later?"

"Do you feel safe at Elaine's?" Stone asked.

"The last time La Biche came to Elaine's, she got arrested," Carpenter said. "I don't think she'll be anxious to return, do you?"

"I guess not," Stone agreed. "Any idea what time you'll be there?"

"I'll call you when I'm on my way. Bye." She hung up.

Stone took a cab to Elaine's, settled in at his table, and ordered a drink and a menu. Elaine came over and sat down.

"You missed all the excitement last night, huh?"

"Yeah, Dino said you alerted him. That was a good call."

Elaine shrugged. "Just watching your ass for you."

"Thanks. I still have possession of it. How did all this happen?"

"She came in and sat down at the bar. One of the bartenders, Bobby, chatted her up a little while she had dinner, and they got along real well. She even gave him her number. Then she pulled out the Page Six clipping, and he mentioned it to me. She wanted to know your name, and he told her. I remembered a conversation in here about that."

"She gave Bobby her number?"

"Yeah, they were going like gangbusters. Bobby's pretty swift with the ladies."

"Excuse me a second," Stone said. He got up and went to the bar. "Hey, Bobby."

"Hey, Stone. How you doing?"

"I'm good. Thanks for your help last night."

"I thought I was helping myself."

"Elaine said the lady gave you her number?"

"Yeah, that's right."

"You still got it?"

Bobby went to the cash register, hit a key, and the drawer slid open. He reached under the currency tray for something and came back with a slip of paper. "Here you go. I don't guess I'll be calling her, from what I've heard about her."

Stone pocketed the paper. "Thanks, Bobby. Have one on me."

"Thanks."

Stone went back to his table and looked at the

paper. The area code was 917, which was reserved for New York City cell phones.

Elaine looked at him. "Jesus, you're not *that* horny, are you?"

"Of course not," Stone said, putting the number in his pocket.

"Where's Felicity?"

"Working. She'll be in later."

"And Dino?"

"We had lunch. We've seen enough of each other for one day."

"Stone, you think you're in any sort of danger from this woman?"

"I hope not, but she's unlikely to come in here again, after what happened to her last night." Stone looked up to see a woman alone come through the front door. She stopped and looked around. Medium height and weight, brown hair, nicely dressed. He started looking for something to throw at her and settled on the wooden Indian standing guard next to his table.

Then the woman seemed to spot somebody at the rear of the restaurant. She walked quickly down the aisle, past Stone, and embraced a man, who had stood up to greet her.

"That's his wife," Elaine said. "Maybe you better have another drink." She waved at a waiter and pointed at Stone.

"I don't mind if I do."

"That one's on me," Elaine said to the waiter when the drink came.

"Thanks," Stone said, raising his glass to her.

"Maybe you ought to get outta town for a few days," Elaine said. "Why don't you go up to Connecticut?"

"I just got back," Stone said, "but that's not a bad idea."

Elaine got up to greet somebody, leaving Stone alone. He ordered dinner, then took out the phone number again. Impulsively, he dialed it.

She answered immediately. "Yes?"

"Ms. du Bois, this is Stone Barrington. Don't hang up," he said quickly, "I just want to talk to you."

There was a brief silence. "All right," she said. "What do you want to talk about?" Her accent was perfectly American.

"First of all, I want to explain why I had you photographed."

"I would be interested to hear this," she said.

"It was a domestic matter: Lawrence Fortescue was married to a woman, my client, who believed he was having an affair. They had a prenuptial agreement that precluded his getting any of her money in a divorce if he was shown to be adulterous. I had no idea who you were."

"Do you now?" she asked.

"I have a better idea," he said, "and I'd just as soon not be on your list of enemies."

She laughed aloud. "Well, Mr. Barrington, you have a well-developed sense of self-preservation, I'll give you that."

"I think it would be a good idea if you and I met," Stone said.

"Come now, you don't really expect that, do you?"

"Are you acquainted with the American principle of the inviolability of the attorney-client relationship?"

"I believe so."

"Then you must understand that if you and I meet for the purpose of your seeking legal advice from me, both the meeting and the conversation would be privileged, and I could not tell the police about either."

"I understand that. Would the attorney-client relationship prevent you from, shall we say, inviting others to this meeting?"

"Yes. I could not ethically inform any authority of our meeting or our conversation unless I had direct knowledge of your intent to commit a crime."

"And what do I know of your ethics, Mr. Barrington?"

"Nothing, except that all American lawyers live by the same code. American attorneys do not turn in their clients, except under the circumstances I have already described."

"I take it you are curious about me."

"Of course, but that's not the principal reason for wanting to meet you."

"And what would the principal reason be?"

"I want to save your life, if I can."

"You wish to persuade me to turn myself in? I was in police custody only yesterday, and they didn't seem to want me."

"I don't represent the police . . . or the British intelligence services."

There was a silence. "You are very interesting, Mr. Barrington, because of who you do not represent. I'm sure you have a cell phone. Give me the number."

Stone gave it to her.

"Tomorrow at six P.M., be at the skating rink in Rockefeller Center. Perhaps I'll buy you a drink. But please don't be so foolish as to ask anyone to join us." She hung up.

Stone was about to put away his cell phone when it vibrated in his hand. "Hello?"

"Hi, it's me."

"Hi."

"Things are going very slowly here, and I'm going to be several more hours. They're ordering in some Chinese, so I'll eat here and see you at home later."

"I'm sorry you couldn't make it."

"Me too. Bye."

Stone put the cell phone away, thinking not about Carpenter, but La Biche. He wondered what he was getting himself into.

37

Marie-Thérèse kept her appointment at Frédéric Fekkai, a fashionable hairdressing salon and day spa on East Fifty-seventh Street. They knew her there by another name.

Mr. Fekkai greeted her warmly. "Mrs. King, how are you? How are things in Dallas?"

"Hey, sugar," Mrs. King replied in a broad Texas accent. "Things are just wonderful. The price of oil is up, so I thought I'd come up here to the big city and spend some of Mr. King's money."

"We are delighted to see you. Let's see, you have a massage and herbal wrap scheduled, and a manicure and an appointment with a makeup artist. We'll do your hair last, is that all right?"

"Of course, baby."

"The girl will order you some lunch."

"I'm famished. Does she have any bourbon?"

"We'll see what we can do."

Marie-Thérèse submitted to half a day of pampering, then reported to Mr. Fekkai at the end of it.

"Now, what shall we do with your hair?" he asked.

"I want it fairly short," she said, running her fingers through it, "and I want a nice blond color, with some streaks."

"I think that will suit you perfectly," he replied. "The colorist is waiting for you, and I'll see you next."

At four o'clock, she left the establishment, quite literally, a new woman. All her identification had been arranged to support the effect. She went into Bergdorf's and bought some clothes, then allowed herself to be fitted for two wigs, charging everything to an American Express card in Mrs. King's name, which would be paid automatically from a bank account in the Cayman Islands. At six o'clock, she stood on the corner of Fifth Avenue and Fifty-seventh Street, took out her cell phone, and made the call.

Stone stood, gazing down at the skaters, one in particular — a pretty blonde in a red outfit with a short skirt, who was far better than anyone else on the ice. He looked around him for a woman alone who might be La Biche. His cell phone vibrated.

"Hello?"

"Good afternoon," she said. "I want you to walk — not ride — to Bryant Park, behind the New York Public Library. You should be there in ten minutes. Walk on the west side of Fifth to Forty-fourth Street, then down the east side of the street to Forty-second, then cross again. Do you understand?"

"Yes."

"I'll call you when you're there." She hung up.

Stone walked to Fifth Avenue and headed toward the library.

She walked over to Madison Avenue, crossed the street, turned left, and entered an electronics shop specializing in spy-type equipment, where she made a quick purchase. She caught a cab and headed downtown, then made another call.

"Hello?" he said.

"Listen very carefully," she said. "I want you to walk west on the south side of Forty-second Street, turn left at the next corner and walk south to Thirty-seventh Street and make another left. There's a bar on the south side of the street called O'Coineen's. Go in there and take a seat in the last of the row of booths on your left. There'll be a reserved sign on the table; ignore it. If anyone questions you, say you're meeting Maeve. Got all that?"

"Yes."

"Be there in ten minutes." She hung up. "Turn right here," she said, "and stop in the middle of the block." She got out of the cab, went into O'Coineen's and then into the ladies' room. She peed, then went into her shopping bag for a wig. She chose an auburn one, very straight, with bangs. She glanced at her watch.

★ ★ ★

Stone found the bar. The place was busy with after-work customers, but the last booth was empty.

A waiter approached. "Sorry, that booth is reserved," he said.

"I'm meeting Maeve," Stone replied.

"It's all right, Sean," said a woman's voice with a very attractive Irish accent.

Stone turned to find a redhead with very straight hair and bangs, beautifully made up. It was not the woman he had seen at the Nineteenth Precinct.

"Stand up, Mr. Barrington," she said.

Stone got out of the booth. "Good evening," he said.

"Hold your arms away from your sides," she said.

Stone complied.

She frisked him in a professional manner, not omitting his crotch, then produced a small black object and ran it over him, head to toe. "Have a seat," she said, pointing to the side of the booth with its back to the street.

"Thank you for coming," Stone said, sitting down.

She slid into the opposite side of the booth, facing the street, and set a Bergdorf's shopping bag on the seat beside her, then she placed a medium-sized handbag on the table, with the open end toward her. She looked around the bar carefully, then at the front windows.

Finally, she turned to him. "What'll y'have?"

"A beer will be fine," Stone said.

"Two Harps," she said to the waiter.

"Right," he said, and went to get them.

"Well, isn't this nice?" she said, keeping the Irish accent.

Stone wasn't sure how to respond to that.

"Come on, Mr. Barrington, I'm here. What d'ya want?"

Stone started to speak, but the waiter came with the drinks, and he waited for him to leave.

She picked up her beer, poured some into a glass, and clinked it against his. "So? Yer not very talkative, Mr. Barrington."

Stone sipped his beer. "I think you should leave New York immediately."

"Oh? And why's that, if you'd be so kind as to tell me?"

"I don't think you should believe that your release from police custody has made you immune," he said.

"Immune to what?"

"To . . . further action."

She glanced at the door, then leaned back into her seat and sipped her beer. "You said on the phone you knew something about me," she said. "Exactly what?"

"It's my understanding that, when you were younger, your parents were killed in an ambush that was meant for someone else, and that after that, you underwent some rather specialized training, then began assassinating various people, with an emphasis on those who were inadvertently responsible for your parents' death."

"My, you are well informed, aren't you?"

"Moderately."

" 'Inadvertently'? Is that what they told you?"

"Who?"

"Whoever told you this rubbish."

"I think it's pretty good information, though it may not entirely conform to your view of things."

She laughed. "Yes, my view of things is somewhat different. I know for a fact that my mother was the target, and killing her husband and daughter, as well, didn't faze them in the least."

Stone said nothing.

"You see, there's two sides to every story."

"Perhaps so. But that doesn't change the fact that they're going to hunt you down and kill you," Stone said.

She looked amused. "Oh? Well, that'd take some doing, wouldn't it?"

"They have no legal recourse, so they're going to use other means."

"And how do you know this?"

"I hear things," Stone said.

She reached into her handbag.

Stone sat up straight.

She came out with a hundred-dollar bill and shoved it across the table. "Put that in your pocket," she said.

Stone put it in his pocket.

"Now you're my lawyer, right? You've been paid for legal advice, right?"

"That's right."

"And this conversation is privileged. You can't disclose it to anyone else."

"That's right."

"Okay, Mr. Stone Barrington, what is your advice?"

"I'd advise you not to spend another night in New York City. I'd advise you not to leave by airline, train, or bus, but to leave by car, and, if you want to leave the country, do that by car, too, or on foot. I'd advise you not to come back for a long time."

"Anything else?"

"I'd advise you to go to ground, establish an identity you can keep permanently, and find a more productive way to live out your life. And to never, ever again identify yourself to anyone as Marie-Thérèse du Bois."

"Well, that's very sound advice, Mr. Barrington," she said. "I'll think it over."

"Don't think too long," Stone said. "And since I'll deny that this conversation ever took place, I'd be grateful if you'd do the same, because it's very dangerous for me to be associated with you in any way."

"Well, I think I can promise you that," she said. She gathered up her handbag and shopping bag. "I'm going to be leaving you now, and I don't expect we'll be meeting again. You finish your beer. Finish mine, too, and take at least fifteen minutes to do it." She stood up.

"Goodbye, then."

Her voice changed to something mid-Atlantic. "Goodbye, Mr. Barrington, and thank you for your concern. I'm very grateful to you."

She walked to the rear of the room and disappeared through the kitchen door.

Stone finished his beer, and hers. He knew from her attitude that he'd set out on a fool's errand. She was going to do exactly what she'd intended to do all along.

38

Stone and Carpenter met at The Box Tree, a small, romantic restaurant near his house. They settled at a table, and Stone ordered a bottle of Veuve Clicquot La Grande Dame, his favorite champagne.

"What's the occasion?" Carpenter asked, when they had clinked glasses and sipped their wine.

"An entire evening, just the two of us, free of the cares of work. What we in America call a 'date.' "

She laughed. "And what were we having before?"

"What we in America call 'wham, bam, thank you, ma'am.' "

"I didn't think American men objected to that sort of relationship."

"It's not a relationship, it's just carnal fun — not that I have any objection to carnal fun."

"So I've noticed."

They looked at the menu and ordered. The waiter poured them more champagne.

"Tell me about yourself," Stone said.

Carpenter laughed again. "Isn't that my line? Why is it that our roles seem to be reversed?"

"Roles are reversible, in certain circumstances."

"What circumstances?"

"When the male has an interest in the female deeper than carnal fun." Stone thought he caught a blush in her cheeks. "Tell me about yourself," he said.

"What you mean is, why do I do what I do. Isn't that right?"

"What people do is often the most important thing about them."

"What I do is *not* the most important thing about me," she said.

"What is?"

"Who I am."

"And who are you?"

She looked at the table, then around the room for a long moment. "All right, what I do is the most important thing about me. It's who I am."

"Imagine that, through no fault of your own, you were unable to continue in your career. Who would you be, then?"

She took a deep draught of her champagne. "That is an unthinkable thought."

"Surely you've seen people sacked from your service, turned out into the cold."

"Occasionally."

"Do you think they were what they did?"

"Some of them, I suppose."

"And what did they do when they could no longer be what they wanted to be?"

243

"One or two of them . . . did themselves in."

"Would you do yourself in?"

"Certainly not," she replied quickly.

"Then what? What would you do? Who would you be?"

"I might ask you the same question."

"You may, after you've answered mine."

"I'd be a barrister," she said. "I read law at Oxford, you know. I could very easily qualify."

"How old are you?"

"Thirty-eight," she said without hesitation.

"Are there jobs for brand-new thirty-eight-year-old barristers in London?"

"I'd have to go to a smaller town, I suppose."

"Are there jobs for brand-new thirty-eight-year-old barristers in smaller towns?"

She shrugged. "I'm not without friends of influence."

"That always helps."

"I don't understand your line of questioning," she said. "What is it you really want to know?"

"I suppose I'm wondering if you and I could have a more permanent relationship —"

"In New York?"

"Of course."

"Why 'of course'? Why couldn't you move to London?"

"Because I couldn't get a job as a barrister anywhere in England, and I doubt if they'd offer me anything at Scotland Yard. And those are the only things I know how to do. I suppose what I really want to know is if you could be happy in an existence where secrets and routine violence — even murder — don't play a part."

"Is that how you see my life?"

"Isn't it how you see it? Don't you ever think about what your work does to you as a human being?"

"There is a long tradition in my family, going back at least five hundred years, of service to one's country."

"No matter what one's country asks one to do?"

"I have always been equal to what my country has asked of me."

"That's what worries me," Stone said.

"That I'm a loyalist?"

"That, where your country is concerned, you're capable of *anything*."

She blinked at him. "What are you talking about?"

"Marie-Thérèse's parents weren't killed by accident, were they?"

"I told you they were. I was there."

"The target was her mother. Isn't that true? Collateral damage didn't matter."

Carpenter set down her glass. "Who have you been talking to?"

"Someone who was there."

"*I* am the only person still alive who was there."

"No," Stone said, "you're not."

She stared at him for a long moment, her face expressionless. "Good God," she said softly.

Stone said nothing, just looked at her.

"I think you'd better stop lying to me," he said finally. "It isn't good for the relationship."

"How did you find her?"

"I'm a good detective. The NYPD trained me well."

"We can't find her, but you could?"

"That seems to be the reality."

"Did you meet her face to face?"

"Yes, but it wasn't the face we saw at the Nineteenth Precinct. I don't know how she changes, but she does."

"Do you have any idea how dangerous that was?"

"It seemed to me more dangerous not to meet with her. She knew who I was and that I had played a part . . ."

"Yes, I suppose that's true. Where did you meet her?"

"In a bar. I'm afraid I can't tell you any more than that."

"Why not?"

"Because, before she would talk to me, she insisted on paying me a retainer. I'm now her attorney."

"That was very clever of her. Can you contact her again?"

"Perhaps."

"You're not sure?"

"No."

Carpenter pushed back from the table. "I have to leave," she said.

"To report to your superiors?"

"Thank you for the champagne," she said. Then she got up and left.

39

Stone's phone rang early the next morning.

"It's Carpenter," she said.

"Good morning."

"Are you free for lunch today?"

"Yes."

"Twelve-thirty at the Four Seasons. There's somebody I want you to meet."

"Who?"

"I'll see you at twelve-thirty." She hung up.

Stone was on time, and Carpenter, with a companion, was already seated at a table in the Grill. The man rose to greet Stone.

"This is Sir Edward Fieldstone," Carpenter said. "Sir Edward, may I introduce Stone Barrington."

The man was six feet, slender, rather distinguished-looking, with thick, gray hair that needed cutting, hair visible in his ears and nose, and a well-cut if elderly suit that could have used a pressing. "How do you do, Mr. Barrington," he said, his voice deep and smooth, his accent very upper-class. "Won't you sit down? Would you like a drink?"

Stone glanced at the bottle on the table: Chateau Palmer, 1966. "That will do nicely," he said.

Sir Edward nodded, and a waiter appeared and poured the wine.

"Thank you so much for coming on such short notice," Sir Edward said. "Let's order some lunch, shall we?"

They looked at the menu, and Stone ordered a small steak, while Carpenter and Sir Edward both ordered the Dover sole, not seeming to care that it might not be the best thing with the wine.

"Lovely weather," Sir Edward said. "We're not used to it. London is always so dreary."

"It can be dreary in New York, too," Stone said, wondering exactly who Sir Edward was. He seemed to be in his mid-sixties, and very un-spylike.

They chatted about nothing until their food came. Stone waited for somebody to tell him why he was there.

"Is there anything you'd like to know?" Sir Edward asked. It seemed a non sequitur.

Stone looked at Carpenter, who kept her mouth shut. "Perhaps you could begin by telling me who you are," he said.

"Of course, of course," Sir Edward said, sounding apologetic. "I'm a British civil servant. Perhaps I shouldn't go any further than that."

"Are you Carpenter's immediate superior?" Stone asked.

"Perhaps a notch or two upwards."

"Are you the head of Carpenter's service?" Stone asked.

"One might say so. Pass the salt, please."

Carpenter passed the salt.

"MI Five or MI Six?" Stone asked.

"Oh, those lines seem so blurred these days," Sir Edward replied. "Let's not be too specific."

"Perhaps I should explain, sir," Carpenter said.

Sir Edward gave her the faintest of nods.

"It is very unusual for . . . a person in Sir Edward's position to meet, in his official capacity, with a person outside his service. In fact, very few outsiders are even aware of his name."

"Would you prefer to be addressed as 'M,' Sir Edward?" Stone asked.

Sir Edward chuckled appreciatively but did not reply.

"That's a little outdated," Carpenter said. "You do understand that this meeting is, well, not taking place?"

"All right," Stone said. "Perhaps you could tell me *why* it is not taking place?"

"Thank you, Felicity," Sir Edward said. "I'll take it from here." He turned to Stone. "Mr. Barrington, I believe you are familiar with recent events involving a young woman by the name of Marie-Thérèse du Bois."

"Somewhat," Stone said.

"And you know that we have been trying to protect certain of our personnel from certain actions of this woman."

"You mean, you're trying to stop her from killing your people?"

Sir Edward looked around to be sure he was not being overheard. "One might say that, though perhaps not quite so baldly."

"Sir Edward, I am an American, not a diplomat, and we are sometimes, as a people, blunt. I think this conversation might go better if you keep that in mind."

"Quite," Sir Edward replied, seeming a little miffed.

"What is it you want of me?"

"It is my understanding that you are representing the woman in certain matters?"

"She has retained me for legal advice."

"Then you are in touch with her?"

"That may be possible."

"I should like to meet with her."

Stone nearly choked on his wine. "You astonish me, Sir Edward, given the history of her meetings with members of your service."

"I am aware that she harbors ill feelings toward us."

"Then you are aware that she would probably enjoy killing you on sight."

"Quite."

"Sir Edward, I think that what you propose is out of the question, given the current state of relations between you and my client."

"It is the relations between us that I would like to discuss."

"Frankly, I cannot imagine a setting where

251

such a meeting could take place, given your separate concerns for security."

"I would be willing to meet with her alone in a place of her choosing, as long as it is a public place."

"Sir Edward, do you intend to propose some sort of truce between your service and my client?"

"Something like that."

Stone shook his head. "For such a meeting to take place, I think there would have to be a level of trust that does not exist on either side."

"I have already said that I am willing to meet with her alone."

"If you'll forgive me, I don't find that a credible proposal."

Sir Edward looked irritated. "And why not?"

"I think my client would view such a meeting as nothing more than an opportunity for your people to kill her."

"Nonsense. I'm willing to give her my word."

"I'm not sure that, given her experience with your service, that would impress her."

Sir Edward looked as if he would like to plunge his fish knife into Stone's chest.

"Surely you can understand that," Stone said.

"Speak to your client," Sir Edward said.

"And tell her what, exactly?"

"Tell her that we are willing to come to an accommodation."

"Make a proposal."

"We stop trying to kill each other. If we can

agree that, then I can arrange for all record of her to be removed from our databases and those of other European services."

"Permanently?"

"We would retain a record, off-line, so that, if she should violate our agreement, we could circulate it again."

"And if *you* should violate it?"

"That, sir, is not in question." Sir Edward shifted in his seat, and his tone became more conciliatory. "Please understand that my service has never before undertaken such an accommodation with . . . an opponent. We are doing so now only because, in you, Mr. Barrington, we suddenly have a conduit to the opposition. You may tell that we respect her motives, but we believe that it is in the interest of both parties to bring a halt to this madness."

"I'll see what I can do," Stone said.

40

Stone walked back to his house, deep in thought. He did not trust Sir Edward Field-stone's intentions, and the man's word was not enough. He had visions of some sniper drawing a bead on Marie-Thérèse's head as she and Sir Edward negotiated in some public place. He got out his cell phone and dialed the number.

She answered immediately. "Yes?"

"It's Stone Barrington."

"Be brief. I don't want to be scanned."

"I need to meet with you again. I have news."

A brief silence. "Go to Rockefeller Center again, at six o'clock this evening. I'll be in touch." She hung up without waiting for a reply.

Stone pressed the redial button.

"Yes?"

"Be very careful. Do you understand? I don't know if I'm being followed."

"I'm always very careful." She cut the connection.

Stone was at the skating rink on time. Ten minutes passed before his cell phone rang. "Hello?"

"Were you followed?"

"Not by anyone I could spot."

"Are you any good at spotting a tail?"

"Fairly good."

"Walk to Central Park. Go up Fifth Avenue, against the traffic. Cross the street at least three times, checking for a multiple tail. There'll be at least four of them. Once in the park, sit on a bench outside the Children's Zoo." She hung up.

Stone walked briskly up Fifth Avenue, stopping now and then to check the reflection in a shop window. He crossed the street four times, looking for a repetition in the faces around him, but he saw none. He strolled slowly through the park to the Children's Zoo and sat down on a bench. His cell phone rang immediately. "Yes?"

"Walk to the Wollman skating rink." She hung up.

Stone walked to the rink, stopping frequently to look at the zoo's animals and checking for a tail. He still saw no one. At the rink, his cell phone rang again. "Yes?"

"Go to the carousel, buy a ticket. Don't ride a horse, you'll look ridiculous. Sit on a bench." She hung up.

Stone did as he was told, mixing among the children and their nannies. The carousel had made three revolutions before she sat down beside him. Her hair was long and dark, and she wore a tweed suit and bright red lipstick.

"Good afternoon," she said.

"Good evening. I assume I wasn't followed."

"Only by me. There was no one else on you. Why did you call?" Her accent was American now.

"Do you know who Sir Edward Fieldstone is?"

"Architect? Of course."

"I had lunch with him today, at his request."

She looked surprised. "And how did this come about?"

"A friend of mine works for him. I told her I had spoken to you."

"I suppose that is not a breach of client confidentiality."

"He wants to meet with you."

She laughed. "I'll *bet* he does."

"I think you should consider this carefully. He says he's willing to meet you, alone, in a place of your choosing, as long as it's a public place. I expect you're thinking there'll be a sniper on a rooftop."

"You're psychic, Stone. What does he want?"

"He wants a truce."

She blinked a few times. "He actually said that?"

"To the extent that you can get an upper-class Englishman to say *anything* explicit, yes."

"On what terms?"

"You stop killing his people, his people stop trying to kill you. He'll remove all traces of you from British and European intelligence computers, keeping only backup files, in case you renege."

"What if *he* reneges?"

"I asked him that, but I didn't get a straight answer. Presumably, you could go back to killing his people."

"I don't get it. Why would he stop trying to kill me?"

"So far, you've killed, what, half a dozen of his people? And he hasn't even killed you once. He's losing, and he knows it."

"It's unlike him to relent," she said. "In Northern Ireland he had a reputation of never giving up until he got his man. Or woman."

"Maybe he's getting old. He's got to be in his mid-sixties. Maybe his fires are cooling."

"Maybe. I doubt it."

"Marie-Thérèse, how long do you think you can continue like this before you end up in somebody's gunsights?"

"As long as I want to."

"Don't you ever get a hankering for a more normal life?"

"What, husband? Children?"

"Whatever you want — being able to live your life without changing your identity every other day; being safe, with no one hunting you."

"Sometimes I think about that, but you don't understand what I'd be up against if I stopped this. There are other people who would not be pleased if I gave up my work."

"I can understand that, but they don't have the sort of facilities at their disposal that the intelligence services have. Granted, they may have large networks of people, but they don't have computers that scan your face every time you cross a border. You could disappear, find a haven where you could live a more normal life — whatever you'd like that to be."

She sighed. "You make it sound very attractive."

"Look, the people you've been working with are going to lose, eventually. They're being hunted, too, and that's not going to stop. They're going up against a group of big nations that have virtually unlimited resources, and they're going to be ground down. Even the countries that have been sheltering them are going to start pulling away, because the cost to them is going to be too great. Eventually, they're going to see that it's easier to do business with the Western powers than trying to destroy them. This is inevitable. When that happens, where do you want to be?"

"You have a point, but it's not going to happen tomorrow. And in the meantime, I'm quite enjoying myself."

"I don't believe that. I think you're getting tired, and if you're tired, you're going to start making mistakes. And you can't afford to make mistakes."

"I may meet with Sir Edward, under the right circumstances, and you're authorized to negotiate those for me. Tell him that if we do meet, it would be a very great mistake to make any move on me."

"I'll relay that."

"Call me when you have something like an agreement, in writing."

"Agreements like this don't get put into writing."

She sighed. "All right, do the best you can, but I want an immediate truce while we're negotiating."

"I'll tell him that."

She stood up, holding on to a bar to keep her balance. "You free for dinner this evening?" she asked.

"Not this evening or any evening," Stone replied. "It's dangerous to be around you."

"Well, if we can make it less dangerous with this deal, maybe later."

"Maybe later," Stone said. But he didn't mean it.

41

Stone went home and called Bob Cantor.

"Hey, Stone."

"Hey, Bob. Where's that nephew of yours?"

"Back running the photo processing equipment at the drugstore."

"What happened to his business plans in Saint Thomas?"

"The boy is — how shall I put it? — mercurial."

"You're a master of understatement."

"What's up?"

"I want my house swept every day for a week. Can you manage the time?"

"Every day? What have you gotten yourself into?"

"Never mind. I just don't want to be overheard while I'm doing it."

"It'd help if I knew what sort of surveillance you're worried about."

"Phones, rooms, the works."

"Who's the opposition?"

"Why do you want to know?"

"If it's some amateur, this is easy. If it's a pro, or a group of pros, it's going to be harder."

"It's a group of pros."

"I'll be there in an hour."

Cantor turned up and began by checking the phone system. After an hour he came into Stone's office, holding up something electronic-looking. "Your phones were bugged, big time," he said, "and this is very sophisticated stuff."

"How sophisticated?"

"They don't have to have a van parked outside your house. This probably has a range of a mile, maybe two. They can leave a voice-activated recorder running and listen to your conversations whenever they get around to it. This device wasn't bought at Radio Shack, or off the shelf anyplace else, come to that. This is custom-designed, custom-made, and it's not a one-off, either. Whoever did this has quality manufacturing at his disposal. Who are these people?"

"An intelligence service."

"Not ours, I hope. I don't want to mess with those people."

"It's foreign."

"How foreign? We're not talking about Arabs, are we?"

"They speak our language; let's leave it at that. Are the phones secure now?"

"Yep — at least, until I leave the house. There are other ways to do this, you know, if they can get access to underground phone company equipment."

"What about the rest of the house?"

"Give me a few minutes."

Cantor came back a while later. "I haven't picked up anything planted, but that doesn't necessarily mean anything. These people could rent an apartment behind your house or across the street and pick up the vibrations from the glass in your windows."

"I have double glazing throughout the house."

"That'll help. Are you planning to have some important conversations in the house?"

"Maybe."

"Then let's go find places where you can defeat surveillance. I wouldn't use this office," he said, pointing at the view of the gardens. "Too easy for them. Let's go upstairs."

They walked around the house, looking at rooms. "The dining room's your best spot; no windows at all. The study is good, too, if you draw those velvet curtains. Your bedroom and the kitchen are not good."

"Okay, Bob, I get the picture. I need some more help."

"What kind?"

"I want you to round up three or four ex-cops and have them tail me."

"You afraid of some sort of personal attack?"

"No, I'm afraid of being tailed. I want your people to look out for other people following me."

"Gotcha," Cantor said, leafing through his address book. "You want to be wired to my watchers?"

"That would be good."

"When do you want to start?"

"I'm going to have a meeting here later. Right after that."

"What time is the meeting?"

"I have to arrange it, then I'll let you know. You start rounding up your guys."

"You've got my cell phone number. Call me."

"Will do." Cantor let himself out of the house.

Stone called Carpenter. "I want another meeting with Sir Edward."

"I'm not sure he has the time."

"*What?* Is he jerking me around?"

"Can you arrange the meeting with La Biche?"

"We can talk about that at the meeting."

"I'll see if he has the time."

"If he wants to get this done, tell him to find the time. We're meeting at my house, as soon as possible."

"He'll want to choose the spot."

"Then tell him to go fuck himself." Stone hung up.

The phone rang ten minutes later.

"Yes?"

"Five o'clock, at your house," she said.

"Just him," Stone replied.

"He wants me."

"I want you, too, when you're not killing people. Tell him I'll frisk him for a wire — you, too."

"He won't sit still for that."

"We're going to do this my way, or not at all," Stone said. "What's it going to be?"

She covered the phone and spoke to someone else, then came back. "See you at five," she said.

Stone hung up and called Bob Cantor. "The meeting's at five."

"That's going to be tough. How long will it last?"

"Half an hour to an hour, is my best guess."

"I'll do the best I can."

Stone went to the dining room. He moved all the chairs back to the wall, except three, then he went to his desk, rummaged through a drawer, and came up with a small scanner. He replaced the batteries and put it into his pocket, then he sat down and called Marie-Thérèse's cell phone.

"Yes?"

"Call me from a pay phone," he said. "I've had my phones checked. They were bugged, but they're clean now."

"Ten minutes," she said, then hung up.

Stone waited as patiently as he could, then picked up the phone as soon as it rang. "That you?"

"It's me."

"I have a meeting with the English gentleman at five."

"Good."

"We have to talk about what you want, so I'll have something to negotiate about."

"I want what he offered me, plus as much else as I can get."

"You mean money? Damages for your parents' death?"

"That would be nice."

"Given the attrition you've caused in his organization, I don't think you'd have a leg to stand on. You've already realized a good deal more than tit for tat."

"All right, I want a written apology for the deaths of my parents."

"I like that. It's good to start with something we know he'll never give us. What else?"

"I don't really care, except I think we need something to punish him with, if he reneges."

"Let me give that some thought. I'll call you when the meeting is over."

"Where is the meeting being held?"

"Oh no, you don't. You're not going to harm a hair on anybody's head while I'm in this, or you'll have to get yourself a new lawyer. I'm not going to be an accessory to a killing."

"Oh, all right, I won't murder anybody for a while," she said, like a child promising to be good.

"Good. Talk to you later." He dictated some notes to Joan and read them as they came off the printer, then read them again. He was ready. He looked at his watch, impatient to get on with it.

42

Sir Edward and Carpenter were on time, and Stone showed them into the dining room. "Would you like some refreshment?" he asked.

"Perhaps later," Sir Edward replied. "Let's get on with it."

Stone sat down. "Marie-Thérèse is willing to meet with you in a public place of her choosing, under stringent security requirements, which she will dictate."

"Agreed," Sir Edward replied. "Subject to my approval of her choice of place."

"You offered to meet at a place of *her* choosing. You won't know the place until you're there. If you become concerned as you make your way there, you can always abort."

"How will she arrange this?"

"You'll go to a public place, then be contacted by cell phone and directed to another public place, then another, until she is satisfied you didn't bring company. Then, and only then, will the meeting take place."

"Agreed," Sir Edward replied.

"She will require a written apology from you, personally, on your service's letterhead, for the deaths of her parents."

Sir Edward grew an inch. "Absolutely out of the question," he said.

"And monetary damages," Stone said.

"That is patently ridiculous," Sir Edward replied hotly.

"Is it? Think about this for a moment, Sir Edward. On your instructions, members of your service lay in wait for her parents, deliberately destroyed their vehicle on a public street, killing her mother and father. That is, of course, a criminal act worthy of life in prison anyplace in the civilized world, but we'll overlook that and keep this a civil matter."

"It doesn't sound very civil to me," Sir Edward said.

"Civil as opposed to criminal. Marie-Thérèse, in return for your written acceptance of responsibility and apology, plus monetary damages, will forgo, in writing, her right to press criminal charges, and she will waive any further civil action."

"Her parents were killed in a war," Sir Edward said.

"Oh? Was there a declaration of war by Britain on Switzerland and its citizens?"

"Of course not."

"Then, under international law, there was no war."

Carpenter spoke up. "Stone, surely you can see that we cannot give her anything in writing. An apology, maybe, but not in writing. She might publish it."

"That's exactly what she intends to do, should you renege on the agreement."

"Ridiculous," Sir Edward said.

"Is it? You have recourse if she breaks the agreement: You can reinstate the computer record of her activities with international law enforcement and intelligence services, and she becomes a fugitive again. She is entitled to recourse, as well, and the ability to publish your letter would be a motive for you to keep the agreement."

"What else does she want?" Sir Edward asked.

"Just those two things."

"How much does she want?"

"Two million dollars; a million for each parent."

"Out of the question."

"Make me an offer."

Sir Edward did some whispering with Carpenter.

"One hundred thousand dollars," Carpenter said.

"If you're going to make jokes, then we don't have anything left to talk about," Stone said, gathering his notes.

More whispering. "All right, half a million," Carpenter said.

"A million," Stone replied.

"Three quarters of a million . . . euros," Sir Edward said, "and that's my final offer."

"I believe I can recommend that to my client,"

Stone said, "though she reserves the right to reject the offer at her meeting with you."

Sir Edward nodded.

"I've drafted some language for your letter," Stone said, sliding a sheet of paper across the table.

Sir Edward shoved it at Carpenter. "Read it to me."

Carpenter picked up the letter. " 'To whom it may concern: On (fill in date) in the city of Cairo, Egypt, agents of this service, at my personal direction, assassinated two Swiss citizens, René and Fatima du Bois, who were innocent of any crime. I wish to apologize personally, and on behalf of this service, to their daughter, Marie-Thérèse du Bois, for this unconscionable act. As a consequence of my actions, this service is paying the sum of (fill in amount) to Mademoiselle du Bois as reparations for the deaths of her parents. Signed.' "

"Will you excuse us for a few minutes?" Sir Edward asked.

"Of course." Stone got up and went into his study. He could hear murmurs and occasionally the raised voice of Sir Edward. Finally, Carpenter came into the study. "All right, come in. And Stone, he will not go one inch further than what you're about to hear."

"Let's hear it," Stone said, getting up and walking back to the dining room.

Sir Edward sat, his jaw clenched, and stared at Stone.

"This is what we have," Carpenter said, reading from a handwritten document. " 'To whom it may concern: Some time ago, agents of British Military Intelligence conducted an operation in the Middle East, during which two Swiss citizens, René and Fatima du Bois, were inadvertently killed. This organization regrets its actions and extends its apologies and sympathy to their daughter, Marie-Thérèse du Bois.' That's it. There will be no mention of reparations in the letter. It will be typed on the letterhead of the Ministry of Defence."

"And I won't change a fucking word of it," Sir Edward said.

"All right," Stone replied, "you may present the letter and your offer to Marie-Thérèse at your meeting."

"Which will be when?" Carpenter asked.

"I'll let you know when I've spoken to my client."

Everyone stood up, and Stone showed them out.

Carpenter hung back for a moment. "Stone, believe me when I tell you, this is an extraordinary concession for Sir Edward. Please tell your client that he will offer nothing further."

"I'll pass that on," Stone said.

"Call me when you have a time for the meeting." The two walked away from the house.

Stone went back inside, called Marie-Thérèse and asked her to call back from a pay phone.

When she did, he read her the text of the letter and told her about the money.

"The letter and the sum are both inadequate," she replied.

"Listen to me, Marie-Thérèse. This is the offer, and it won't change. It's more than you ever expected to get, and I advise you in the strongest terms to accept it."

She was quiet for a moment. "All right, but Sir Edward will have to apologize to me in person when we meet."

"We can make that demand at the meeting, but don't expect it to happen."

"All right. Now, how are we going to prevent these people from trying to kill me at the meeting?"

"I have some ideas about that," Stone said, and he explained.

"I like it," she said. "Tell Sir Edward to be at the Rockefeller Center skating rink tomorrow at three P.M."

"All right," Stone said, and hung up. Then he called Dino.

43

Stone was halfway through his first bourbon when Dino arrived at Elaine's.

Dino gave Elaine a kiss and settled into a chair opposite Stone. "A Laphroaig on the rocks," he said to a waiter.

"You're drinking single malts now?" Stone asked.

"Only when you're buying," Dino replied. "And it's better than that corn whisky you drink."

"Corn liquor aged in oak barrels for ten years," Stone said. "And bourbon is a patriotic American libation."

"Then you ought to get the Medal of Honor. What's going on?"

"I need your help."

"So what else is new?"

"You'll be preventing a killing on the streets of New York, so just think of it as doing your job."

"I'm real anxious to hear what your idea of doing my job is."

"All right, pay attention, this is complicated."

"I'll try to follow," Dino said, "if you'll keep it to words of two syllables or less."

"Actually —"

"That's four syllables."

"Dino, shut up and listen."

"Can I have another Laphroaig on the rocks?" Dino asked a passing waiter.

"You haven't finished the one you're drinking," Stone pointed out.

"Yeah, but you're going to talk for a long time, and I don't want to interrupt you by ordering another drink."

"You just did."

"After this. Go."

"I've arranged a meeting between the head of Carpenter's service and La Biche, and —"

"Whoa, whoa, whoa!" Dino nearly shouted. "How the fuck could you do that when you don't know either one of them?"

"We've all met since I saw you last."

"Last I heard, you were upset about their trying to kill her."

"I still am. I'm trying to stop it from happening. That's why I need your help."

"Okay, just a minute, there's something I want to know."

"What?"

"What are four retired NYPD cops doing outside in the street and at the bar right now?"

"They're making sure I'm not being followed."

"Stone, have you come over all paranoid?"

"Dino, if you'll just let me talk uninterrupted for a few minutes, all your questions will be answered, I promise."

"I'm listening."

"No, you're not, you're asking questions."

"No, I'm listening." Dino rested his chin in his hand. "See? This is me listening."

"To begin again, I've arranged a meeting between La Biche and Sir Edward Fieldstone —"

"Where do the Brits get these names?" Dino asked, shaking his head.

"Dino, shut up and listen."

Dino drew an imaginary zipper across his mouth.

". . . who is the head of Carpenter's service. He has proposed a truce between his people and La Biche — in short, they stop killing each other."

Dino shook his head in wonder and laughed.

"Dino . . ."

"I didn't say a word, but that was funny."

"The participants in this situation don't think it's funny."

"Yeah, I'll bet. How many of this Fieldstone guy's people has La Biche got on the scoreboard?"

"Too many, that's why he wants the truce. So I've arranged a meeting between them."

"Is the girl bananas? If she shows up at a meeting, the Brits will waste her."

"That's what I'm trying to prevent, and that's why I need your help."

"You want me to get her some body armor to wear?"

"That's not the worst idea you've ever had, but no, I don't think that will be necessary."

"Well, I don't want to be anywhere nearby when this meeting happens."

"That's exactly where I want you to be."

"Not anywhere nearby?"

"No, nearby. In fact, *very* nearby."

A look of incredulity spread across Dino's face.

"Just hear me out."

"You want me to take a bullet for this broad?"

"No, but if you're there, nobody will take a bullet."

"And how do we know that?" Dino asked. "Really, I'd like to know why my presence would stop them from pulling her plug."

"Dino, you're a lieutenant in the NYPD. It's not in their interests to kill such a person. That's why they won't shoot if you're close to her and they know it."

"And where is this meeting going to take place?"

"I don't know."

"What?"

"I don't know *yet*."

"Let's backtrack a minute here," Dino said. "How is it you happen to be in touch with La Biche?"

"I got her number from Bobby, the bartender."

"From Bobby, the bartender *here?*" Dino pointed down.

"Yes."

"Let me get this straight: If you want to get in

touch with an international terrorist and assassin, the guy to see is Bobby, the bartender at Elaine's?"

"In this case, yes. You see —"

"Boy, I've been underestimating Bobby. I thought all he did was pour drinks, but all the time, he's a clearinghouse for spies and assassins."

"You remember the night you arrested her here?"

"I seem to have some recollection of that."

"She was at the bar talking to Bobby. He asked her for her number, and she gave it to him. Her cell phone number."

"Man, I wish I'd thought of that when I had her in custody. It would make it so much easier to get in touch with her the next time she kills somebody."

"Dino, that's how it happened. I called her and met with her —"

"And why the fuck would you want to do a stupid thing like that. After that thing in the *Post* . . ."

"That's *why* I wanted to talk with her, to explain that I had nothing to do with trying to kill her. I didn't want her breathing down my neck."

"And she took your word for that? She's not as smart as I thought she was."

"She is very, very smart, believe me, and I can pull off this meeting and stop this killing, if you'll go along with me."

"Sure, sure, I'll go along. It'll make a nice

change. I haven't done anything this crazy in years."

"All right," Stone said, "this is how we're going to do it."

Dino listened, rapt. When Stone had finished, he burst out laughing.

"Jesus, I love it. And what are you going to do if World War Three breaks out in this public place?"

"Trust me, Dino, this is going to work."

"I hope to God you're right," Dino said, "because if you're not, it's going to be my ass."

"And mine."

"Never mind yours," Dino said.

44

Sir Edward Fieldstone stood in the middle of Rockefeller Center and tried to watch the skaters. He did not like being in the midst of all these . . . *people* . . . these foreigners, these colonials, these Americans with what he assumed were Brooklyn accents. His idea of New York accents had been formed by watching a great many World War II movies, American ones, mostly. His idea of a New Yorker was William Bendix.

He had stood there, increasingly annoyed, for twelve minutes before the cell phone in his hand vibrated. He opened it and put it to an ear. "Yes?"

"Good afternoon, Sir Edward," Marie-Thérèse said.

"If you say so."

"Now, now, mustn't be unpleasant."

His annoyance, and the thick body armor he wore under his jacket, caused him to begin to perspire. "May we get on with this, please?"

"Of course. You are to walk west on West Fiftieth Street, to your right. When you come to Sixth Avenue, cross and turn left."

"What . . ." But the connection had been broken.

"I'm to walk west on Fiftieth Street, cross Sixth Avenue, and turn left," he said, lowering his head and hoping the microphone pinned to the back of his lapel was working.

"The van won't be able to follow you," Carpenter replied, "because the traffic on Sixth Avenue moves uptown, and you'll be walking downtown, and I don't think we can take the risk of backup on the ground. But the chopper will keep you in view."

Sir Edward looked up.

"Don't look up," Carpenter said, "and don't lower your head when you speak. The microphone can pick up your voice. Speak as little as possible, and when you do, try not to move your lips."

What was he, a ventriloquist? He hated that he had allowed Carpenter to talk him into this nonsense, but he had to agree that it was their only chance to get at La Biche. He began walking. At Sixth Avenue, he crossed and walked downtown at a leisurely pace. He didn't like Sixth Avenue; it was full of taxicabs and grubby people and those awful street vendors with their kebobs and foreign food stinking up the atmosphere. His cell phone vibrated. "Yes?"

"At the next corner, cross the street, then continue downtown."

He followed her instructions, resisting the urge to look behind him. There was no one there anyway, unless La Biche had accomplices.

Stone's cell phone went off. "Hello?"

"It's Cantor. The Brit is crossing Sixth and heading downtown. None of my guys have been able to spot a tail yet. He may be clean."

"Good," Stone said, then closed his phone.

Sir Edward had walked for nearly eight blocks with no further word. He did not enjoy walking, especially in New York; he preferred his car and driver. His cell phone vibrated. "Yes?"

"Cross Forty-second Street, then turn left into Bryant Park, behind the New York Public Library. Ten paces into the park, stop and wait for another call." She cut the connection.

"She's directed me into the park behind the library," Sir Edward said to the air around him.

"I can't believe we're that lucky," Carpenter replied, "unless it's not the final meeting place."

"She told me to stop when I get into the park. Do you think she'll fire?"

"I don't believe she will. Now listen, when she's clear, your signal to fire is to take off your hat, smooth your hair, and put your hat back on."

"I believe I remember that," Sir Edward replied. "Just be sure your man doesn't miss."

"His weapon mount is gyro-stabilized," she replied. "The copter's movement won't muss his aim." She glanced at Mason, who was standing beside her wearing a harness that held him in the helicopter and a baseball cap backwards. She thought he looked ridiculous.

"I hope to God you're right." Sir Edward crossed Forty-second Street, walked another few yards, then turned into Bryant Park. He counted off ten paces and stopped. His cell phone vibrated. "Yes?"

"Very good, Sir Edward. Do you see the line of park benches to your right? The ones in the center of the park?"

"Yes."

"Go and sit on the fourth bench, at the end closest to Sixth Avenue."

Sir Edward looked at the benches: They were strung out in a line with a few feet between them. He counted, then went and sat on the bench as he had been instructed. He looked around.

"What's happening?" Carpenter asked.

"She told me to sit on this bench."

"Nothing else?"

"No."

"Then let's wait for something to happen."

"I don't see any alternative," Sir Edward said, "unless she's drawing a bead on me now." Someone sat down beside him on the bench.

"Who is that? The man in the hat?" Carpenter asked.

"Good afternoon, Sir Edward," the man said.

"Barrington? What are you doing here? The meeting was to have been with Miss du Bois."

"Stone Barrington is there?" Carpenter asked.

"Yes," Sir Edward replied.

"Yes, what?" Stone asked.

"I wasn't talking to you," Sir Edward said.

"Who were you talking to?"

"Ah, myself. Where is Ms. du Bois?"

"She will arrive in due course," Stone replied.

Sir Edward looked around him. The park was fairly crowded with all sorts of people. Which one could be the woman? The bag lady pushing a shopping cart? The woman in a business suit with a briefcase? The girl on Rollerblades?

"Where is she?"

"Relax, Sir Edward," Stone replied.

On the sidewalk behind the benches, a man in a suit and hat pushed a wheelchair bearing an old woman, who was hunched over, a large handbag in her lap. Sir Edward kept looking, trying to identify La Biche.

The wheelchair came to a halt between Sir Edward's bench and the next. The man bent over the woman, apparently his mother. "There, dear, is that comfortable for you?" he asked her.

"Very comfortable," she replied in an old lady's voice. She reached over and plucked the tiny receiver from Sir Edward's ear. "Good afternoon, Sir Edward," she said. Her voice was no longer old, and her accent was as British as Sir Edward's. "I am Marie-Thérèse du Bois. May I introduce Lieutenant Dino Bacchetti of the New York Police Department."

"How do you do, Sir Edward?" Dino said. He was still bending over the wheelchair. His head close to that of Marie-Thérèse.

45

Sir Edward looked around himself. "I'm surrounded," he said, lowering his head to be closer to the microphone behind his lapel.

It took Marie-Thérèse only a moment to locate it and pull it free. "Sir Edward is quite safe," she said into the microphone. "And I wish to point out that an attempt on me is very likely to hit either Lieutenant Bacchetti or Mr. Barrington. If that should happen, the *New York Times* will have the story before the ambulances arrive." She picked up Sir Edward's earpiece, which was resting on his shoulder, and put it into her own ear. "Did you read that loud and clear?" she asked.

Sir Edward removed his hat, ran his fingers through his hair, and put the hat back on.

Carpenter, in the helicopter, looked at Mason, who shook his head. "No shot," he said. "And we don't want to knock off one of the local constabulary, do we? Never mind your mate."

"I read you loud and clear," Carpenter said into her own microphone.

"Then kindly go and park that chopper over

the East River," Marie-Thérèse responded. "You'll still be able to read our transmissions, but you don't want to make me nervous by hovering, do you?"

Mason switched off his headset. "How soon can we have men in the park?"

"I estimate four minutes, if they run," Carpenter replied.

"Looks like we're stuck with the situation, doesn't it?"

Carpenter switched on her headset again. "Pilot, head for the East River and hover there," she said, so that La Biche could read her. She switched to her channel two. "Everybody converge on Bryant Park, behind the New York Public Library. Subject is seated next to Architect. Use extreme caution, and don't fire unless certain of success without collateral damage."

"Thank you so much," Marie-Thérèse replied. She watched as the helicopter moved east, along Forty-second Street, then she leaned forward in her wheelchair so that she could see Stone. "Let's get on with it," she said.

"We won't have long before Sir Edward's cavalry arrives."

"Sir Edward," Stone said, "did you bring the letter?"

Sir Edward reached into an inside pocket, produced an envelope, and handed it to Stone.

Stone read the letter and handed it to Marie-Thérèse. "It's as advertised."

She looked over the letter. "And the money?"

Sir Edward produced another envelope. "Here is a deposit receipt from Manhattan Trust. Call the number at the top of the page, use the code word 'structure,' and the bank will wire the funds to any account in the world. The transaction is irrevocable from my end."

"I certainly hope so, for your sake, Sir Edward, because if there is any problem with the transfer, you will be in violation of our agreement."

"I believe I'm due a signed document from you," Sir Edward said.

Stone handed him a letter. He looked at it and put it into a pocket. "It is satisfactory," he said.

"All right, let's go," Marie-Thérèse said. "Sir Edward, you will push my wheelchair."

"What? I'm not going anywhere."

"We're all going into the library. It's a lovely building, you'll be impressed."

"We'll be done in a couple of minutes, Sir Edward," Stone said. "Please don't make a fuss."

The four set off together, Sir Edward pushing the wheelchair, Stone and Dino walking on either side of Marie-Thérèse. They entered the library through a side door and took an elevator to the main floor.

"Stop here," Marie-Thérèse said. "Sir Edward, you will accompany these gentlemen to the main entrance of the library, then you will be free to go." Grabbing the wheels, she maneuvered the wheelchair through a rest room door bearing a handicapped-use sign.

"Let's go," Stone said, indicating the way for Sir Edward.

Marie-Thérèse locked the door, shed some clothes, and produced others and a wig from her large handbag. A quick check in the mirror, and she left the rest room, abandoning the wheelchair and her other clothes. She returned to Bryant Park and headed toward Sixth Avenue. As she reached the sidewalk, half a dozen men ran past her as she hailed a cab.

Stone paused at the top of the library's front steps. "That concludes our transaction, Sir Edward."

"I should bloody well hope so," Sir Edward replied.

"You couldn't just play it straight, could you? So much for the word of an English gentleman."

"Oh, go roger yourself," Sir Edward said, sweat rolling down his face.

"You should get out of that body armor before you have a heart attack," Dino said. "Let's go, Stone." He led the way down the front steps, and they got into Dino's car, which was waiting at the curb. "Where to?"

"Home, I guess." The car moved off.

"And where is Marie-Thérèse now?" Dino asked.

"I don't know," Stone said, "and I don't want to know."

★ ★ ★

Marie-Thérèse opened her cell phone and dialed the number on the bank receipt Sir Edward had given her.

"Wire transfer department," a woman's voice said.

Marie-Thérèse read off the account number from the sheet in her hand.

"What is your code?"

"Structure."

"Accepted. What are your instructions?"

"Wire the full amount to the following number at Saint George's Bank, Cayman Islands." She recited an account number.

The woman repeated the number for confirmation. "The funds will be in your account tomorrow morning," she said.

"Why not today?" Marie-Thérèse asked.

"Transfers must be made before two P.M., or they go out the following business day."

"Make an exception," Marie-Thérèse said.

"I'm afraid it's a nationwide banking rule," the woman replied. "Good day." She hung up.

Marie-Thérèse dialed Stone's cell phone number.

"Yes?"

"The bank won't wire the funds until tomorrow morning."

"That's normal. Transfers have to be made by two P.M."

"All right," she said. "I'll check with my bank in the morning, and if the funds are not there . . ."

287

"Please, don't tell me," Stone said.

"You'll hear from me if the money isn't there."

"I'd rather not hear from you again, Marie-Thérèse."

"What about your bill?"

"Consider my services pro bono," Stone said. "Now please disappear, and have a happy life."

"Check your coat pocket," she said. "And thank you for your help, Stone." She hung up.

Stone felt his pockets. There was something in one of them. He reached in and pulled out an envelope. Inside was a thick wad of one-hundred-dollar bills.

"Looks like about ten grand," Dino said. "Don't forget to report it on your tax return. And you're buying dinner tonight."

46

Stone and Dino had just sat down at Elaine's, when Carpenter walked in.

Dino waved her to a seat. Stone ignored her greeting.

"Whatever Dino's having," she said to a waiter.

"A nice single malt, on Stone," Dino said.

"Quite a day, eh?" Carpenter said. The waiter set down her drink, and she raised her glass. "To a job well done by the firm of Barrington and Bacchetti."

Dino raised his glass. "I'll drink to that."

Stone left his glass on the table.

"What's the matter with you?" Dino asked.

"She was in the chopper," Stone said to Dino. He turned to Carpenter. "Who was the shooter? Mason?"

"Mason was the best shot in the Royal Marines, a few years back," she replied. "He keeps his hand in."

"But you were calling the shot, weren't you?"

"No, Sir Edward did that, when he took off his hat. I called it off."

"But you wouldn't have, if Dino hadn't been there, would you?"

"If Dino and *you* hadn't been there. That

was very clever of you."

"I knew it was the only way I could keep her alive."

"It was."

"Well, I've learned something from this experience," Stone said.

"What's that?" she asked.

"Never trust an English gentleman, or an English gentlelady, for that matter."

"It's like they say in your Mafia," she replied. "It wasn't personal, it was business."

"Forgive me if I take it personally."

"That's up to you."

"Stone and I take a different view of this," Dino said. "I understand your position. I may even have some sympathy for it."

"Thank you," Carpenter replied. "It's nice to get a little understanding from *somebody*."

Stone picked up a menu. "Anybody want some dinner?"

"I'm starved," Carpenter said. "I'll have whatever Dino's having."

"Smart girl," Dino said. "We'll try the osso buco," he told the waiter.

"Same here," Stone said, "and tell Barry to make it with polenta, instead of pasta. And bring us a bottle of the Amarone."

"Why do you prefer the polenta to the pasta?" Carpenter asked.

"My necktie prefers it," Stone replied.

"Tuck your napkin into your collar, the English way."

"I intend to, even with the polenta."

"So," Dino said, "what are your plans now, Felicity?"

"Oh, I may stick around New York for a while. It's time I got back to the work I came here to do, before La Biche so rudely interrupted it."

"And what work was that?"

"I'm afraid I can't tell you, Dino."

"She's afraid the NYPD might interfere," Stone said. "During the past few days Carpenter and her people have broken more New York laws than a Mafia family."

"Well, as long as they don't do it in the Nineteenth Precinct, and frighten the patrol cars."

Elaine came and sat down. "So?"

Stone shrugged.

"It's a pity you weren't here a minute ago," Dino said to her. "You missed Stone's display of moral outrage."

"Yeah? We don't get a lot of that around here, except when the Yankees or the Knicks lose."

Their dinner came, and Elaine moved on to another table.

"This is delicious," Carpenter said.

"The best in New York," Dino replied. "Better than I've had in Italy, come to think of it."

Stone ate half his dinner and stopped.

"What's the matter with you?" Dino asked. "I never saw you leave osso buco on a plate."

"I'm still thinking about this afternoon, I guess, and it's not doing my appetite any good."

He waved at a waiter. "Wild Turkey on the rocks."

"You haven't finished your wine," Carpenter said.

Stone poured his glass into hers. "You finish it for me. Wine isn't strong enough tonight." The bourbon came, and he took a large swig.

"Uh-oh," Dino said. "I'm going to have to send him home in a patrol car tonight."

"Does it happen often?" Carpenter asked.

"Couple of times a year, maybe. Usually, it's a woman."

"It's a woman tonight," Stone said.

"Anybody we know?" Dino asked.

Stone looked directly at Carpenter for the first time that evening. "She's not a hundred miles from this table."

"Oh, I like the thought of driving a man to drink," Carpenter said.

Stone stared into his bourbon.

"You don't get it, do you?" Carpenter said.

"No, I don't."

"It's a war, and we've got to win it."

"You won the First World War and lost a million men, a whole generation of leadership. You won the Second World War and had your cities and your industry reduced to smoking rubble and lost your empire. What do you hope to win this time?"

Carpenter shrugged. "Some sort of peace."

"At what price?"

"Whatever it takes."

"I admire your commitment, but not your tactics," Stone said.

"In every country, even in this one, there are a few who are willing to do what's necessary to achieve greater good. The public doesn't care, they look the other way, while we clean up the mess left by foreign policy."

"Oh, thank God for the few," Stone said, raising his glass. He took a large swig. "The few make me sick."

"You're not going to throw up in my police car, are you?" Dino asked.

"I may throw up on this table if I hear any more of this."

"Dino," Carpenter said, "can't you explain this to him?"

"He wouldn't understand," Dino said.

"Oh, I understand, all right," Stone replied. "It's just that what I understand makes me ill."

Carpenter threw her napkin on the table and drained her wineglass. "Well, I don't think I'll go on making you sick." She stood up.

"Do you have any idea what's going to happen tomorrow?" Stone asked.

"What's going to happen tomorrow?"

"Marie-Thérèse is going to find out that the money Sir Edward promised her isn't in her bank — that's my guess, anyway, having dealt with Sir Edward this once. And if he's as duplicitous as I think he is, there's going to be blood in the streets — your blood, and Sir Edward's and Mason's, and whoever in your service is foolish enough to stick his head out of doors."

"You think we should all leave town, then? Run?"

"I think you should leave the planet, if you can, because you still don't grasp how determined this woman is and what she's capable of. You wronged her once, and you lost half a dozen people. If you've wronged her again . . . Well, there'll be no end to it, until all of you are dead — her, too."

"Felicity," Dino said, "is the money going to be in her bank tomorrow morning?"

Carpenter looked at Dino. "Yes," she said, turning toward Stone. "I made the banking arrangements myself. Now I'm getting out of here. I'm sick of Stone's moral superiority."

"It's easy to feel morally superior to some people," Stone replied.

She picked up her handbag and walked out.

Dino turned to Stone. "She says they paid the money. Maybe this is going to be all right."

"She's lying," Stone replied. "That's all they do, these people, is lie and kill. This is going to be a disaster, you wait and see."

"Ever the optimist," Dino said.

47

Marjorie Harris arrived at her desk at Manhattan Trust half an hour early, as she usually did. She switched on her computer and opened the wire transfer file. She had prepared a list of transactions that had been ordered too late for the two P.M. deadline the previous day, and now all she had to do was press the send key, verify the instruction twice, and tens of millions of dollars were automatically wire-transferred to banks all over the world in a matter of seconds.

She waited for the confirmations to come back, and, one by one, each transaction was confirmed by a computer in another bank somewhere. Human hands were not involved, though in some cases the instructions were received by fax.

Marjorie, her first duty of the day accomplished, opened the bag from the deli, removed a warm cheese Danish, which was not on her diet, and a black coffee, then turned to the *New York Times* crossword puzzle. The rest of her day would not begin until she had finished it.

At that same moment, in the Cayman Islands, south of Cuba, Hattie Englander let herself into

St. George's Bank and went to her desk in the wire transfer department. She placed her coffee and ham-and-egg sandwich on her desk, then went to the fax machine, bent over, and removed a stack of faxes that had arrived during the night or earlier that morning.

As she was about to straighten up, she heard a small, chirping sound behind her. She smiled and maintained her position.

"There it is," Jamie Shields said, running a warm hand over her buttocks. "Shining like the morning sun." He lifted her skirt and pulled down her panties. "Is it wet this morning?" he asked Hattie.

"You know it is," she replied, moving to the touch of his hand, then to the touch of something even warmer.

He slid into her from behind. "What a wonderful way to start the day," he breathed, as he established a rhythm.

Hattie shortly did what she did two or three times a week: She came in a series of snorts and cries, grabbing hold of the fax machine for support. The papers in her hand fell and scattered as Jamie joined her chorus.

Five minutes later, when the other workers began to arrive, Jamie was at his desk at the other end of the room, and Hattie was on her hands and knees, scooping up the stack of faxes that had slipped from her grasp.

"What's going on?" her boss asked sharply.

"Nothing, Mr. Peterson," Hattie said, her

search interrupted before she could see the single sheet of paper that had landed under the fax machine. "I just dropped the morning faxes."

"Deal with them at once," Peterson said grumpily.

"Yes, sir," Hattie replied, taking her seat at her desk. Coffee would have to wait. She stacked the papers evenly and ran through them quickly. All were copies of transfers wired that morning or during the night from banks around the world. Except one sheet, which was a request for notification. One hour after opening time, she was to fax a number in Switzerland, to report receipt of a transfer of 750,000 euros from Manhattan Trust in New York. If the funds were received into the St. George's account, she was to immediately forward them to an account in the Swiss Bank, holding out only the fifty-dollar transfer fee. If the transfer from New York had not arrived, she was to report that fact to the Swiss Bank.

She went through the other sheets again; the transfer had not arrived. She checked her watch: twenty minutes before nine. She opened her coffee. Plenty of time to have breakfast before checking the fax machine again at nine. She began to munch her sandwich and sip her coffee.

At nine o'clock, she checked the fax machine again. A number of other transfers had arrived, but not the one from Manhattan Trust. She opened a fax form in her computer and typed a short message: "Subject: wire transfer, 750,000 euros, from Manhattan Trust not received. Please inform client." She moved the cursor to the send button and clicked. This whole business would have been easier if her bosses had completed the computer setup that would handle everything automatically, but they were waiting for the end of the fiscal year to spend the money.

Five minutes later, she received an e-mail from Switzerland. "Please confirm receipt or lack of receipt of Manhattan Trust transfer at your 2:00 P.M. cutoff time."

Hattie logged in wire transfers all morning, getting hungry as one o'clock passed. She could not have lunch until the two-o'clock cutoff time. At two, she checked the fax machine once more and found it empty. She grabbed her handbag and headed for the door. Then, as she was about to leave, she remembered.

She returned to her desk, checked the transfers once more, then tapped in a message to Switzerland. "Manhattan Trust transfer of 750,000 euros not received this day. Please inform client." Then she went to lunch.

Marie-Thérèse was having breakfast in her suite at the Carlyle when her cell phone rang. "Yes?"

"Good morning, it's Dr. von Enzberg, in Zurich," a deep male voice said.

"Good morning, Dr. von Enzberg," she replied. "I'm glad to hear from you."

"Saint George's Bank has informed us that the transfer from Manhattan Trust has not been received," he said. "However, it will almost certainly come later in the morning. I've asked them to contact me at their two-P.M. cutoff time, to let me know if it has arrived."

"Thank you, Dr. von Enzberg," she said. "I'll expect your call." She closed the cell phone and went back to her breakfast. Then she stopped, nervous. She found the sheet of paper Sir Edward had given her and dialed the phone number at the top.

"Wire transfer room," Marjorie Harris said.

"Yesterday I gave instructions for a transfer to Saint George's Bank in the Caymans," Marie-Thérèse said. She gave the woman the account number.

"Oh, yes," Marjorie replied, checking the number on her computer. "That went out first thing this morning. It should be in your account now."

"Thank you," Marie-Thérèse said, then hung up, feeling better. She finished her breakfast, then drew a bath and got in. Where would she go? she asked herself. The world was her oyster now. Even the countries where she had been a fugitive were now open to her, as long as she had a good European Union passport, and she could manage that in a day. She thought about England: perhaps a nice, little Queen Anne house in the country, not too far from Heathrow. The Cotswold Hills were appealing, and she liked the irony of living in Sir Edward's own country. The thought made her laugh. Some shopping before leaving New York would be in order.

Marie-Thérèse was trying on a dress in the Armani shop a little after two, when her phone rang again. Finally. "Yes?"

"It's Dr. von Enzberg. I've had notification from Saint George's Bank that no funds were received into your account from Manhattan Trust."

"They're certain?"

"I asked for confirmation and received it. What are your instructions?"

"None," Marie-Thérèse replied. "I will handle this myself." She closed the phone. "I'll take this dress and the tweed jacket," she said to the saleslady.

"They'll both be wonderful for traveling," the woman said.

"Oh, I'm not traveling just yet," Marie-Thérèse replied. "I have a few things to do in New York over the weekend, before I leave." Clearly, the phone number for Manhattan Trust was manned by someone from British Intelligence. They would not fool her again.

Just at closing time, a cleaning woman came into the wire transfer department of St. George's Bank and made ready to mop the floor. You going to be long?" she asked the young woman still seated at her desk.

"I'll be out of your way in a moment," Hattie replied.

The cleaning woman took hold of the cart that held the fax machine and rolled it away from the wall. A single sheet of paper lay on the floor where the cart had been. She picked it up and handed it to the woman at the desk. "This yours?"

Hattie examined the document. "Oh, yes," she said. "Where did you find it?"

"It was under the fax machine."

"I was waiting for it all morning," Hattie said, laughing. She checked her watch: after closing time in Switzerland. She typed a message confirming receipt of 750,000 euros from Manhattan Trust and clicked on the send button. It was Friday night in Switzerland. They would receive the e-mail when they opened on Monday morning.

48

Marie-Thérèse yawned. It was boring, this sort of surveillance, but at the moment, it was her only way to keep track of these people. She had been waiting for nearly two hours in that most anonymous of vehicles in New York City, a black Lincoln Town Car.

"How much longer?" the driver asked. He had been provided by her friend at the embassy.

"As long as it takes," she replied. "Read your paper."

"I've read it."

"Then do the crossword."

"I can never do those things in English."

"Then shut up."

He was silent.

They were parked in a legal spot on Third Avenue, near the anonymous building that housed the people she wanted. She had a good view of the front door, and her eyes rarely left it. Then, finally, something happened. Three large, black SUVs with darkened windows passed her car and turned left into the street. They drew up to the front door of the building, and immediately, four men came out the front door and began looking up and down the street.

"Now," she said aloud. "Wait until the three black vehicles move, then start the car."

"Right," her driver replied.

A man and a woman emerged from the building and quickly got into the middle SUV, and the three cars began moving.

"Let's get going," she said. "Stay as far behind them as you can without losing them."

The driver did as instructed, and the trip was short. The three cars drove to Park Avenue, turned, then turned again into Fifty-second Street and stopped at an awning protruding from the lower level of the Seagram Building. Four men emerged from the first and third vehicles, had a good look around, then, at a signal from one of them, the rear doors of the middle SUV opened, and three men and a woman got out and went inside. The three SUVs drove off, no doubt to find a convenient parking spot.

Marie-Thérèse, whose car was waiting on Park Avenue, spoke. "Drop me at the awning, then drive around the block and park where you can see the doors. If the police hassle you, show them your diplomatic passport, but don't move from the spot until I appear."

The car stopped before the awning, and Marie-Thérèse got out, smoothing her little black dress and pulling on a pair of short, black kid gloves. Her hair was long and dark for the occasion. She went inside and started up the broad staircase. Her quarry was only yards ahead, and as she emerged on the second floor, his group, along with two bodyguards, were disappearing down a hallway toward the pool room of the Four Seasons.

This was not good. There was no way in or out of that room except by a hallway, perhaps ten feet in width, except maybe a kitchen door that she didn't have access to. She took a seat at the corner of the large, square bar, facing east, with the hallway on her left. One of the bodyguards returned after a couple of minutes, presumably having completed his scan of the large dining room, while his companion had stationed himself there. The man took up a station across the bar from Marie-Thérèse, facing west, so that he could watch the hallway from his seat. He ordered a mineral water and sipped it slowly.

He was not British, she thought. His suit was wrong, and his hair cut too short. He looked like a very boring young businessman.

Marie-Thérèse put a fifty-dollar bill on the bar and glanced at her watch. "I'm early," she said to the bartender. "A very dry Tanqueray martini, straight up, please."

"Yes, ma'am," the bartender replied, then went to work.

How long would this take? Her man was in his mid-sixties, so probably not all that long. Before the main course was served, was her guess.

The young man sitting across the bar from her picked up his drink, walked around the bar, and sat down next to her, facing south. Now his back was to the hallway he was supposed to be

304

watching. "Good evening," he said. Yes, American.

"Good evening," Marie-Thérèse replied coolly.

"I hope I'm not intruding," the man said, "but I find you very attractive. May I buy you a drink?"

"Thank you, I already have a drink. And my date will be arriving in a few minutes."

"May we talk until then?"

"All right."

"My name is Burt Pence," he said, offering his hand. "And yours?"

"Elvira Moore," she replied, shaking his hand.

He moved the fifty away from the bartender, toward her purse. "Please put this away," he said. "This is on me."

Marie-Thérèse picked up the fifty and stuck it into her large handbag, which rested on the stool next to her. "Thank you, Burt. Tell me, what sort of work do you do?"

"I'm an FBI agent," Burt replied.

"Oh, sure. I've heard that one before."

Burt reached into an inside pocket, produced a wallet, opened it, and laid it on the bar.

"Oh, my, you're telling the truth," she said, picking up the wallet and examining it. "What on earth are you doing at the Four Seasons? I hope you're on an expense account."

"Actually, I'm not dining this evening," Burt replied. "I'm on duty."

"Really?" She tried to look very interested. "What sort of duty?"

Burt looked slyly from side to side, as if he feared being overheard. "I'm protecting the director of the FBI and the head of British intelligence."

Marie-Thérèse looked around. "Where are they?"

"In the other dining room, down the hallway. My partner is on duty in there."

"What are you protecting them from?"

"Oh, nothing in particular. I mean, there's no specific threat at this time, but the director always has a bodyguard."

"I see. What about those people there?" She nodded at a couple who had come up the stairs and were being escorted down the hallway. "Would they be a threat?"

Burt looked down the hallway at their backs. "Probably not, but my partner will observe their actions in the dining room." He suddenly stood up. "Uh-oh, you're going to have to excuse me."

Marie-Thérèse looked down the hallway to see Sir Edward Fieldstone walking briskly toward them.

"That's my British subject," Burt said out of the corner of his mouth. "Probably going to the can."

"Well, you'd better go and hold his . . . hand," she said, laughing.

Sir Edward started down the stairs, and Burt fell in behind him.

Marie-Thérèse put her fifty back on the bar and hopped down from her stool. She began walking down the stairs and stopped on the landing. Sir Edward was standing outside the men's room, and Burt was nowhere to be seen. Then Burt came out the door, nodding, and held it open for Sir Edward, who disappeared inside. Burt took up his station outside the door.

Marie-Thérèse walked quickly down the stairs and over to Burt.

"What, you're leaving?" he asked. "I'll be right back."

"My date called me on my cell phone and canceled," she replied.

"I'm off in a couple of hours," he said. "Want to meet somewhere?"

Marie-Thérèse looked around. The coat-check girl had momentarily disappeared. "Are you carrying a gun, Burt?"

Burt grinned and opened his jacket, revealing a 9mm semiautomatic.

"Oh, good," she said, sticking her silenced pistol into his ribs and backing him against the wall. "I'll have that, Burt." She pulled his pistol from its holster. "Now, let's go to the men's room." She shoved him with her gun barrel.

"Hey, lady, what's going on?" Burt asked, as if she were joking. But he went through the door into a little vestibule.

Marie-Thérèse hit him, hard, in the back of the head with his own pistol, then tossed it onto his crumpled form. "Sorry about that, Burt." She pushed open the door to find Sir Edward standing at a sink, washing his hands. An attendant stood by with a towel. She shot the attendant first, to get Sir Edward's attention.

Sir Edward stood up straight, holding his wet hands out before him. "No, no," he said. "I paid the money, really I did."

"A liar to the end," she said, and shot him once in the chest. He fell to the floor, then she walked over and put a round into his head.

She dropped the pistol into her bag, left the men's room, stepping over Burt's inert form in the vestibule. He began to stir. She thought about it, then picked up his pistol and hit him with it again. "This is your lucky day, Burt." Then she peeked out the door. The entrance hall was empty. She walked casually from the men's room and out the front doors, looking for her car. Spotting it near the corner, she beckoned, then waited, and the driver drove quickly up and stopped.

"Slow down, for Christ's sake," she said as she got into the car. "Just drive away in a leisurely fashion." She looked back at the three SUVs parked at the curb. They remained where they were.

"That went very well," she said, removing her gloves. "Drop me at Madison and Seventy-second Street."

She got out of the car and began window-shopping her way back toward the Carlyle.

49

Carpenter sat in the pool dining room of the Four Seasons with the director of the FBI and his deputy. Their main course arrived, and Sir Edward had not returned from the men's room.

"I'd better go and check on him," she said to the director.

"Keep your seat," he replied, and waved over his bodyguard. "Find the men's room and check on Sir Edward," he said to the man. "He may be ill."

"I'm sure it's nothing," Carpenter said. "He probably ran into someone he knew. I think we should start without him." She picked up her knife and fork and cut into the venison on the plate before her.

"How long have you been an intelligence officer, Felicity?" the director asked.

"Twelve years, sir," she said. "I read law at Oxford, then joined the service."

"Sir Edward tells me your father was also in your service."

"That's correct," she said, "and my grandfather, as well." Something across the room caught her attention. The director's bodyguard was crossing the big room, walking fast, nearly running. He arrived at their table.

"What's wrong?" the director asked. "Is it Sir Edward?"

"Yes, sir," the agent replied. "Please follow me, and let's move quickly."

Everyone left the table and followed the agent from the dining room, drawing stares from other patrons. They entered a kitchen area, then came to a large door with an EXIT sign above it.

"What's happened?" the director asked.

"Please wait here just a moment, sir," the agent said. He walked out the door and returned a few seconds later. "Please hurry, your car is waiting."

Carpenter followed the three men into one of the black SUVs, and it drove away quickly.

"Now tell me what's happened," the director said.

Carpenter thought she knew what had happened. She got out her phone.

Stone and Dino were finishing dinner at Elaine's when Dino's cell phone went off.

"Bacchetti," he said into the phone. He listened for a moment, then spoke. "I'm on it. You on your cell phone? Don't go back to where you came from, go somewhere else. I'll get back to you." He hung up.

Stone looked at Dino. "What's wrong? You don't look good."

"It looks like . . ." His phone rang again.

"Bacchetti. . . . Yes, sir, I've just heard. I have men on their way. . . . Yes, sir, I understand how this looks. I'll be there personally in ten minutes. . . . Yes, sir, I understand." He hung up. "Come on," he said to Stone, and they both ran for the door.

They were in the rear seat of Dino's car, headed downtown with the siren going before Dino spoke again. "Don't let anybody slow you down," he said to the driver, then he got out his cell phone again.

"Wait a minute, Dino," Stone said. "What's going on?"

"Looks like your client just popped Sir Edward Fieldstone in the men's room at the Four Seasons." Dino dialed a number. "This is Bacchetti. I want four homicide detectives, a crime-scene team, and twelve uniforms at the Four Seasons, on East Fifty-second Street, *now*. Close the block, don't let anyone into the restaurant, but let the patrons out as they finish dinner. Screen off the men's room, and don't let anybody in there until I'm on the scene and say so. I arrive in six minutes."

"Oh, Jesus," Stone said, sinking back into the seat.

"So you had this all fixed, huh?" Dino said.

"At the *Four Seasons*?" Stone moaned. "Holy shit."

"That about sums it up for me," Dino said. "I just had the commissioner on the phone, and if he ever finds out that I was involved in that little

311

business of yours in Bryant Park I'll be walking a beat in the far reaches of the Bronx for the rest of my career."

"I don't believe this," Stone said. "It was all fixed — everything."

"I like your idea of all fixed," Dino said. "Call your client."

"What?"

"Call her. You've got her cell phone number."

"What am I supposed to say to her?"

"Ask her what she's going to do next."

"Why do you think she'll tell me?"

"Just ask her. Go ahead, call." Dino handed Stone his cell phone.

Stone dialed the number, which he now knew by heart, while Dino stuck his ear next to Stone's.

"Yes?" she said.

"It's Stone. What have you done?"

"They didn't send the money."

"Of course they sent it. I confirmed it. Didn't you call the bank?"

"Yes, but it wasn't the bank. It was obviously one of Sir Edward's people. They lied to me and to you, Stone. I had it confirmed twice that the money never arrived."

"You've got to stop this, Marie-Thérèse," he said.

"I've no intention of stopping," she replied. "They broke their agreement, and now they're fair game." She hung up.

Dino snatched his cell phone back and

pressed redial long enough to get the number.

"What are you doing?" Stone asked. "That was a conversation with a client."

"A client who has just announced her intention of committing a crime," Dino replied. "Your obligation now is to report that to the police and render whatever assistance you can, which you have just done." He called another number. "This is Lieutenant Dino Bacchetti at the Nineteenth Precinct," he said. "I want a wall-to-wall surveillance on the following cell phone number." He read out the number. "Nail it down in a hurry and call me back with a location. Highest priority. Do not — repeat — *do not* attempt to detain the holder of the cell phone." He hung up. "I'm going to nail the bitch," he said.

"What else can I do to help?" Stone asked.

"Think. Think of another way to get to her. Do you know where she's sleeping?"

"No."

"No idea at all? Hotel? Apartment? Safe house?"

"I have no idea. The only thing I have is the cell phone number, and you have that now."

"I hope to God it's enough," Dino said. "Did I mention that at the time she shot Sir Edward, he and Carpenter were having dinner with the director of the FBI?"

"Oh, shit."

"That's right, pal."

The car was waved through a roadblock at

Fifty-second and Park, then screeched to a halt in front of the Four Seasons. Stone and Dino got out of the car.

"Stay with me," Dino said, "and keep your mouth shut."

"What could I possibly say?" Stone replied.

50

Dino and Stone walked into the downstairs lobby of the Four Seasons to find a phalanx of uniformed police officers standing in front of the men's-room door. A man in a pin-striped suit was yelling at them. "You don't understand! I've got to get into that men's room *right now!*"

Dino tapped the man on the shoulder, spinning him around. He flashed his badge. "Sir," he said, "go upstairs and ask the headwaiter to direct you to the other men's room."

"What other men's room? There isn't one."

"Believe me, he'll find you one," Dino said. He pointed at an officer. "You. Escort this gentleman upstairs."

The cop took the man's elbow and steered him up the staircase.

"Out of my way," Dino said to the uniforms, who parted like the Red Sea. He pointed a thumb at Stone. "He's with me." Then he led the way into the men's room. A team of EMTs were bent over two bodies, one of them in a dark suit.

"Are they dead?" Dino asked.

"Yep," an EMT replied, "both of them."

"Then get the hell out of my crime scene."

The EMTs gathered their gear and left.

Dino bent over Sir Edward. "One in the chest, one in the head. Very professional." He looked at the men's-room attendant. "Poor schmuck," he said. "Wrong place at the wrong time."

A uniform stuck his head through the doorway. "Lieutenant, we got an FBI guy up at the bar. He's the only witness."

"Let's go," Dino said to Stone. He marched up the stairs and to the bar, where an EMT was doing something to the back of a young man's head. There was a glass of brown liquid before him, no ice. He took a big swig.

Dino removed the glass from his hand and set it on the bar. "This is how the FBI recovers from a tap on the head?" he asked. "I'm Bacchetti, NYPD. What happened, and get it right the first time."

"I was sitting here, watching the people entering the hall to the dining room. My partner was in the dining room with the director, his deputy, and his guests."

"Who were . . . ?"

"Deputy Director Robert Kinney, Sir Edward somebody or other, the dead man, and a woman who works — worked for him."

"Go on."

"Sir Edward came down the hall looking for the men's room. I went with him, and then the woman —"

"Wait a minute, what woman?"

316

"There was a woman sitting next to me at the bar."

"She was sitting next to you, or you were sitting next to her?"

"Well . . ."

"I'm glad we got that cleared up."

"Anyway, I went down with Sir Edward and checked out the men's room. There was nobody in there but the attendant. I was waiting outside the door for him to finish when the woman came downstairs."

"Describe her."

"White female, thirty to forty, five-six or -seven, a hundred and thirty pounds, long, dark hair, wearing a black cocktail dress and black gloves." He looked longingly at the glass on the bar. "A real looker."

"Very good description," Dino said. "At least you learned *something* at the academy. What happened next?"

"She asked me if I was armed, and I showed her my gun. She pulled a black, small-caliber pistol with a silencer from her handbag, took my gun, and pushed me ahead of her into the vestibule inside the men's-room door. She must have clocked me with either her weapon or mine. I passed out. When I came to, she hit me again. I only woke up five minutes ago, and I got on my radio."

"So where are all your people?"

"On the way."

Dino looked at the back of the man's head.

"Get him to a hospital," he said to the EMT. "He's going to need lots of stitches."

The EMT and his partner escorted the agent down the stairs; Dino and Stone followed. They had only just seen him into an ambulance when a procession of dark vans drove into the block, and men in body armor and helmets, carrying automatic weapons, began spilling out of them, "FBI" emblazoned on their backs.

Dino stood in front of the door and held up his badge. "NYPD," he said. "Who's in command?"

A man in a suit got out of the front seat of a van and walked over, flashing his ID. "I'm Jim Torrelli, agent-in-charge of the New York office of the FBI," he said. "You're in the way of my men."

"No, I'm not," Dino replied. "*They're* in the way of this city's traffic. Please get them out of here."

"We have a crime scene to secure," the man said.

"It's an NYPD crime scene, and it's already secured," Dino replied, not budging.

"We have an injured FBI agent in there," Torrelli said.

"No, you don't. He's already on the way to a hospital. There are no other FBI personnel inside, just two murder victims, and murder, if I may remind you, is not a federal crime. Now, if you want to hang around and see what happens, you may do so at my invitation, but don't get in my way, and get these storm troopers out of here, *now*."

Torrelli thought about it for a moment. "Everybody back in the vehicles," he said. "Return to base and wait for my call." The men got back in the vans and drove away. "Now, Detective . . ."

"*Lieutenant* Bacchetti," Dino said, "commander of the detective squad at the Nineteenth Precinct."

"Can you tell me what happened here?"

"Yeah. The director of the FBI and his deputy took the head of British Intelligence and his colleague out to dinner, guarded by two FBI agents. The Brit went to the men's room, and a young woman hit one of the agents over the head and shot the Brit and the men's-room attendant. She left the premises. That's all I've got, at the moment, but when we're done here, there ought to be enough embarrassment for the FBI to last for years."

Torrelli's jaw began to work, but he managed to get a few words out. "Has the young woman been apprehended?"

"No, and I don't expect she will be right away."

"Has she been identified?"

"Yes."

"Who is she?"

"I'm not at liberty to give you that information at the moment. Maybe later."

"Lieutenant, if I have to go to the commissioner or the mayor himself, I'm going to know everything there is to know about this case."

"I'll send you a copy of my report," Dino said. "Now why don't you go up to the bar and have a drink. We don't need you right now."

"Can I see the bodies?"

"They're dead. Two slugs in the Brit, one in the attendant. That's all you need to know."

"I'd like to put the FBI crime lab at your disposal," the agent said.

"From what I've heard about the FBI lab, I think I'd rather handle it in-house," Dino said.

The man, who was much larger than Dino, looked as if he wanted to beat him into the ground. "I'll be in my car," he said, and returned to his van.

Dino and Stone walked back into the restaurant.

"You're going to hear about that," Stone said.

"Don't worry about it." Dino got out his cell phone and pressed a speed-dial button. He held the phone to his ear. "Sir, it's Bacchetti. This is where we stand." He gave a concise report to the commissioner. "And the FBI is already trying to horn in on our scene. I'd appreciate your help in keeping them off my back, so I can get this thing cleared and make an arrest." He listened for a moment. "Thank you, sir." He hung up and turned toward Stone. "I don't think we have to worry too much about the Feds."

"What next?" Stone asked.

Dino's phone went off. "Bacchetti." His eyes widened. "Location?" He snapped the phone shut. "We've got a fix on her cell phone."

51

Dino reached into the front seat and picked up a handheld radio. "Remind me what's at Madison and Seventy-third," he said to Stone.

"A lot of very expensive shops," Stone replied.

"Listen up," Dino said into the radio to the four detectives in the car behind him. "Get out at Sixty-fifth and Madison and work your way north, shop by shop. I'll be working south from Seventy-sixth Street. We're looking for a good-looking white woman, probably alone, thirty to forty, five-six or -seven, a hundred and thirty pounds, wearing a black cocktail dress and black gloves. She may be wearing a coat, too. It's nearly ten, and nothing's open this time of night, but we had her standing still at Seventy-third and Madison for a couple of minutes, so she may be window-shopping. Detain and identify anybody of that description, alone or accompanied. Until you do, try not to look like cops. Be careful, because she's armed and very dangerous." Dino released the talk button on the radio. "This isn't going to work," he said.

"Why not?" Stone asked. "We may get lucky."

"I don't get this lucky," Dino said. "You get

this lucky. Anyway, if we catch her, she's going to kill at least one cop before somebody shoots her."

Stone didn't comment on that.

"Remind me," Dino said. "How did I get mixed up in this?"

"There was a murder on your beat," Stone said.

"Oh, yeah. Next, you're going to remind me that I had her in custody and let her go."

"I wasn't going to, but, of course, that's true."

"I'm going to be lucky to get out of this with my badge."

"Dino, all you have to do is blame it on the Brits and the FBI."

Dino brightened. "Yeah, you're right." He tapped his driver on the shoulder. "Right here."

Dino and Stone got out of the car. "You take the east side of the street, I'll take the west," he said to Stone. "Are you carrying?"

"No."

Dino handed him a .32 automatic. "Take my backup."

"Thanks," Stone replied.

The two men began walking south on Madison. It was well after dark, but there were still a lot of people on the street.

Stone looked carefully at every woman he saw, looking for something familiar. She may have already changed clothes, he thought, but he might be able to recognize her. Then, half a block away from him, walking slowly uptown, he saw her. She wasn't wearing gloves, but her dress was black, and her hair shoulder-length and dark. The face? He couldn't tell; each time he had seen her she had looked so different. His hand closed over the gun in his pocket. She stopped and looked into a shop window for a moment.

Stone looked across the street at Dino and nodded toward the woman. Dino began making his way across Madison Avenue, through heavy traffic, not waiting for the light.

Stone walked up to her. "Excuse me, haven't we met?" he asked.

She turned and looked at him. "No," she said with a little smile. "But I certainly have no objection."

Dino stood directly behind her. "Miss," he said, "I'm a police officer. Please stand perfectly still."

She looked over her shoulder. "What is this, a gang bang?"

"Let me see some ID," Dino said.

Stone grabbed the bag before she could reach into it, then handed it to Dino, still looking into her eyes.

She looked back, with interest. "So, this is how the NYPD amuses itself in the evenings?"

"When the weather's nice," Stone said.

"What's your name?" Dino asked, looking at the driver's license in his hand.

"Donna Howe Baldwin," she said.

"Social Security number?"

She recited it. "But you won't find it on my license. They don't do it that way in Florida."

"Why do you carry a Florida driver's license?" Dino asked.

"Because I live in Miami. My address is on the license."

"Why are you in New York?"

"Because I heard what a lot of fun the police are here."

Stone looked at Dino and shook his head. "It's not Marie-Thérèse."

"I could be, if you wanted me to," the woman said. "Are we done here?"

"Yes," Dino said, handing back her handbag. "I'm sorry to have detained you. We're usually nicer to out-of-town visitors."

"You still could be," the woman said. "I've no objection to two dates. Who's buying the drinks?"

"Perhaps another time," Stone said.

She handed him a card. "I'm at the Plaza for two more days. Anytime at all." She looked at Dino. "And be sure to bring your friend." She continued walking uptown.

"Well," Dino remarked, "I said you would be the one to get lucky."

"Looks like we both did," Stone said.

Dino went back across the street, and they continued their walk downtown, inspecting every woman they encountered. Once, Dino showed his badge and asked a woman for ID, then she continued uptown, apparently livid.

At Seventy-second Street, they met the four detectives coming the other way, and Dino's car caught up with them.

"Why do I think she was going uptown?" Dino asked.

"Because she was walking away from the Four Seasons," Stone replied.

"What's uptown from Seventy-third?" Dino asked.

"A couple of hotels: the Westbury and the Carlyle."

"It's worth a try," Dino said. "You four guys take the Westbury. Get the manager to give you a list of every single woman staying in the hotel and question every one of them who even remotely matches the description. Stone, you and I will take the Carlyle." They got into Dino's car and started uptown.

"This isn't the worst idea you've ever had," Stone said. "She's got to be sleeping somewhere, and the Carlyle is about the last place you'd look."

"The worst idea I ever had was showing up with you in Bryant Park yesterday," Dino said.

The car stopped, and they got out.

"You know anybody here?" Dino asked, as they went in through the Madison Avenue entrance of the hotel.

"The manager," Stone replied. "He won't be here this time of night, but I can drop his name."

"Never mind, I'll just drop my badge," Dino

replied as they approached the front desk.

Stone's cell phone vibrated, and he flipped it open. "Hello?"

"It's Carpenter," she said.

52

Stone was surprised how glad he was to hear from her.

"Where are you?"

"With the director of the FBI at a government flat in the Waldorf Towers."

"Stay there. It's dangerous everywhere else."

"I intend to, for the moment. Have you spoken to Dino?"

"I'm *with* Dino."

"Is Sir Edward dead? Is it confirmed? These people won't tell me anything."

"It's confirmed."

"Oh, shit," she said.

"Well, yes."

"Ask Dino where I can claim his body."

"At the city morgue, but after a post-mortem."

"Is there any way to avoid that? I'd like to get him home."

"Ask the director. He can probably call somebody."

"He's very annoyed at everyone in the New York City government, from Dino to the mayor."

"That's because Dino wouldn't let him play

in his pond, and the commissioner and, presumably, the mayor backed up Dino."

"Something like that. Apparently, he has all
these men in black with guns, and he can't use
them."

"That always annoys the FBI."

"Will you come and see me here?"

"The FBI would probably shoot me if I
tried."

"I want to see you. I need to see you."

"Don't you think it would be a little crowded
in a hotel suite with you, me, and the director all
there?"

"I'll figure something out."

"Tell me, was Mason on the scene when
Marie-Thérèse's parents were killed?"

She paused. "Sort of. He was in a van nearby."

"Then you'd better tell him to watch his ass.
Who else was there, who's still alive?"

"Just the two of us."

"If I were you, I'd order up an airplane to an
airport other than Kennedy and get out of the
country. She knows where you've been camp-
ing out in New York. You'd be safer in London."

"I'll think about it. Does she know I've stayed
at your house?"

"Not that I'm aware of."

"I'll call you later, on your cell phone."

"Promise?"

"Yes, but I don't know when."

"Whenever, just call." Stone hung up. "Carpenter's a little stressed," he said.

"Who wouldn't be?"

The duty manager came to the front desk.

Dino showed him a badge. "I'm Lieutenant Bacchetti. I need a list of all the women staying in the hotel who are traveling alone."

"What for?" the man asked.

"There may be a lady murderer in your hotel, and I'd like to arrest her before she kills some of your guests or staff."

"Just a minute," the man said, then went to a computer terminal. "We've got three."

"Do you know them by sight?"

"I know Mrs. King, from Dallas. She's stayed here before. And Ms. Shapiro, from San Francisco. I don't know Mrs. Applebaum, from Chicago."

Dino gave him the description.

"Both Mrs. King and Ms. Shapiro fit the general description," the manager said.

"I want to speak to both of them, but I don't want them to know we're the police," Dino said. "And find me somebody who knows Mrs. Applebaum by sight."

"Just a minute." The manager went away for a moment and came back with another man. "This is the concierge. He knows Mrs. Applebaum, and she's in her sixties."

"All right, here's what we do," Dino said. "You make up a story that gets both women out of their rooms for long enough for us to get a look at them."

"I could tell them we have a small fire in a

suite near them, and ask them to leave their rooms for a few minutes."

"Where will you move them?"

The manager checked his computer. "I have empty suites near both of them," he said.

"Get us some hotel coveralls and a toolbox," Dino said. "Let's start with Ms. Shapiro."

The manager took Dino and Stone into his office and ordered coveralls for them, then he picked up the phone and called the room. "Ms. Shapiro, this is the duty manager speaking. I'm sorry to disturb you, but we have a small electrical fire in the suite below you, and I'm going to have to move you temporarily to a room down the hall while the electrician checks your room. . . . Yes, I'm really very sorry. May I bring him upstairs? . . . Thank you." He turned to Dino. "Ready?"

Dino and Stone stood on either side of the manager while he rang the doorbell. Each had his hand on a gun.

The door opened and a woman in a dressing gown greeted them.

"Thank you for your cooperation," the manager said.

"Glad to help," she replied.

She had a very large, and quite beautiful nose, Stone thought. He looked at Dino and shook his head.

Dino put his cell phone to his ear. "Yes? Thank you." He turned to the manager. "The problem's been fixed," he said. "We won't have

331

to disturb Ms. Shapiro."

"That's good news," the manager said. "Again, I'm very sorry, Ms. Shapiro."

She smiled and closed the door.

Dino handed the man his cell phone. "Now, Mrs. King," he said.

The manager called the front desk and asked for Mrs. King's suite. "No answer," he said. "She must be out."

"You got a passkey?" Dino asked.

"Yes, but you realize it would be an illegal search."

"Not with your permission."

The man handed over the key. "It's two floors up — nineteen-seventeen."

"Thanks," Dino said. "I'll return this to you. Let's go, Stone."

Downstairs, in the Café Carlyle, Marie-Thérèse was deep in conversation with a man at the bar.

Musicians began taking their places at the opposite side of the room, and a voice came over the sound system. "Ladies and gentlemen, the Café Carlyle is proud to present, in his thirtieth season at the Carlyle, Mr. Bobby Short!"

The music began, and Marie-Thérèse and her new acquaintance turned toward the stage.

53

Carpenter dialed Mason's cell phone and he answered immediately. "Speak," he said.

"It's Carpenter. Where are you?"

"At a restaurant called La Goulue, on Madison Avenue, at Sixty-fifth Street."

"Are you alone?"

"No."

"I have news, but don't react."

"Go."

"Architect is dead."

"Really?" he drawled, in his Etonian accent. "Anyone we know involved?"

"La Biche shot him in the men's room at the Four Seasons."

"Goodness gracious. Who's next in line?"

"You and I."

"Well, I wouldn't like that much."

"I didn't think so. I think she followed him from the firm offices, so don't go back there."

"Makes sense. Any suggestions?"

"Don't go back to your hotel, either."

"Well, I suppose I'll have to seek shelter elsewhere," Mason said, sighing.

"Good idea."

"Do you have any plans?"

"I think we should get an RAF airplane over here and get out. I'd feel more comfortable at home."

"Would you? I'm not sure I agree. After all, our, ah, friend is here, isn't she? I should think we'd have more luck making a connection with her right here in the Big Apple."

"You might not like the connection."

"Leave that to me."

"I'll be on my cell phone. Let's stay in touch."

"Where are you?"

"At the Waldorf Towers, in the director's company flat."

"How cozy."

"Don't make bad jokes. Stay in touch."

"Righto."

Mason hung up and gazed at the young FBI agent sitting across the table from him. "There's been a spot of bother. My governor is deceased."

"Well, at his age . . ."

"It wasn't a coronary."

The young man dug out a cell phone.

"Oh, don't do that," Mason said. "They'll just put you to work. They'll get in touch if they need you."

The agent smiled and pocketed his cell phone.

Mason leaned forward. "It's been suggested that I shouldn't go home. Mind if I bunk with you tonight?"

The agent smiled. "I'd be delighted."

★ ★ ★

Carpenter went back into the suite's living room, where the director and his deputy were on separate phones.

"I'm getting zero cooperation from the New York police and the local administration," the director was saying. "It might help if you called the mayor, sir." He took the phone away from his ear when the reaction came. "Sir, I think you should consider the reaction in the press when they find out that a high figure in British intelligence has been murdered while in the company of a high American official. . . . Well, you have a point. The press will never have heard of Sir Edward, unless, of course, the NYPD decides to tell them who he is. I think that if you called the mayor, we might be able to keep this as the murder of a foreigner in a restaurant, nothing more. . . . Thank you, sir." He hung up and sighed.

"Problems, Director?"

"Call me Jim, Felicity." He patted the sofa next to him. Carpenter took a nearby chair, instead. "Jim it is."

"The attorney general doesn't want to get involved," the director said.

"One can hardly blame him," Carpenter replied. "I don't think you need be concerned about the press's treatment of this event. We go to some lengths to see that our own management's names are never published, and the only member of the NYPD who knows who he is is Lieutenant Bacchetti, at the Nineteenth Precinct. I don't think he'll be loose-lipped."

"Bacchetti, yes. I've heard of him. Somebody recommended that I recruit him in a management position. What do you think?"

"He's a good man."

"Maybe this would be a good time to broach the subject with him."

"I wouldn't know about that."

The director stood up, an empty glass in his hand. "Can I get you a Scotch?"

"No, thank you, sir. Officially, I'm still on duty."

"What has London had to say about all this?"

"I have a call in to the home secretary, but he hasn't gotten back to me. It's the middle of the night there, and I doubt if his duty officer has the nerve to wake him. There's not much he can do, anyway, and I'd rather be free to act without his orders inhibiting me."

"Are you planning something?"

"I'm planning to react, if I get the opportunity. I don't know if I will."

"Well, you're safe here with me," the director said, pouring himself another Scotch.

"Thank you, sir, that's very reassuring."

"How well did you know Sir Edward?"

"I've known him all my life. He and my father served together."

"Then I suppose my personal condolences are in order."

"Not really, sir. Sir Edward was a shit, and I won't miss him."

Stone and Dino stood outside the door of Suite 1917.

"Ready?" Dino asked.

"Whenever you are," Stone replied, gripping the gun in his pocket.

Dino rang the bell. No answer. He rang it again. "What the hell," he said, slipping the passkey into the lock.

54

Stone followed Dino into the suite, gun in hand.

"Hello?" Dino called. "Hotel maintenance. Anybody home?" He walked quickly to the bedroom door, flattened himself against the wall, and nodded to Stone.

Stone pushed the door open with his foot and stepped tentatively into the room. "Hotel maintenance. Anybody there?"

Dino put a foot against his backside and pushed him into the bedroom.

"Just like old times," Stone said. "First through the door again."

"You have a lousy memory," Dino said, following him into the room.

They looked around. Everything seemed perfectly normal.

"Check the closet," Dino said.

"You think she's in there? *You* check it."

Dino opened the closet door, and the light came on. Inside hung half a dozen outfits. "She travels pretty light, for a woman."

Stone pointed at the upper shelf, where three wigs rested on plastic forms. "Not every woman travels with that much hair."

"Okay," Dino said, "let's turn it over, but leave everything exactly as it is."

"What are we looking for?"

"Evidence. I'd love to find the weapon she's been using."

"It's probably tucked into her bra."

"I'm willing to look there."

They went to work.

Downstairs in the Café Carlyle, Bobby Short's performance was drawing to a close. The applause was long and warm.

"Well," the man next to her at the bar said. "Can I buy you a nightcap?"

"I'm staying here," she said. "Why don't you let me buy you one upstairs? There's a bar in my suite."

He held out a hand. "I'm Jeff Purdue. You're on."

"I'm Darlene King. Right this way."

They fell in with the crowd leaving the café.

"I take it you're not a New Yorker?" he said.

"I'm a Texan, sugar."

"Dallas?"

"Sometimes."

"What do you do down there?"

"My husband's in the oil business."

"You have a husband? I hope he's in Dallas."

"He sure is. If I know him, he's in bed with his secretary right this minute."

His hand dropped from her waist to her ass. "What you need is a little revenge," he said.

"Believe me, I know the deep satisfactions of revenge," she replied.

Stone stopped looking. "That's it. There's nothing more."

"There's a safe in the closet," Dino said. "I'll call the manager. We'll get it opened."

"It's late," Stone said, looking at his watch. "We don't want her to walk in on us."

"I need some evidence."

"She's obviously carrying the weapon."

"We don't even know this is her suite," Dino said.

"It's her suite," Stone said.

"How do you know?"

"Because when I met her the first time, she was wearing a red wig that's now on the shelf of her closet."

Dino looked at his watch. "Let's get out of here and set up surveillance."

"Okay."

They let themselves out of the suite and headed for the elevators.

Marie-Thérèse and her new friend had made their way out of the café crowd and into the lobby. As they rounded a corner, headed for the elevators, she stopped and stepped back. She had just seen Stone Barrington and that police lieutenant step off the elevator into the lobby, and they were wearing workmen's coveralls.

"Something wrong?" Purdue asked.

"I just remembered what a mess my suite is. Where are you staying?"

"At the Waldorf, five minutes from here in a cab."

"Why don't we go there?" she asked.

"Fine with me."

She led him back past the café and out the Madison Avenue exit, where a couple of cabs waited at the curb. In a moment, they were driving away.

He leaned over and kissed her on the neck, cradling a breast in his hand.

She didn't react, just looked straight ahead, thinking fast. The cab turned onto Fifth Avenue.

He pinched a nipple hard. "What do I have to do to get your attention?" he asked.

"I'm sorry," she said, patting him on the knee. "My mind was elsewhere for a moment. What do you do, Jeff?"

"I'm with the State Department, on the U.S. delegation to the United Nations. I spend two weeks a month in New York."

"How very interesting," she said, turning toward him with new interest. "So your wife's back in Washington?"

"She usually comes with me, so she keeps some clothes here. But she had some meetings this week."

"Well, isn't that convenient," she said, kissing him.

He ran his fingers through her hair, and it came away in his hand.

"Well, there's a surprise," he said, holding the wig in his hand and looking at her short blond hair.

"I'm just full of surprises, sugar," she said, running her hand up his thigh.

55

Stone and Dino sat in Dino's car outside the Carlyle, while Dino made a phone call. "Sir, it's Bacchetti. We've found out where the woman is staying. She's in a suite at the Carlyle. . . . Yes, sir, she certainly has good taste. I've ordered in a surveillance team. In very short order I'll have the place covered and a couple of men in the suite next door with a listening device. . . . No, sir, I don't want to take her in the street or in the lobby. There's sure to be weapons fired, and we don't want a mess. I want to let her come home and go to bed. We'll know when that happens. Then, when she orders breakfast in the morning or leaves her suite, we'll be waiting. I think we can take her clean. . . . Yes, sir, I know how important that is. I'll call you the minute anything happens." Dino hung up. "He's not going to get any sleep tonight," he said.

"I expect not," Stone replied.

Dino's driver returned with a paper bag holding coffee.

"We may as well make ourselves comfortable," Dino said.

"I had a thought," Stone said. "Suppose she's in the café, listening to Bobby Short?"

Dino snorted. "Not everybody has your weird taste in music, Stone."

The ride up in the elevator seemed a long one.

"I'm in the Towers," Purdue explained. "The government rents an entire floor, where the UN delegation stays, and there are apartments for visiting dignitaries, including a presidential suite."

"How interesting," Marie-Thérèse said. "Who's in residence at the moment?"

"I'm the only one of the delegation in town. Most of the others arrive tomorrow, for the opening of the Security Council session. I saw the director of the FBI in the elevator earlier, though, so I guess he's staying. I'll bet he's commandeered the presidential suite."

Marie-Thérèse laughed aloud.

"What's so funny?"

"It's just that I never thought I'd be this close to the director of the FBI."

The elevator stopped, and they got out. A man in a dark suit holding a clipboard stopped them.

"It's all right," Purdue said, "the lady's with me."

"I'm afraid I'll have to see her ID, sir," the guard said.

"No problem," Marie-Thérèse said, digging out her wallet and her Texas driver's license.

The man wrote her name down and noted the time, then returned the license to her. "Sorry for the inconvenience, ma'am," he said.

"Right this way," Purdue said, taking her elbow. They walked a few steps and he led them into a suite, tossing his keycard onto a table in the entrance hall.

"Very nice," she said, looking around. It wasn't big, but it was certainly elegant. "Where's the bedroom?"

"A woman after my own heart. Right this way." He led the way into the bedroom.

She unzipped her dress. "I want to hang this up," she said, "since I'll be wearing it tomorrow morning."

"Right over there," he said, pointing at a closet, then he went into the bathroom. "Excuse me a second."

Marie-Thérèse opened the closet door to find a small collection of outfits. She plucked one off the rack and held it up to her. "Not bad," she said aloud.

"Don't mess with my wife's things," he said, coming out of the bathroom. "She'd notice, believe me."

"Don't worry, sugar," she replied, hanging up the dress. "I won't disturb a thing. Tell me, have you got an early day tomorrow?"

"Nah, the session doesn't open until after lunch. We can sleep in, if you like."

"Oh, good," she said, hanging her dress in the closet and shedding her underwear. "You ready for me, sugar?"

"Oh, yeah."

She slid into bed with him. This wouldn't take long, then she could get a good night's sleep.

Stone's cell phone vibrated. "Hello?"

"It's Carpenter."

"Hi, there."

"Turns out we're in the presidential suite, but I've managed to get a room with a lock on the door that opens into the hallway. Why don't you join me?"

"I can't, but you're going to like my news."

"What's that?"

"She's staying at the Carlyle. Dino's people have got her suite staked out now. They'll wait for her to come home and go to sleep, then take her in the morning."

"God, that's a relief," Carpenter said. "Are you sure you wouldn't rather wait her out in the presidential suite?"

"I want to be here. You sleep well, and we'll talk in the morning." Stone hung up. "Carpenter's staying in the presidential suite of the Waldorf Towers, with the director."

Dino laughed.

"She says there's a lock on her door."

Carpenter called Mason.

"Hello," he panted, on the fourth ring.

"You sound a little winded," she said.

"What is it, Carpenter? I'm busy."

"The director wants a meeting tomorrow

morning at eight. Think you can manage that?"

"I expect so. Can I go now?"

"I should have talked with the home secretary by then."

"How nice for you. Good night." He hung up and returned to his FBI agent.

The following morning at eight o'clock, Carpenter took her seat at the suite's dining room table. Mason had been on time, though he looked a little worse for the wear, and he was wearing the same suit and shirt as the day before.

"All right, let's get started," the director said.

Carpenter's phone rang. "Excuse me, sir." She stepped away from the table and opened the phone. "Yes?"

"It's Stone."

"What happened?"

"She didn't come home last night."

"Oh. I'll report that and call you later." She closed the phone and sat down.

"Anything?" the director asked her.

"I'm afraid there's bad news, sir. As I mentioned earlier, the NYPD had her located in a suite in the Carlyle hotel. They staked it out, but she didn't come home last night."

"Shit," the director said. "I thought we had her."

"So did I, sir."

"I wonder where she is at this moment," he mused.

56

At that moment, Marie-Thérèse was looking at the top of the head of a member of the U.S. delegation to the UN. He performed with enthusiasm and considerable skill, she thought, and she told him so.

They were interrupted by the doorbell. Purdue grabbed a robe and signed for breakfast, then wheeled the cart into the bedroom.

"Sorry for the interruption," Purdue said.

"You should have told him you'd already eaten."

He laughed and handed her a plate of sausage and eggs. "How much longer are you in New York?" he asked.

"Why?"

"Since my wife isn't along on this trip, I thought we might see more of each other."

"It's hard to know how we could see more of each other than we already have," she said, laughing.

"You have a point," he agreed. "Stick around for a while? I'm here through next week."

"And then, back to the wife."

"It's a tough job, but somebody's got to do it."

"Tough?"

"Being married to a rich woman is a hard way to make a living," he said.

"So, get a divorce."

"I've learned to like my lifestyle, but I can't afford it on a State Department salary."

"So, if you want the lifestyle but not the wife, get somebody to kill her."

He laughed. "You Texans," he said. "I don't want to end up the subject of some TV movie-of-the-week."

It occurred to her that Washington might make a nice change of scene, at the moment. She could rent a car and drive down. "Oh, it can be done quite discreetly," she said. "I can arrange it."

"*What?*"

"You'd be at a Security Council session, or someplace with a lot of witnesses. She'd be the victim of a burglary gone wrong, or something like that. No one would ever be able to connect you to it."

"*You* can arrange it?"

"I'm a resourceful person. I was thinking of traveling to Washington, anyway. It would be my pleasure."

"That sounded as if you wanted to do it yourself."

"I have some experience at these things."

"What sort of experience are you talking about?"

"I lied to you, Jeff. I'm not a Texas matron, I'm a professional assassin."

Purdue laughed heartily. "I'm not sure I can afford you," he said.

"I'll work cheap. Tell you what: Allow me the use of your suite through the weekend, and she'll be dead by the middle of next week."

"You sound serious," he said.

"And you sound interested."

He stopped eating. "All right, I'm interested," he said warily. "Tell me why we wouldn't get caught."

"Because you and I have no history together that could be discovered later, and because I have no motive to kill your wife. Also, when I leave New York for Washington, I'll no longer be Darlene King, but someone else, who will disappear the moment she's dead."

He set down his plate. "Ah, the stuff that dreams are made of," he said wistfully.

"I imagine you'd be a very eligible man as a widower — handsome, well connected, and, finally, rich."

"That's perfectly true. But, if you're what you say you are, why are you confiding in me? I could walk down the hall, rap on the door of the presidential suite, and tell the director about you. I'll bet he would be interested."

"Oh, you couldn't do that, Jeff: You'd have too much to explain. You'd end up having to explain it to your wife, and she might react badly. You might find yourself living on your State Department salary. No, I'm perfectly safe confiding in you."

"Convince me you're what you say you are," he said.

Marie-Thérèse set her plate on the room-service cart and got out of bed. She walked over to where her purse rested on a chair, dug out her little silenced pistol, walked back to the bed, and pointed it at Purdue's head.

Purdue's face froze.

"Oh, relax," she said, "I'm not going to shoot you."

"What kind of gun is that?" he asked, fascinated.

"An assassin's weapon. It was made by your very own CIA," she said.

"And how did you come into possession of it?"

"By means too convoluted to explain."

"If you shot my wife with that, could the gun be connected to other murders?"

"No, it could not. You'll have to trust me on that."

"Well, I'll be damned," he said.

"You think it over," she replied. "I'm going to have a shower." She walked into the bathroom, taking her purse and the pistol with her.

Carpenter closed her phone. "The NYPD has given up on La Biche's returning to the Carlyle suite, so they're going to concentrate on our local headquarters," she said to the meeting, "in the belief that she might watch the place again. They're stationing snipers on the rooftops nearby."

"I don't see what else can be done," the director said. "My people are watching the airports, train and bus stations. We've circulated her description to the car rental agencies, too. What identity was she using at the Carlyle?"

"Mrs. Darlene King, of Dallas, Texas," Carpenter replied. "She's apparently stayed there before under that name."

"I don't suppose she'd be so foolish as to use it again," he said.

"I doubt it. She's abandoned the suite at the Carlyle, and I expect she has abandoned that identity for another."

Mason leaned over. "Look, if you don't need me anymore, I want to go back to the office and pick up some fresh clothes."

"Go ahead, but watch yourself," Carpenter said.

Marie-Thérèse checked herself out in the mirror. She looked very good in Mrs. Purdue's Armani pantsuit, she thought, and she felt clean and fresh in her underwear, too. She walked back to the bathroom, where Purdue was shaving.

He looked at her reflection in the mirror. "Hey, you can't wear that," he said. "That's my wife's."

"She's not going to be needing it, is she?"

He continued shaving. "Let's drop this little game," he said. "You're no assassin, and my wife is not going anywhere. Now put on your own

352

clothes and get out of here. You're a great fuck, but we're not going to be seeing each other again."

His tone annoyed Marie-Thérèse, not to mention that he was talking with his back to her.

"Well, Jeff, I was going to do you a favor, but since you take that attitude, I think I'll do your wife one, instead." She took the pistol from her purse and fired once into the back of his head. The soft-nosed bullet splattered his face all over the bathroom mirror.

She hung her dress carefully in the closet, so as to blend in with Mrs. Purdue's things, dropped her dirty underwear in the hamper, and walked out of the suite, closing the door behind her. The guard from the night before was still on duty. "Good morning," she said sweetly.

"Good morning, ma'am," he replied, pushing the elevator button for her.

Another man came down the hall and stood with her, waiting for the elevator. When it arrived, they both got on.

"Good morning," he drawled.

"Good morning," she said, looking at him for the first time. "Well, upon my word, if it isn't Mason!" She laughed aloud.

He squinted at her. "How do you know that name? Have we met?"

"No," she said, "but your reputation precedes you." She fumbled in her handbag, as if she were looking for her lipstick. When her hand was on the pistol, she pressed the emergency stop button on the elevator.

"What are you doing?" Mason demanded, then his face fell as he realized who she was.

"I'm getting off here," she said, withdrawing the pistol from her bag. "You're going all the way down." She shot him twice, then stepped off the elevator, reached back inside, and released the car.

57

The meeting in the presidential suite was just breaking up, when an FBI agent walked quickly into the room and whispered something in the director's ear.

The director's eyebrows went up. "You cannot be serious," he said.

"I am perfectly serious," the man replied.

The director turned to Carpenter. "Your man, Mason, has just been found dead in the elevator, shot twice."

Carpenter stood up; she wasn't sure why. Before she could say anything, her cell phone rang. Automatically, she answered it. "Yes?"

"It's Stone. Dino and I have just arrived at the Waldorf. We'd like to meet with you and the director."

"Stone, she's in the hotel."

"Who's in the hotel?"

"La Biche. She just shot Mason in the elevator."

"Don't leave the suite, and tell the director not to, as well. I'll call you back." He broke the connection.

"What is it?" Dino asked, as they walked up

the steps from the drive-through under the hotel, headed for the Tower elevators.

"Marie-Thérèse is in the building," Stone replied. "She's just killed Mason in an elevator."

Dino ran back to his car and retrieved a handheld radio. "This is Bacchetti," he said into it. "La Biche is at the Waldorf. Pull everybody off the Brits' offices and get them over here. Call hotel security, too, and get every available patrol car to the hotel. I want every woman alone stopped and ID'ed, then held if there's the slightest suspicion."

Marie-Thérèse waited impatiently for an elevator to stop, but none did. Then she realized what had happened. She had been on an express elevator to the Towers, one that stopped only because she had pressed the emergency button. The elevator to this floor was not an express, but stopped at any floor that had requested it, and at this hour of the day, it was receiving many requests. She had planned to reach the lobby while there was a commotion over the discovery of Mason's body, before anyone had time to begin searching for his killer, but now her time was running out while she waited for an elevator. And at this moment, the security guard on the Tower floor was giving her description to her hunters. She looked around for an exit, a stairway, and found it. The door was plainly marked, sixteenth floor. If she took the elevator, someone would very likely be waiting at the bottom. How long would it take her to walk down sixteen flights of stairs?

She looked in the other direction and saw an open door, with linens and supplies stacked inside. She ran down the hallway into the closet and closed the door behind her. She found a maid's dress, freshly laundered, on a shelf, and quickly got into it, buttoned it closed over her suit. She rolled up her pant legs, so that they disappeared under the skirt, and she found a maid's cap and put it on. Then she heard a key in the lock, and the door opened.

A maid stood in the hallway beside a cart laden with supplies. Before she could speak, Marie-Thérèse asked, "Excuse me, where is the service elevator? I'm lost."

"Down there," the woman said, "but you'll need a key." Then she realized that something wasn't right. "What are you doing in here? I don't know you."

Marie-Thérèse grasped her wrist and yanked her into the closet. She hit her sharply on the back of the neck with the heel of her hand, and the woman collapsed in a heap. Marie-Thérèse searched her for her keys and found them in a pocket. She left the closet, closing the door behind her, and began pushing the maid's cart toward the service elevator, placing her handbag in the cart's hamper. As she walked, she grabbed a towel and wiped her face vigorously, removing her makeup.

Stone called Carpenter's cell phone again.
"Yes?"

"Dino and I are at the Tower elevators, and hotel security has it roped off. If she comes down in one of the other elevators, we'll stop her."

"Good."

"Now, you're going to have to organize a search of every floor between you and the ground, knocking on every door and checking out every woman who even vaguely fits her description."

"The FBI is already working on that," she said.

"Dino has called his people off your offices and is bringing them here, but if Marie-Thérèse has already made the ground floor, they're going to be too late to stop her. Our only chance is if she's still somewhere upstairs."

"We have a new description," Carpenter said. "She's wearing a pantsuit, color undetermined, and she has short blond hair and is carrying a large handbag."

"Got it," Stone said. "Call me with any news." He hung up. "She's now got short blond hair," he said to Dino, "and she's wearing a pantsuit."

Marie-Thérèse found the elevator key, slipped it into the lock, and turned it. She looked up at the floor lights. The car was three floors above her and headed down. After a long moment, the

358

door opened, and she pushed the cart aboard. She looked at the buttons on the control panel and discovered that the hotel had a basement and two subbasements. She inserted her key and pressed the basement button. The doors closed, and the car started down.

To her alarm, it stopped again almost immediately, and the doors opened. A busboy pushed a room-service cart aboard, but her cart was between him and the control panel. "Push SB-one for me, will you?" he asked.

She inserted her key again and pressed the button. The elevator began moving down again.

"Man, this day is a bitch," the busboy said in Spanish-tinted English. "I got half a dozen carts to get downstairs, and somebody's stopping me every two seconds."

"Why are they stopping you?" she asked, alarmed.

"They're looking for somebody upstairs," he said, "some woman. That's all I know. Security is all over the place, and there's lots of other guys I don't know, guys in suits."

"I'm new here," she said. "What's in subbasements one and two?"

"Kitchen on SB-one, laundry on SB-two," the man said. "Hey, I buy you a cup of coffee sometime in the lounge, okay?"

"Sure," Marie-Thérèse said. She was starting to sweat under the two layers of clothing. And she was frightened.

58

Marie-Thérèse changed her mind and pushed the elevator button for SB-2.

"I thought you were getting off at the basement," the busboy said.

"I meant to go to the laundry," she said. "I got confused."

"Yeah, it takes a while to learn your way around this place." He got off at SB-1. "See you later."

"Yeah, sure." The door opened again at SB-2, and she pushed the cart out ahead of her. And there before her was something she had been looking desperately for: a sign saying EXIT, with an arrow pointing to her left. She pushed the cart in that direction, then followed another sign, turning down a long hallway. At the end was a door with an EXIT sign over it, but there was a uniformed, armed security guard standing in front of it. This shouldn't be too difficult, she thought.

She pushed the cart nearly all the way to the door, then stopped and took her handbag from the hamper.

"I'm afraid you can't get out this way, lady," the guard said. "I got orders."

She adopted the Spanish accent of the busboy. "Oh, I just want to have a cigarette outside," she said. "They give you a hard time if you smoke inside." She rummaged in her handbag, as if she were looking for her cigarettes.

"Yeah, I'm a smoker, too, so I know how it is, but I still can't let you out this door. It's orders from upstairs." He rested a hand nonchalantly on the butt of his pistol.

Marie-Thérèse stopped rummaging in her bag. If she tried to shoot him, he'd have a head start. "Oh, well," she said, "I'd better get back to work. I can have my smoke later." She turned the cart around and pushed it back the way she had come, looking for another way out. She found another exit, but there was another security guard standing in front of it, and he looked less friendly than the last one. Finally, with nowhere else to go, she went back to the elevator, put her key into the lock, and pressed the button. She'd try another floor.

Carpenter showed her ID to the guard and took the express elevator to the lobby. As she stepped out, Stone and Dino approached.

"She hasn't come this way," Stone said. "How's the search upstairs going?"

"Slowly," Carpenter replied. "She could have knocked on the door of any room and got herself inside, and it's a big hotel."

361

"Dino," Stone said, "if you can get a cop or two to watch the elevators, we could work our way up."

Dino spoke into his radio, and a moment later, two uniformed officers approached. Dino gave them instructions, then turned to Carpenter. "Okay, let's go upstairs."

"We'll take the other elevator, to the lower floors," Carpenter said, "and just do a sweep of each floor. We won't knock on every door. We'll leave that to the search teams and just hope to get lucky."

Stone and Dino followed her onto an elevator and rode up a floor. They got off and began walking the halls.

Marie-Thérèse got off at the basement level; at least it was closer to the street. But to her surprise, the floor contained staff offices for the hotel. A security guard down the hallway spotted her and began walking toward her. Quickly, she got back onto the elevator, hoping he didn't have a key. The ground floor would be crawling with cops, so she pressed three. At least she could walk down quickly from that level.

Carpenter and her two companions completed their patrol of the second floor, and she started toward the stairs.

"No," Dino said. "If we get into the stairwell, we won't be able to get out on another floor;

we'll have to walk downstairs, and we just came from there. We'll have to take the elevator." He pressed the call button.

"Do you really think she's still in the hotel?" Stone asked.

"I don't know," Carpenter replied, "but it's the only place we've got to look for her at the moment. If she got out of the hotel, she could be anywhere."

"Let's just keep at it," Dino said. "It's called police work, Stone, remember?"

"I remember," Stone said. They got on the elevator and pressed the button for the third floor.

Marie-Thérèse got off on the third floor, pushing the cart ahead of her, her handbag back in the hamper. She rounded a corner, looking for an exit, in time to see two men and a woman get off the elevator. They turned and began to walk toward her. She recognized them immediately and fought the urge to run. "Good morning," she said in her Spanish accent, as they passed her.

"Good morning," the three muttered.

They had gone a dozen steps when Carpenter held up a hand to stop them. A gun was suddenly in her hand, and she held the barrel to her lips. Silently, she pointed the weapon at the maid disappearing down the hallway.

Stone and Dino turned to look at the woman.

From under her white uniform skirt, a black pant leg had fallen to her ankle.

"Pantsuit," Carpenter whispered.

Stone and Dino drew their weapons.

59

Marie-Thérèse knew she had been made. She had the maid's passkey in her hand, and, crouching behind the cart, she grabbed her handbag from the hamper and opened the door to the room nearest her, ducked inside, and slammed the door behind her.

A man emerged from the bathroom. He was enormous — six and a half feet tall, three hundred pounds, she estimated. He was dressed in trousers and a white shirt, and a necktie hung loose at his neck. "Yeah?" he asked.

She dug into her handbag and came out with the pistol. "Stand over there," she said.

"What the fuck is going on here?" he demanded.

Marie-Thérèse tossed her maid's cap on the unmade bed and began unbuttoning the uniform dress. "You look like you once played football."

"Yeah, so what?"

"Ever have a knee injury?"

"Yeah."

"Remember how much it hurt?"

"Yeah."

She pointed the pistol at his right knee. "This

is going to hurt a lot more," she said.

He held his hands out in front of him in a pacifying motion. "Okay, okay, whatever you say."

Marie-Thérèse walked to the window, keeping the gun pointed at him, and looked out. She was only three floors above street level, and she had thoughts of tying the bedsheets together, but there were two police cars parked in the street, their lights flashing. She turned back to her captive.

"Just tell me what you want," he said.

"I want a ride out of here," she replied.

Stone, Dino, and Carpenter stood in the hallway, their backs against the wall, on either side of the door.

"Kick it in," Carpenter said. "That's what cops do, isn't it?"

"That kind of door don't kick," Dino said, "unless you want to break an ankle." He put the handheld radio to his mouth. "This is Bacchetti. We've got the suspect cornered in a room on the third floor. I want a SWAT team with a battering ram up here *now*."

"Lieutenant, it's Sergeant Rivera," a voice came back. "We don't have a SWAT team on site — you didn't ask for one earlier. I'll have to call it in, so it's going to be a few minutes."

"She isn't going anywhere," Stone said.

"Okay," Dino said into the radio, "tell them to shake their asses."

"What do we do now?" Carpenter asked.

"Let me see if I can talk her out," Stone said.

"Feel free," Dino replied.

Stone moved closer to the door and rapped on it sharply. "Marie-Thérèse, it's Stone Barrington."

"Well, hi there, Stone," her muffled voice came back. "What brings you to see me?"

"I want to get you out of here alive," Stone said.

"Sounds good to me. How do we go about that?"

"It's simple. You open the door, toss out your weapon, and walk out with your hands on your head. I guarantee you'll be safe."

"Carpenter's out there, isn't she?"

"Yes, she's here."

"Can you guarantee I'll be safe from her? After the lie about the money transfer, I don't trust her."

"I sent the money!" Carpenter shouted. "It's in your account!"

Stone motioned for her to be quiet. "Carpenter is not going to shoot you, but a SWAT team is on the way, and unless we get you out of there now, they're going to be battering the door down, and anything could happen."

"Well, we don't want that, do we? All right, I'm coming out. Everybody stand away from the door."

The three of them backed across the hallway and waited.

"We're out of the way," Stone said.

"Okay, here I come."

The knob turned, and the door swung inward.

Stone blinked. A man stood there, a man so big that he filled the whole doorway. His fingers were interlaced across his belly, and from under his arms protruded two female feet, in heels. Marie-Thérèse peeked over his shoulder, an arm around his neck, and her pistol was against his temple.

"Giddyup," she said, "but take it slow."

The man moved slowly through the doorway.

"Just don't turn your back on them," Marie-Thérèse said.

Dino spoke up. "Hey, I know you, don't I?" he said to the man. "Weren't you a linebacker for the Jets a while back?"

"Yeah," the man replied.

"Billy Franco, The Freezer!"

"Yeah, right, now could you just please do whatever it takes to get this lady offa my back and outa my life?"

"I'm sorry to interrupt this sports chat," Marie-Thérèse said, "but we're going to do a little dance now. Everybody is going to rotate counterclockwise until we've changed places."

The three began moving in that direction, and Franco moved at the same time, until his back was to the opposite wall, and they were standing in the doorway of the room.

"Now, everybody back into the room and

close the door, and then I won't have to splash Mr. Freezer's brains all over the place."

"Then what?" Franco asked.

"Then I'm going to ride you out of this hotel and into the nearest car."

"I got a better idea," Franco said.

"What?"

He took a quick step backward and slammed Marie-Thérèse against the wall, then dove sideways.

Marie-Thérèse made a sound like air rushing from a blown tire and ended up in a sitting position on the floor. Then, with the last of her strength, she raised the pistol, pointed it in the general direction of the three, and pulled the trigger. There was a soft click as the hammer fell on the empty chamber.

For a moment, no one moved, then Carpenter fired two bullets into Marie-Thérèse.

Stone swung an arm, knocking Carpenter off her feet. "Stop it!" he yelled.

Franco, who had been lying facedown in the hallway, his hands covering his head, turned and looked. "Did somebody get shot?" he asked.

Stone bent over Marie-Thérèse and held his fingers to her throat. "Yes," he said. "Shot dead."

60

Stone got back to his house around noon. There was a courier package on his doorstep, and he took it inside and dumped it on the hall table. He was exhausted and dispirited, and he was in no mood to read anything. What he needed was sleep.

He left a trail of clothing from the elevator to the bedroom and climbed into bed, pausing only to press the privacy button on his telephone.

When he awoke it was dark outside. The bedside clock said just after eight. He got his feet on the floor, stood up, and walked to the bathroom. Five minutes of hot shower on the back of his neck made him feel nearly human again.

He went back into the bedroom, thinking of food. He hadn't had anything to eat since the night before. He switched off the privacy button on the phone, and it rang immediately.

"It's Dino. Get your ass up to Elaine's."

"I don't know, Dino. I just woke up."

"Carpenter's leaving. She tried to call you, but I guess you had the phone turned off. She's stopping by on her way to the airport."

"All right, I'll be there." He hung up, then

shaved and got into some clean clothes, still a little fuzzy around the edges. As he was about to leave the house, his eye fell on the package on his front hall table. The return address was the Carlyle hotel. He opened it. Inside were several sheets of paper and a fairly thick envelope.

Stone:

I have the very odd feeling that I am at the end of something, maybe of everything. I wish I could stop, but I can't, not until I've done what I set out to do. I know you think I'm a fool, and you had me convinced of that, until I was faced with the duplicity of the people I oppose. If things go well, I will probably be out of the country by the time you read this. If things go wrong, as I fear they might, then you have your instructions. I have enclosed the name of my lawyer in Zurich. When he is notified, he will know what to do. I wish to be cremated and have my ashes sent to him. Thank you for what you tried to do.

Marie-Thérèse

Stone looked at the attached document, which was neatly typed and notarized. It authorized him to act as her attorney in the United States, before and after her death. Another sheet of paper was a copy of a letter to her Zurich attorney, apprising him of Stone's involvement in her affairs. He ripped open the envelope to find a stack of one-hundred-dollar bills, the same as the last time she had paid him. He tossed the package onto the table, left the house, and looked for a cab.

Dino was alone when Stone arrived. He sat down, and without a word, Dino shoved a copy of the *New York Post* across the table, open to a story inside.

STATE DEPARTMENT OFFICIAL MURDERED AT WALDORF

Jeffrey Purdue, a member of the U.S. delegation to the United Nations, was found shot to death in a suite in the Waldorf Towers this morning. Police sources said that he had picked up Darlene King, a high-priced prostitute, the evening before and had taken her to his suite, and that, after a night together, she had robbed and murdered him.

A maid discovered the body early in the morning and notified police and hotel security. The hotel was locked down and a search conducted, resulting in a confrontation between Ms. King and police. When she pointed a pistol at them, she was shot to death.

"That's it?" Stone asked. "No reference to what happened at the Four Seasons or to Mason?"

"It's the clean version," Dino said. "Only

Purdue gets his name in the papers." Dino threw up his hands. "Don't look at me. This came from a lot higher up the food chain."

"Speaking of food," Stone said, reaching for a menu. A waiter set down a Wild Turkey on the rocks. "Want to share the porterhouse for two?"

"Why not?" Dino said. "I haven't eaten. Mary Ann is at her father's."

"The porterhouse, medium to medium rare," Stone said to the waiter.

"Make that rare," Dino said.

"Make it rare on *his* side," Stone countered, and the waiter went away.

Carpenter suddenly appeared, looking businesslike in a suit. She sat down.

"Drink? Dinner?" Dino asked.

"Neither. I'll eat on the airplane."

"There's a flight to London this time of night?" Stone asked.

"There's an RAF airplane waiting for me at Teterboro," she said. "I'm taking back two bodies as hand baggage."

"Oh, yes."

"What will happen to La Biche's remains?" she asked Dino.

"Potter's field is my guess."

"No," Stone interjected. He told them about the package from Marie-Thérèse. "She wants her ashes sent back to Switzerland."

"Why don't you just flush them down the toilet?" Carpenter asked.

"Shut up, Felicity," Stone said.

"You liked her, didn't you?" she asked.

"No, I didn't. I admired . . . some of what she was — determined, even principled, in a way."

"And you don't like me anymore?"

"I like you, but I don't admire you," Stone said.

"I did what had to be done."

"No, you did what you had to do; there's a difference."

"At least I know that she's not after me anymore. I can relax now."

"I don't know how you can ever relax again," Stone said.

"I'm quitting, you know."

"Are you really?"

"I'm thinking about it."

"Don't think about it, just quit. You can't be a human being again until you do."

"I wish you understood," she said.

Stone shrugged. "Like you said, it's a war; what's to understand?"

She stood up. "I have to go." She gave Dino a hug, then turned to Stone.

"I don't feel like kissing you," she said.

"Then don't."

"Call me when you're in London?"

"After you've retired."

She gave him a little wave, then left.

They were quiet for a while, sipping their drinks, then Dino finally spoke. "You were too hard on her."

"Was I?"

"We all have our dirty work to do — Carpenter, me, and you."

Stone downed the rest of his bourbon and signaled a waiter for another. "I think you'd better order a police car to take me home tonight."

"It's waiting outside," Dino said.

Mount Desert, Maine, June 26, 2002

ACKNOWLEDGMENTS

I am grateful to my editor at Putnam, David Highfill, for his continuing fine work on my manuscripts and his shepherding of my books inside the publishing house, as I am to all the people behind the scenes at Putnam who do so much to make my work a success.

I am grateful, too, to my literary agents, Morton Janklow and Anne Sibbald, for all their work in the management of my career over the past twenty-two years. They have always made me feel I am in good hands.

AUTHOR'S NOTE

I am happy to hear from readers, but you should know that if you write to me in care of my publisher, three to six months will pass before I receive your letter, and when it finally arrives it will be one among many, and I will not be able to reply.

However, if you have access to the Internet, you may visit my Web site at www.stuartwoods.com, where there is a button for sending me e-mail. So far, I have been able to reply to all of my e-mail, and I will continue to try to do so.

If you send me an e-mail and do not receive a reply, it is because you are among an alarming number of people who have entered their e-mail address incorrectly in their mail software. I have many of my replies returned as undeliverable.

Remember: e-mail, reply; snail mail, no reply.

When you e-mail, please do not send attachments, as I *never* open these. They can take twenty minutes to download, and they often contain viruses.

Please do not place me on your mailing lists for funny stories, prayers, political causes, charitable fund-raising, petitions, or sentimental claptrap. I get enough of that from people I already know. Generally speaking, when I get e-mail addressed to a large number of people, I immediately delete it without reading it.

Please do not send me your ideas for a book, as I have a policy of writing only what I myself invent. If you send me story ideas, I will immediately delete them without reading them. If you have a good idea for a book, write it yourself, but I will not be able to advise you on how to get it published. Buy a copy of *Writer's Market* at any bookstore; that will tell you how.

Anyone with a request concerning events or appearances may e-mail it to me or send it to: Publicity Department, G. P. Putnam's Sons, 375 Hudson Street, New York, NY 10014.

Those ambitious folk who wish to buy film, dramatic, or television rights to my books should contact Matthew Snyder, Creative Artists Agency, 9830 Wilshire Boulevard, Beverly Hills, CA 90212-1825.

Those who wish to conduct business of a more literary nature should contact Anne Sibbald, Janklow & Nesbit, 445 Park Avenue, New York, NY 10022.

If you want to know if I will be signing books in your city, please visit my Web site, www.stuartwoods.com, where the tour schedule will be published a month or so in advance. If you wish me to do a book signing in your locality, ask your favorite bookseller to contact his Putnam representative or the G. P. Putnam's Sons Publicity Department with the request.

If you find typographical or editorial errors in my book and feel an irresistible urge to tell someone, please write to David Highfill at Putnam, address above. Do not e-mail your discoveries to me, as I will already have learned about them from others.

A list of all my published works appears in the front of this book. All the novels are still in print in paperback and can be found at or ordered from any bookstore. If you wish to obtain hardcover copies of earlier novels or of the two nonfiction books, a good used-book store or one of the on-line bookstores can help you find them. Otherwise, you will have to go to a great many garage sales.